THE GONE SISTER

THOMAS FINCHAM

The Gone Sister
Thomas Fincham

Copyright © 2017
All Rights Reserved.

Visit the author's website:
www.finchambooks.com

Contact:
finchambooks@gmail.com

Join my Facebook page:
https://www.facebook.com/finchambooks/

LEE CALLAWAY SERIES

1) The Dead Daughter
2) The Gone Sister
3) The Falling Girl
4) The Invisible Wife
5) The Missing Mistress
6) The Broken Mother
7) The Guilty Spouse
8) The Unknown Woman
9) The Lost Twins

ONE

Several Years Earlier

Anthony "Fatboy" Carvalho lit up a cigarette and took a long drag. He had earned his nickname back when he used to weigh almost three hundred pounds. After a heart attack at the age of thirty-five, however, he changed his diet and started exercising. He lost close to a hundred pounds in two years, and he planned to lose another twenty by the end of this year.

He had also stopped drinking, but he could not kick smoking. Cigarettes were his constant companion during his weight loss. He would light up a cigarette whenever he had a craving for food. His smoking was probably worse than his excess weight, but he would take things one step at a time. First, he would finish losing weight, and then he would quit smoking.

Fatboy was sitting at a table on a restaurant's outdoor patio. He could feel the sun beating down on him, making his neck burn, but he did not mind it. Vitamin D was good for him. His shirt and jacket hung loosely over his slimmer frame. His belt was on its last notch to keep his pants from falling off. He had still not upgraded his attire. He wanted to hit his target weight and then do a complete overhaul of his wardrobe. *Why waste money on clothes before that?* he figured.

The waitress brought over his espresso. She was young and blonde. He felt an impulse to get her number, but he quickly decided not to. He was not presentable yet. He still had more work to do on his body.

There was, however, another reason for hesitation.

He was a marked man.

Fatboy worked as the right-hand man for Paolo Beniti. Beniti imported heroin from the Balkans and Eastern Europe, and then he sold the drug through a network of dealers in the city. He also wholesaled heroin, which enabled him to keep the peace with other distributors. If they ran short, he was more than willing to sell the drug to them. He was also involved in selling counterfeit brand-name goods, and he owned retail properties and small businesses throughout the city.

Beniti valued obedience above everything else, and if one of his subordinates deviated from his instructions, Beniti's reprisals were ruthless.

Several months earlier, Fatboy had gotten into an altercation with the son of a casino owner. The altercation had left Fatboy with a black eye, a swollen cheek, and a bruised ego. If Fatboy was not in the process of losing weight, he would have used his bulk to win the fight. Beniti had ordered Fatboy not to retaliate, as Beniti was friends with the casino owner.

Fatboy did not listen.

When he saw his opportunity, he attacked the casino owner's son with a baseball bat. He broke several of the boy's bones and walked away, feeling satisfied.

The boy had to spend a month in the hospital.

Naturally, Beniti was not pleased. Fatboy apologized and swore he would never disobey his commands again, but he knew he had crossed the line.

Fatboy was notorious for his temper. His bad attitude made him feared in the organization, but his anger had put him in the position he was in now. Had he let bygones be bygones, he would not be sitting here drinking espresso, wondering if this would be the last drink he ever tasted. But what was done was done. Sooner or later, someone would come for him.

But Fatboy would not go down without a fight.

He always kept a watchful eye on his surroundings, making sure nothing caught him by surprise. This survival tactic had kept him alive before, so why not now?

He was also proactive.

Fatboy had done what his dead associates never did. He had gone to the feds. He promised the FBI valuable information on Beniti and his associates in return for immunity and protection.

He took a sip of his espresso and checked his watch. His FBI contact would be here any minute.

He heard a commotion. A male customer two tables down was arguing with the pretty blonde waitress. The man was loud and rude. Fatboy felt an urge to get up, go give the man a hard slap and say, *That's no way to speak to a lady*.

He got ready to rise to his feet when he heard a rumble. Fatboy turned to see what it was.

A motorcyclist pulled up next to the patio, stopping five feet from Fatboy. The rider—a man—was dressed in black. Black leather jacket, black pants and boots, and a black helmet. He looked like the Grim Reaper.

Fatboy knew what this was. *My time is up,* he thought.

Fatboy and the hitman went for their guns.

The hitman whipped out a 9mm and fired first.

A bullet ripped through Fatboy's shoulder, spinning him in his chair. Fatboy fell to the deck and pulled his table in front of him as a shield.

The hitman blazed away at Fatboy, but his bullets smacked into the metal table instead.

Pandemonium broke loose as café customers and employees fled the patio, screaming and ducking as they fled.

Fatboy finally drew his gun—a revolver—and fired back.

He caught the shooter off guard. He turned to flee, but he slipped and fell.

Fatboy felt a surge of rage. He got up from behind the table and fired again. His bullet struck the shooter in the back, but the shooter was able to turn and fire off one more burst.

One of his shots hit Fatboy squarely in the chest.

He dropped to the deck.

The shooter hopped on his motorcycle and rode away.

Fatboy clutched at his chest as blood covered his shirt. His ears rang, and he felt disoriented.

He glanced off to his right and saw people huddled around someone on the deck. He could not tell who.

Why aren't they checking on me? he wondered. *I'm also hurt.*

He realized he was still gripping his revolver. He let the gun slip from his fingers. His eyelids suddenly felt heavy, and his entire body was on fire with pain.

His breathing became labored as he shut his eyes and fell into a sea of darkness.

TWO

Present Day

Her legs ached as she made her way up the narrow street. The predawn glow filled the eastern horizon, but the streetlights were still lit.

The woman wore a light-colored hoodie and track pants. Rock music blared through her earbuds, giving her the energy to keep pushing even when she was on the brink of exhaustion.

Dana Fisher loved to go for a run early in the morning when everyone was still asleep. There were no people, cars, or pets to contend with. She felt like she was on a solitary journey. Her destination was not important, nor was finishing her run by a certain time. The only thing that mattered to Fisher was getting in a good workout.

She checked her athletic watch. She had a good heartbeat, a high burned-calorie count, and the miles run were more than on her last sprint.

She smiled and resumed her run, pushing herself even harder. She raced down the street, cut through a park, went over a railway line, and then made her way back to her apartment building.

As Fisher entered the lobby, she pulled off her soaking wet hoodie, revealing her dark shoulder-length hair. She was five-five and weighed close to a hundred and ten pounds. Her nose was thin and pointed upwards, and it moved whenever she opened her mouth. Her green eyes were large and expressive, and they were staring at her reflection in the lobby's mirrored wall.

She was a member of the Milton Police Department. She had ambitions to become a captain one day. So far, she was enjoying her time as a detective. Being a police officer was gritty and gruesome work, but it gave her invaluable experience. She had learned to be better focused, patient, and to compartmentalize her tasks: all skills she would need when the time came for her to run her own police precinct.

She had no doubt she would one day.

While she waited in the lobby, she saw that one of the three elevators was not working. There was always something wrong in her building. If it was not the elevators, it was the hot water shutting off in the middle of a shower, or the heating system not producing enough air to warm a room. Or worse, the fire alarms malfunctioned when there could be a potential emergency.

She had thought about moving out, but with the rent so high in the city, it was almost impossible to find something affordable. With rent control, she was secure in not having to worry about her rent increasing exorbitantly. If she went to another location, the landlords could charge her whatever they wanted, as the rent control laws did not apply to new tenants. On top of that, there were the moving costs.

Until she could save enough money or get a promotion, she was staying put.

The other two working elevators were on the top floors. She decided to take the stairs instead. Unfortunately, she lived on the sixth floor.

Her apartment was brightly colored. She could not stand looking at the beige walls that had turned yellowish after years of dirt and grime, so she had given her place a new coat of paint right after she moved in.

The bedroom was on the right, the living room and kitchen on the left. At the far end was her favorite spot. The balcony had been enclosed by the previous tenants, giving her an extra room. She had converted the space into her meditation room.

The apartment walls were covered in family photos. In each picture, she was the one girl with three brothers. Maybe that explained why she was comfortable with butting heads with her male colleagues. Her parents were both professionals, and they had hoped their daughter would get a nine-to-five job behind a desk. She knew she was not ready for that at this stage of her life. She wanted to see the city, and as a detective, she saw more than what most people did.

Her cell phone buzzed. She thought about not answering.

Her phone continued to buzz.

She gritted her teeth, put her phone to her ear, and said, "Fisher." She listened. "It's my day off. Call Detective Holt." She listened some more. She sighed. "Okay, fine. I'll be right there."

THREE

Fisher's hair was still wet from the cold shower as she drove twenty-five minutes to her destination. She was wearing a white top, blue jeans, brown boots, and a black jacket. She did not even have time to put on makeup. She was not big on cosmetics, but a simple eyeliner and lipstick would have been nice. She might have to make a statement to the press.

She took a sip from the thermos. The coffee was piping hot.

She had her entire day planned out. After her morning run, she was going to have a long bubble bath. She would then make herself pancakes for breakfast. Not a healthy choice, but after a good workout, she needed to reward herself.

There was a book on her coffee table that she was looking forward to reading. The novel was a Harlequin romance. She would never let anyone at work know this. The teasing would never stop. The book was one of her guilty pleasures. The premise was straight out of dozens of romance novels: a working-class girl somehow meets and falls in love with a real-life prince. The twist was that the girl was also a princess, but she wanted to see if the prince would marry a commoner.

Afterward, she was going to go out for lunch with a friend. She had been postponing the meeting for months, and she hated having to cancel at the last minute. She would find a way to make it up to her friend later.

Her night was supposed to have been spent watching a light romantic comedy. She needed some lightness in her otherwise dark life. Detectives were faced with gruesome deaths, destroyed families, and other unimaginable horrors. The last thing she wanted was to end her day by watching a gut-wrenching drama, a tense thriller, or a murder mystery.

She spotted a police cruiser parked by the side of the road. She slowed down when the officer waved her through. A yellow strand of police tape had been arranged to secure the area. The officer held the tape up to allow her to drive underneath.

She was in the parking lot of a retail store whose sign read *Elegant Furniture*. A car was parked in one of the empty spots. Fisher did not park next to that vehicle. Instead, she found a spot further in the corner.

She got out when the officer approached her. "Detective Fisher?" he said.

"You're the officer who asked for me specifically?" she asked.

"I did."

She was annoyed. "I was scheduled to be off today, you know. I booked vacation time weeks ago."

"I'm sorry, ma'am, but I figured you'd want to be here."

"And why is that?" she replied. She was still thinking about the pancakes she was supposed to have for breakfast.

"You should take a look."

They walked to the parked car. The sun had begun to rise, illuminating the car. She could tell the vehicle was a Chrysler sedan just by looking at it. The paint was silver with alloy rims. As she got close, she saw broken glass scattered on the asphalt next to the driver's side door.

She also saw blood.

A man was slumped in the seat. His head bowed with his chin resting on his chest. The strap of the seatbelt was preventing him from falling on the steering wheel.

Fisher put her hand over her mouth when she saw who the victim was.

FOUR

He pinched his nostrils and tilted his head back. He grimaced as pain shot up through his nose and into his brain. His fingers were covered in blood, but when he checked his hands, he saw the blood had dried.

Great, he thought. *I managed to stop the bleeding.*

Lee Callaway was tall and in relatively good shape. He was tan, and he had strands of silver around his temples that made him look far more mature than he was.

Callaway was seated on a park bench. He was wearing a t-shirt that was stained red. Fortunately, the t-shirt was black, so his blood was not easily visible. His jeans were tattered, and his boots were scuffed. His leather coat was the only thing that did not look like it had been purchased from a used clothing store, even though Callaway had purchased the coat from just such a place. He was proud of the low price he had paid for the coat.

His eyes watered when he touched the bridge of his nose. He had already snapped the bone back in place, but he knew it could take days for the swelling to come down.

He could not believe he had put himself in this situation.

His reckless behavior had once again gotten him in trouble.

A client had hired him to follow his wife. He believed she was cheating on him. The case was straightforward; one Callaway had tackled dozens of times. Callaway did not expect he would get intimately involved with the wife. She was beautiful, lonely, and vulnerable. She was much younger than her husband by almost twenty years. She was a mail-order bride. The client was a brute of a man, twice Callaway's size. During a stakeout, Callaway caught the wife weeping in her bedroom. In a moment of sympathy, which he now regretted, he knocked on the front door. They talked. She told him how much she missed her family back in Russia. He felt sorry for her. And then one thing led to another, and he found himself at the end of the husband's fist.

He had to return the fee he had charged the husband for his services. He also had to pay extra to stop the husband from hurting him more.

Callaway did not think this was fair. Did the wife's involvement with him not prove she was cheating on her husband? He should have gotten a bonus instead of being subjected to a beating.

The sun was up, and he squinted as the light hit his eyes. The night had been a total failure. After extricating himself from the situation, the only thing Callaway had in his mind was to get as far away from the husband as possible. In his haste, he forgot his car was still parked across from the client's house.

He was walking for a couple of hours when his feet started to hurt. He spotted a park bench and decided to take a rest.

He pulled off his shoes and rubbed his toes and heel. He was certain he had blisters.

A man approached him. His hair was gray, his skin was wrinkled, and he sported a heavy mustache. "Do you mind if I sit here?" he asked.

"Help yourself," Callaway said, giving him space on the bench.

The man gingerly sat down. He pulled off his wool cap and wiped his forehead with a handkerchief.

"Nice morning for a walk," he said.

That's all I've been doing, Callaway thought.

The man squinted. "You okay, son?"

"I am," Callaway replied, not making eye contact with him.

"You don't look so good. You need help?"

"I'll be fine. Thanks."

"Woman trouble?" the man asked with a grin.

Callaway finally looked at him. "How'd you know?"

The man tapped the end of his nose. "It's been broken eight times. Twice during a bar fight. Once during a car accident. And the rest by boyfriends and husbands." The man smiled wistfully. "I gotta say, those were the happiest times of my life."

Callaway did not know how to respond.

"Was it worth it?" the man asked.

Callaway thought for a moment. "I guess it was."

"The pain will go away, but the memories will last forever."

The last thing Callaway wanted was to remember what happened the night before. He got up. "Nice talking to you."

"Your nose looks pretty bad, son. You should get it checked out by a medical professional," the man suggested.

I should get my head checked instead,
Callaway thought, and walked away.

FIVE

Fisher debated whether to make the call. She knew she had to. If she did not, she would never be forgiven.

After she hung up, she shut her eyes. She wanted to be anywhere, but here. She almost wished she had taken a cruise to the Caribbean like she had wanted to. Had she done so, she would not have to endure what she was about to go through.

She could not believe she was being selfish at a time when she was needed more than ever. Tragedy had struck, and as a friend and colleague, she would be relied upon to hold everything together. She could not imagine what she would do if something terrible happened to those she loved.

She opened her eyes and found the officer staring at her.

"Are you okay?" he asked, concerned.

"I'm fine, thanks," she said, composing herself. "Did you touch anything?"

The officer shook his head. "No, ma'am. After arriving at the scene, I called dispatch and told them to contact you."

"You did the right thing," she replied. She suddenly felt guilty for being annoyed at the officer. His request for her was out of courtesy. His duty was to secure the area and wait for the investigator to take charge of the scene, which he did.

Fisher glanced at the officer's name tag. It read *McConnell*. The name rang a faint bell in her memory.

She smiled. "Have we met before?"

McConnell nodded. "Yes, we have. I'm Officer Lance McConnell. We met at the annual police challenge."

Each year, the department held an event that tested officers in a variety of exercises that ranged from disarming an assailant to running obstacles to accuracy with a handgun. Fisher was not sure which event he competed in.

As if reading her mind, McConnell said, "I won the hundred-meter track."

Right, she thought. *That's why he looked familiar.*

His flowing blonde hair was covered by his police cap. He had deep blue eyes and a prominent chin. He was tall, and his uniform clung tight to his body.

He smiled.

She blushed, but she did not know why.

"How'd you know who the victim was?" Fisher asked, getting back to the case. "You didn't check his ID, did you?"

"I didn't have to. I'd seen him in the papers, and it's no secret whom he's related to. That's why I thought you'd want to be here first."

"I appreciate what you did."

"No problem."

A car pulled up to the curb. Officer McConnell rushed over and held the police tape so the car could pass through.

Fisher took a deep breath to steady her nerves.

Detective Gregory Holt stepped out of the car. He was six-four and weighed close to two hundred and fifty pounds. He had thick arms, thick hands, and a thick neck that was too large for his shirt collar. The skin on his shaved head was wrinkled. His small black eyes darted from one spot to another as if sizing everything up around him.

Holt walked toward Fisher as if he was in no hurry. His belief was not to rush unless he had to, and if things could wait, they did.

"I was surprised when you called me," he said. "I thought you were looking forward to your day off."

"I was, but this is important."

Holt stared at her. "Okay, so where's the victim?"

"Greg…" she started to say, but she stopped. Her eyes welled up.

"What's going on?" he asked, alarmed.

"I'm so sorry…"

Holt's face darkened. He tried to move past her, but she put her arm out to block him. Even though he could have pushed her aside with one finger, he held up.

"I need to tell you something," she said.

"What?" Holt asked.

Tears flowed down Fisher's cheeks.

"It's Isaiah."

SIX

Isaiah Whitcomb was six-foot-eight, weighed over two hundred and ten pounds, and he was a rising college basketball star.

He was also Holt's nephew.

The Milton Cougars had made it to the NCAA tournament twice, and it was all due to Isaiah. He was not a good shooter, but he was a great passer and a demon on defense. There was a belief amongst coaches and scouts that if Isaiah continued playing the way he did, he could make it to the NBA.

Over the years, the professional game had changed, going from an inside game to an outside game. Seven-footers who played with their backs to the baskets were no longer as coveted as before. Players who could play along the perimeter were more sought after. The ones who could shoot three-pointers and also defend against the opponent's three-point shooters were the new stars.

Isaiah was quick on his feet. It had something to do with his desire to be a soccer player as a kid. But then, at age sixteen, when he shot up six inches in height, basketball became the next option. He would hound every player on the opposing team, even the point guards. He had an abundance of energy. He never wanted to be taken out of a game even for a minute's rest.

He was also very competitive. Whenever his team lost a game, he would lock himself in a room and watch footage of the game. He always strived to get better, and he wanted his teammates to succeed too. He was very vocal when they made a mistake. He was also supportive when they needed a boost. He was his team's biggest cheerleader.

Holt stood frozen as he stared at the young man who held so much promise for himself and his family. The bright future that was before him was now gone.

Isaiah is no more.

Holt shut his eyes, hoping that when he opened them, he would not see Isaiah but someone else. He was used to seeing dead bodies of strangers. He never expected that one day a victim would be someone close to him.

Not Isaiah, he thought. *Not the little boy that used to call me "Uncle G" because he couldn't say my name.*

He opened his eyes and saw the dead body of his nephew. His eyes welled up, and he almost wished no one saw him.

Holt wanted to reach through the window and hug Isaiah. He wanted to tell him everything would be okay. But he knew things would never be okay. Not for him, not for his family, and not for everyone who loved and adored him.

He felt Fisher next to him. She placed her hand over his and gripped tightly. Her eyes were moist as she stared into his eyes. "Why don't you go home to your family, and I'll take care of this?" she said.

How do I go to my family? he thought. *What do I say to them?*

His chest tightened, and he felt like he could not breathe.

He clenched his jaw and inhaled deeply through his nostrils. *This is no time to fall apart*, he thought.

"Isaiah's family," he slowly said. "And I want to stay here with him."

"Okay," Fisher said.

SEVEN

Callaway stood before his beloved Dodge Charger with a tear in his eye. The black car's side doors had key marks, the windshield had cracks, and the taillights had to be replaced.

He sighed, and his shoulders sank. What did he expect the husband would do the moment he saw Callaway's car sitting across from his house?

Before returning, Callaway made sure the husband had left the house. Callaway hid behind a tree and watched until the husband and his soon-to-be ex-wife had driven away in their Hummer. There was no telling what the husband would do if he saw Callaway near his house again.

Callaway felt for the wife. She must have borne the brunt of his wrath. He doubted the husband had gotten physical with her. During Callaway's long talk with the wife, she admitted the husband had never hit her once. If he did, she would return to Russia on the next available flight. Callaway had a feeling that was what she would now do. She missed her family, and the only reason she was in the U.S. was to start a new life with her husband. The marriage was now over—Callaway was partly to blame for that—but she was not happy here anyway.

He put his hands over his face and quickly regretted it. His nose was still tender and would be so for a couple of days. *I should avoid touching it*, he thought.

He suddenly felt like sneezing, but he quickly put his finger near his nose to prevent it from happening. One sneeze and his nose would flare with pain, and blood would flow anew.

Callaway pulled out his car keys and unlocked the door. He grabbed the handle and suddenly sneezed violently. A sharp, stabbing pain shot up into his brain. He covered his nose and felt hot liquid on his fingers.

Damn, he thought.

He tilted his head back to stop the blood. He shut his eyes and pinched his nostrils again. He waited until the bleeding stopped.

He opened the car door and got behind the wheel. From the glove compartment, he pulled out a box of tissue and stuffed a bunch into his nostrils.

He saw his reflection in the rearview mirror and wondered why he kept putting himself in positions like this.

He used to be a deputy sheriff in a small town. He was married, he had a daughter, and he had a house to call his own. He still had his daughter, although he hardly saw her. But he was divorced, and he was relying on other people's kindness for lodging.

A very wealthy client had let him stay at her beach house until she returned from her trip to Switzerland. She was back, and she had brought with her a much younger man. Callaway had to quickly make himself scarce.

Fortunately for him, he did not have much to move. Most of his belongings were in his ex-wife's garage. After his last big case, he and his ex-wife were on much better terms. The payout was more than Callaway had expected. Instead of holding on to the money, which he would burn through in no time flat, he gave it to his ex. He was already way behind on his child support, and she could do more good with the money than him, although he could use the money about now. The Charger would need a new paint job, a new windshield, and new taillights. It would cost a pretty penny, but Callaway saw no other option. He could not see his prized possession in this condition.

He placed his hand on the dashboard. "I'm sorry, darling," he whispered. "It's my fault you had to suffer. I promise I'll get the money somehow to make you good as new."

He placed the key in the ignition and turned it. The Charger roared to life. The damage was cosmetic. The car was still in running condition. The cracks in the windshield were not so bad, and he could still make out what was in front of him. The taillights would be a problem. Not for him, but for the drivers behind him. *A minor inconvenience*, he thought.

He grinned. No matter what life threw at him, he would find a way to get through it with a smile on his face and his middle finger raised high.

He put the car in gear and pulled away from the curb.

He heard a loud bang, almost like the sound of a shotgun. He shut off the engine and got out. He walked around the vehicle and saw his right rear wheel was flat.

So much for the smile and the raised middle finger, he thought.

EIGHT

Fisher glanced at Holt and saw the strain on his face. *I'd prefer it if you went home*, she thought. Her partner was in mourning, and she worried his emotions could cloud his judgment. As investigators, they were supposed to be impartial, but this case was personal, Fisher knew, even for her. She had met Isaiah a few times, and she found him polite, respectable, and full of energy. He seemed like he could not sit still in one place for long. There was always something that needed his immediate attention.

Holt's gaze did not move away from Isaiah's Chrysler. He was not going to leave Isaiah, and Fisher was not going to try to make him leave. If someone she cared for had been brutally victimized, she would damn well do everything in her power to find out who did it.

The crime scene unit would soon be going over the area with a fine-tooth comb, and the medical examiner was on her way too. Holt and Fisher had to conduct their preliminary examination before anything was touched or moved.

Fisher placed her hand on Holt's shoulder. He slowly turned to face her.

"You up for it?" she asked.

Holt took a deep breath and let it out.

He nodded.

Fisher pulled on a pair of latex gloves and handed a pair to Holt. He put them on.

They approached the body together.

Isaiah was wearing a Milton College sweatshirt. He had dark curly hair and olive skin. He was a handsome kid, the product of a white mother and a black father. He had full lips, an aquiline nose, and emerald eyes. His eyes were closed, but Fisher remembered how bright and full of life they once were.

The front of Isaiah's shirt and the side of his neck and head were covered in thick red blood. The smell was overpowering.

Fisher gently pulled the driver's side door open. Shards of glass fell by her feet. She scanned the car's interior. Glass was everywhere—on the seats, the floor, and the dashboard. The glass was from the passenger's side window, which was completely shattered.

The Chrysler was an older model that lacked the technology that came with the latest models. No GPS, no back camera, no lane assist. For a moment, Fisher wished the car had GPS. They could have used the device to track Isaiah's movements the night he died.

"It's not his car," Holt said.

She looked up at him. He, too, was leaning into the vehicle. "How do you know?" she asked.

"Isaiah was saving up to buy a brand-new Dodge Ram. I was supposed to go with him after the semester was over."

Fisher's eyes narrowed. "We need to find out whose car it is then."

NINE

Even with a cracked windshield and broken taillights, Callaway made it to his destination after putting on his spare tire. As he pulled into the auto shop, he felt grateful no police cruiser had passed by him on the way over. The cops would have ticketed him for equipment violations.

He stepped out when a Hispanic man appeared from the garage. He had smooth dark hair, a pencil-thin mustache above his upper lip, and scruffs on his chin. He was wearing blue overalls. He wiped the grease off his hands with a cloth and smiled. "Lee Callaway, to what do I owe the pleasure?"

"Hello, Julio," Callaway said sheepishly.

Julio's smile faded when he saw the condition the Charger was in. "What happened?" he asked.

"It's a long story."

"Let me guess. You slept with your client's wife, and he hurt you and your baby."

Callaway frowned. "How'd you know he did anything to *me*?"

"Your face, man. Those tissues stuffed in your nose makes you look like a warthog."

Callaway pulled out the tissues. His nostrils stung. "I need you to fix the Charger," he said.

"Sure, that's what I'm in business for," Julio said. "The only question is, do you have the money to pay for the repairs?"

Julio was aware of Callaway's money troubles. In fact, Callaway still owed him for the last two oil changes he had done for him.

"You know I'm good for it," Callaway said.

"That's what you always say," Julio said, sounding exasperated. "And I believe you, but then you disappear until *you* need me again."

"Listen, I've been busy. You hear about the Gardener case?"

"I read it in the papers. I heard you got a nice chunk of change out of it."

"How'd you hear that? It wasn't printed anywhere."

"People talk when they are waiting for their cars to be fixed. I'm a good listener, you know." Julio gave him a crooked smile. "You still have any of that money left over?"

Callaway's shoulders drooped. "No."

"I figured that. You can't help yourself, can you? It must have been a very special horse you bet on."

"Actually, I gave most of it to Patti."

Julio's eyes widened. "You did?"

"Yeah, I figured the temptation of a special horse would be too much for me."

Julio laughed. "I never thought I'd see the day when you put other people over yourself."

Callaway was not amused.

"But, I'm still going to need cash upfront to fix your ride," Julio said.

"Come on," Callaway pleaded. "Do me this one favor."

"Sorry, Lee. Not this time."

"How about we barter?"

"Barter what?"

"My services for your services. You fix my car, and I follow your wife to make sure she's not cheating on you."

Julio almost keeled over laughing. "You do know my wife and I have been together for over fifteen years, right? And we got three daughters that we love more than anything in the world. There's no way in hell my wife's doing anything behind my back."

"You sure about that?"

"More than you'd ever be certain of anything in *your* life."

Callaway smiled. He knew Julio and his wife were high school sweethearts. They got married right after graduation.

"That's why it'll be the easiest job I ever take," Callaway said, his smile still not fading.

Julio sighed and shook his head. "Fine. I'll see what spare parts I've got in the shop and work on your baby, but you still have to pay me when you get the money, got it? I've got a family to feed and a business to run."

"Deal," Callaway said. "Make sure it's like new."

"I always do," Julio said.

"Oh, and I need one more favor."

TEN

Holt thought he could handle the sight of Isaiah, all bloodied and dead. His years of experience had taught him to disassociate his feelings from the task at hand. In this case, he found the task was too much.

"I'll go survey the area," he said to Fisher.

She nodded and went back to examining Isaiah's body.

Holt had to get away. He should not have stayed. But he could not leave Isaiah like this. He felt like he was abandoning him at a time when he needed him the most. But Isaiah was gone, and he was not coming back. There was nothing Holt could do to change that.

He loosened his tie and unbuttoned his shirt collar. He was suffocating. He broke into a cold sweat. The back of his shirt stuck to his body.

Holt's emotions were all over the place. He had gone from initial shock to anger, and now sadness was hitting him hard.

He walked to the back of the furniture store. He pushed himself up against the wall. He wanted to cry. He wanted to scream. He wanted to punch something or someone.

He wanted to hurt the person who had hurt Isaiah.

He took deep breaths to calm himself.

He could not afford to fall apart now. If Fisher saw him like this, she would report him to her superiors. But she would do so out of love and concern.

The last time tragedy hit him, he had nearly lost his mind.

He had flown to another country to punish those whom he felt were responsible for what happened. He returned a broken and disappointed man.

He never imagined he would go through this again.

He shut his eyes tight. Tears flowed down his cheeks.

When Isaiah was born, Holt was at the hospital. Until then, his family had not had a birth in years. The excitement in the waiting room was palpable. He could not believe he was going to be an uncle. He remembered hearing the cries of a child when his brother-in-law, Dennis, burst into the room and announced the baby was a boy. Dennis was in tears. So was Holt. They hugged like they had won an NBA championship.

Isaiah was so tiny when Holt first laid eyes on him. He was pink all over, and he was huddled into a ball. He looked so scared of the world around him. Holt was petrified when his sister, Marjorie, asked him to hold the little boy. Holt worried he might crush his nephew with his big hands, but his sister encouraged him to hold Isaiah. She knew he would never harm this boy. She also knew he would never let anyone else harm this boy either.

Holt suddenly felt like he had failed Isaiah and Marjorie.

ELEVEN

The Chevy Impala was not much to look at. The exterior was dented and covered in rust spots. The interior was outdated, and there were tears in the seat fabric. The car was a late-nineties model, and it had over three hundred thousand clicks on the odometer. But despite all that, the engine had started up right away, and the car drove smoothly. There was an odd noise in the engine, but Julio assured him it was nothing.

Callaway could not really complain. He had not paid for the car. It was a loaner. Julio used it to run errands, such as picking up parts from manufacturers or driving to customers whose cars had broken down and were pulled off on the side of the road.

The radio did not work properly, and the air conditioning and heating were not functioning at full capacity, but again, this was something Callaway could ignore. Had it not been for Julio's generosity, Callaway would be taking public transit about now. Taking the bus or train would make his job as a private investigator impossible. How could he tail a cheating spouse while he was on a subway train? What if he had to extricate himself from a dangerous situation? He could not make a run for it only to be stuck at a bus stop waiting for the next bus. But public transit would save a lot of money. The Charger was not cheap to service and to maintain. The car did not just eat gas—it swallowed it by the mouthful. He was constantly filling up.

He could get an economical vehicle, maybe even a hybrid or one of those electric cars, but the Charger was his prized possession. The one thing he never risked losing.

There were times he owed money to the wrong people. They offered to take the Charger off his hands in exchange for wiping out his debt. He always turned them down. The Charger was not for sale or for barter. He would somehow find the money to pay the loan sharks back, but he would not let anyone else drive his "baby."

It irked him that someone had taken out their anger on the Charger because of him. The only consolation was that they did not do more harm to *him*. His health came first, and then the Charger's.

Julio would make the Charger as good as new, but Callaway still had to find a way to pay him. He hated taking advantage of others. Julio was a good person, and he had a family to feed. Callaway would never stiff him willingly if he had the money, which he almost never did.

Why couldn't I just get a job with a steady income? he thought. *Why do I have to be so stubborn and be a private eye?*

He knew the answer: he was addicted to chaos and danger.

He knew full well the repercussions of sleeping with a client's wife, but he still did it. It was dumb, reckless, and immoral. The latter Callaway never cared much for, though.

How did he expect the husband to react once he found out? Callaway was lucky he walked away with only a broken nose. Something far worse could have happened to him.

As he pulled into the parking lot of a restaurant, he vowed he would change his ways and live a more responsible life.

Deep down, he knew it was an empty promise, one he would break the moment he got the chance.

TWELVE

Holt went back to the Chrysler when he saw the medical examiner leaning into the vehicle.

Andrea Wakefield had short, cropped hair and round prescription glasses. Her petite body was covered in a white lab coat.

She must have come straight from her office, Holt thought.

Wakefield was known for arriving early at work and leaving late. If there was something that was puzzling her, she would work all night until she solved it.

She stood up the moment she heard him approach.

"Detective Holt," she said. "I'm so sorry for your loss."

"Thank you," he said.

Wakefield stood there for a moment as if unsure of what else to say to Holt. She spent more time with the dead than the living, but she preferred it that way. The living could hide who they really were, but the dead were like open books to her.

Wakefield asked, "Should I do this with Detective Fisher, or would you like to be privy as well?"

"I want to know," he replied.

"What we discuss may be troubling to you."

"I'm a professional," he said. "This is what I do. I solve murders, and right now, I want to know what happened to my nephew."

Holt did not realize he had raised his voice.

Wakefield looked over at Fisher.

Fisher nodded.

"Very well," Wakefield said. "Perhaps it might be better if you observed from the other side of the vehicle. There is only so much room in here."

Holt walked around the Chrysler and leaned into the passenger's side window.

Wakefield pulled out a small penlight from her pocket. She flashed the light on Isaiah's temple. "From my initial assessment, the victim died of gunshot wounds to the neck and the right side of the head." Wakefield moved the light over two black holes—one in the lower neck and the other in the temple. "If it's any consolation, the victim died immediately."

"It's not," Holt said sternly.

Wakefield coughed to clear her throat. "Moving on, the shots were fired from the passenger's side of the vehicle. The wounds are on the right side of the body, which confirms this premise."

Fisher asked, "Why did the shooter not attack from the driver's side? It would have been much more efficient."

"That's a good question," Wakefield replied.

"The shooter didn't want Isaiah to see him coming," Holt said. "He was ambushed."

They were silent for a moment.

"What else can you tell us?" Fisher asked.

Wakefield's eyes darted over the body, recording and analyzing even the smallest details.

"I noticed the victim's left ring finger is swollen and discolored," she said.

"Isaiah broke it," Holt said. "He was going up for a block and his hand hit the backboard."

Wakefield looked confused. "Going up for a what?"

"The victim is a basketball player," Fisher explained. "It's a sport injury."

"Okay, that would explain it. Other than that, there are no contusions or lesions visible on the body that I can see. Naturally, once I conduct a full autopsy, I will give you a definitive answer."

"Why do you think he was still wearing a seatbelt?" Holt asked.

Wakefield shrugged. "Maybe he was waiting for someone."

Fisher pointed at the keys still in the ignition. "It looks like he was ready to drive away at a moment's notice."

Who were you waiting for, Isaiah? Holt thought. *Did they have something to do with what happened to you?*

THIRTEEN

Callaway went inside the restaurant and walked straight to a booth in the corner.

A waitress came over. She had blonde hair that was pulled back in a ponytail. She wore a tight-fitting t-shirt and an apron tied around her waist.

"Don't tell me," she said. "You slept with a client's wife and he beat you up."

How do people know what I did? he thought. *Is it that obvious?*

"Actually, there was a terrorist threat that involved blowing up an airplane. Had it not been for my quick intervention, a million lives would have been lost as a result of it," Callaway said.

She raised an eyebrow. "I didn't know a plane could hold a million people."

"You didn't let me complete my story," he said, feigning disappointment. "The terrorists were planning to crash the plane into a nuclear plant."

"I thought you said they were going to blow it up?"

"They were going to blow it up inside the nuclear plant."

"After they had crashed it?"

"What can I say? These terrorists aren't that bright."

Joely Paterson finally smiled. "So, what really happened, Lee?"

"I just told you."

"You told me a plot from an action movie."

"Was it good? Maybe I can write the screenplay and sell it for millions of dollars."

"Good luck with that. After you get your millions, maybe you can pay me back for all the lunches I've given you."

"Speaking of lunches…"

"No."

"You didn't even let me finish."

"You have to pay if you want to eat here," she said. "If Bill sees me give you any more freebies, he'll throw you out and fire me."

Bill was the restaurant's owner, and he had come to despise Callaway.

Callaway was always finding a way to avoid paying for his meal. He was no better than a beggar on the street.

"How's your son?" Callaway asked, changing the subject.

She smiled. "He's growing up fast."

Joely was a single mom. Her then-husband was an equipment manager for a rock band. He went on the road for a tour and never came back. He did call, but only to say he did not see himself being married or a father.

"And what's going on with the music producer?" Callaway asked.

Joely's dream was to become a singer. After she posted her songs online, a producer contacted her. The last time Callaway was at the restaurant, she was going to record a song with the producer.

She frowned. "It didn't work out."

"Why not?"

"Let's say, he was more interested in other things than my singing career."

Callaway's eyes narrowed. "I'm guessing he didn't want a professional relationship?"

She shook her head. "And if I went along with it, he promised he would make me a star."

Callaway knew men with power were always using this tactic to get women to go to bed with them. It was one of the oldest tricks in the book. Make outlandish promises, and when you get what you want, you break those promises.

"I'm sorry," Callaway said.

Joely shrugged. "It's okay. So, why does your nose look like a ripe tomato?" she asked.

"It's that bad, huh?" he replied, not touching his nose. The pain was still fresh in his mind.

"You still haven't seen it?"

"I'm trying not to."

Joely grinned. "If you ask me, it looks really nasty. Must hurt like hell."

"You're enjoying this, aren't you?" Callaway asked.

"Oh, definitely. I bet you deserved it," she replied.

"I didn't."

She stared at him.

"Okay. I fully deserved it." His stomach grumbled. "Can I get a bite to eat?" he asked.

"Money first."

"Come on," he pleaded. "I gave the husband everything I had on me to stop him from hurting me more."

Joely crossed her arms over her chest. "Sorry, Lee. I can't risk losing this job. I need it. You can always go to a homeless shelter down the block. I'm sure their kitchen is still open right now."

"I'm not homeless," he said, waving a finger at her. "I'm Lee Callaway, private investigator extraordinaire. Wait here."

He got up and left the restaurant. He went to the Impala and looked through the glove compartment. He then checked the middle console. They were both empty.

Callaway then flipped the cigarette lighter panel and smiled. The small slot held a bunch of loose coins.

Julio must have left spare change for when he needed it for an emergency.

Callaway hated taking the coins, but he was hungry, and he had no money on him. He had full intention of returning it, though, and that was not considered stealing but more like borrowing.

He scooped out the change and went back inside the restaurant.

FOURTEEN

Fisher cupped her hands over her eyes and peeked through the front window. The furniture store was empty. She was not expecting anything different. There was a for-rent sign taped to the glass, and by the looks of things, the building had been vacant for quite some time. Graffiti was sprayed across the window in various colors. Profanity and crude images were painted for everyone to see.

"I'm not sure if it has surveillance," Fisher said.

"It does, but take a look," Holt said, pointing up with his index finger.

There was a camera at the upper right corner of the front windows, but the camera was tilted at an awkward angle and looked like someone had taken a baseball bat to it.

"I doubt it caught anything," Fisher said.

Holt was thinking the same thing.

"We should contact the owner. He needs to know something… tragic happened on his property," Fisher said, choosing her words carefully. With Holt's emotions raw, saying "death" or "murder" would only hurt him further.

She pulled out her cell phone and dialed the number on the for-rent sign. She was greeted with the voice message of a real estate firm. The owner must have listed the property with the real estate firm in order to find a tenant. By the looks of things, there were no takers.

This isn't surprising, Fisher thought.

The area did not give off the vibe that businesses thrived in this neighborhood. When she drove here, she had seen other stores with closing-sale signs or for-lease signs, and some stores were boarded up with plywood.

Fisher wondered why Isaiah, a kid from a nice family and neighborhood, was in a seedy place like this so early in the morning.

Her thoughts were broken when Holt asked, "Who called it in?"

She blinked. "What do you mean?"

"Who found the body? Someone had to have reported it for the officer to arrive at the scene."

"That's a good question." She punched in a number that took her directly to the 9-1-1 command center. After providing her badge number, she asked the person on the line to replay the call. Fisher put it on speaker so Holt could hear it too.

"9-1-1, what's your emergency?" the operator asked.

"Yeah, there's a guy dead in a parked car in front of *Elegant Furniture*." The voice sounded young and rough.

"Did you say a person is dead?"

"Yeah, he's dead."

"Are you certain?"

"Listen, lady, the brother looks like he got shot up by some bad dudes. He's Isaiah Whitcomb, the basketball player. I've seen his games on TV."

"And where is the body?"

"At the corner of Fairwood and Elm."

"I'll send an officer over. Please stay where you are to answer any questions the officer may have."

"Sorry, lady. I gotta go."

The line went dead.
Holt and Fisher looked at each other.

FIFTEEN

Fisher shut her cell phone as she pondered what she had just heard. Officer McConnell had not seen anyone at the scene. Could the person who called 9-1-1 be responsible for Isaiah's death? Fisher did not think that was likely. Why would he call it in if he was the killer? It just did not make sense. But then again, stranger things had happened before. Regardless of his innocence or guilt, they had to find him. He might know something that could shed light on what happened here.

Holt shut his eyes and rubbed his temples. Fisher could tell the pressure was getting to him. He had a job to do, but he also had his family who was now going to look to him for answers.

"You need to go talk to your sister," Fisher said.

Holt grimaced. She could tell he did not want to leave the scene. He was also delaying facing Marjorie.

"We've got everything we need," she added. "The press is going to want a statement soon. I don't think it's a good idea for you to be in front of the cameras. And I especially don't think it's a good idea for Marjorie to find out about Isaiah via the news."

Holt's shoulders sank and he let out a loud sigh.

"If you want, I'll do it," she said.

He shook his head. "Isaiah was family. It's my duty."

"Do you want me to come with you?"

"No, I'll be fine."

"Okay."

Holt pulled out his cell phone. "I have to call Nancy first. If she found out from someone else, it would devastate her."

Fisher understood. Holt's wife had seen her share of trauma, and it had left her mentally unstable. Even the most trivial setback could send her spiraling into a deep depression.

Holt's devotion to his wife was unlike anything Fisher had ever seen. He protected her as if she was the most fragile thing in the world. If Fisher could describe them, Holt was a granite rock while Nancy was a delicate flower.

To an outsider, their relationship was baffling. Even Fisher wondered how they were still married to each other. But over the years, she realized Nancy gave Holt the hope he needed to keep going.

Holt's work made him see the evil side of human nature. Nancy made him see the beauty in an otherwise bleak world.

They were sort of like Yin and Yang, and they complemented each other in ways no one fully understood, not even Fisher.

As Holt walked away, Fisher could not help but feel sorry for him. He not only had to break the news to his sister, but he also had to break it to Nancy.

Fisher did not want to be in his shoes right now.

SIXTEEN

After a breakfast that consisted of a cup of coffee, a slice of toast, and one egg—all he could afford from the spare change he had found in the Impala—Callaway drove to his new digs, a hotel room he had booked for a month. He could have found something more permanent, but he was never sure when his next assignment would come. There was also the matter of providing the first and last month's rent. He just did not have the money. The hotel was much cheaper by comparison. And if he ever fell behind, he did not need to worry about being evicted. He would just go someplace else, maybe even a rooming house if it came down to it.

The hotel was not five-star by any means. The place was barely two-star, but it was the only place he could afford at the moment. The hotel had running hot water, functioning plumbing, and he was assured the heating worked. Since the weather was still warm, he would take their word about the heating system. He had seen a few cockroaches, but so far, no rodents. If he ever saw mice or a rat, he would vacate the unit in an instant. Callaway could not stand the sight of those little creatures. He shivered at the mere thought of them.

When Callaway came to check-in, he had seen a long line of people at the elevators. He had specifically requested a unit on one of the lower levels so he could take the stairs. He was booked a room on the third floor.

He unlocked the door and entered the cramped room. It had a bed on the right, and a futon sat beside the bed. A TV stand was across from the futon. The room had a bathroom, but no kitchen. Callaway did not know how to cook, so a kitchen would have been useless. A tiny fridge would have been nice, but the room did come with a tiny microwave. Callaway could always re-heat his takeout leftovers.

He pulled off his coat and dropped it on the bed. He made his way to the bathroom. He braced himself and turned on the lights.

He looked far worse than he imagined.

The reflection in the mirror was not a pretty sight. His nose had swollen into a lump. The redness in his eyes had not dissipated, and there was still puffiness underneath the eyelids. He turned on the taps and tried to wipe off the blood on his shirt. He realized his cleaning attempt was futile. Even though the t-shirt was black, the stain would be there forever.

He pulled the shirt off and threw it in the garbage.

He then took a long, hot shower. He savored cleansing his body of all the filth from the last twenty-four hours.

Feeling somewhat refreshed, he went out and sat on the bed. He grabbed a bottle of painkillers from the side table, dropped two pills into his palm, and downed the pills with a glass of water.

He pushed himself up on the bed and rested his head on the wall. He closed his eyes and waited for the painkillers to take effect.

He felt like crap, and he looked it too.

Why can't I be more like my parents? he thought. They were good people who went to church every Sunday. His father never drank, gambled, or womanized. The only thing that mattered was God and family.

Callaway was the opposite. He had not stepped inside a church in decades, and his actions and vices had led to the dissolution of his marriage.

I'm a perfect example of how to screw up your life, he thought.

His eyes snapped open when he realized he did not have his digital camera. In his rush to get away, he had left his camera at the client's house. The camera did not have any incriminating photos, only what he took of the client's wife when he was on a stakeout at the house. But now he would have to go and purchase a new camera, another expense he could not afford.

He felt a migraine coming on.

He reached for more painkillers.

SEVENTEEN

Holt watched as Marjorie sobbed into her hands. Dennis stood silently by the kitchen sink.

At first, Marjorie did not believe him. She had even slapped him for saying something so terrible, but when she saw the pain in his eyes, she knew he was telling the truth.

Compared to him, Marjorie was half his size. She looked more like their mother while he looked more like their father.

Marjorie was seven years older than him. There was a brother in between, but he was born with cerebral palsy and died before the age of two. His mother thought having another baby would make her get over the grief of losing a child, but Holt's birth reminded her of the boy she lost. She began to experience mental breakdowns. By the time Holt was four, she had been in and out of mental institutions over half a dozen times.

His father was a proud man, but after seeing his wife fall apart, he began to hit the bottle. He eventually drank himself to death, leaving Marjorie to take care of Holt and raise him. With the help of relatives—particularly his grandparents—Holt and Marjorie made it to adulthood.

This life experience was why he was so gentle and understanding with Nancy. Holt and his wife had adopted a little boy from Ukraine. The boy was supposed to complete their family. He did not live to see his first birthday, dying from a rare form of cancer.

His death had hit Nancy hard. The loss hit Holt harder. But instead of tearing their relationship apart, the loss made them closer.

Unlike his father, who was a product of the time when men did not share their feelings with their spouses, Holt shared everything with Nancy. He discovered that by sharing how he felt, he became extra sensitive to her needs.

As he watched Marjorie weep for her lost child, he could not help but feel like tragedy somehow followed his family wherever they went. There was a brother he never got to meet, then there was a child he never got to see grow up, and now there was Isaiah.

"Where's Brit?" Holt asked. Britney was Isaiah's younger sister. She was a senior in high school. If Isaiah excelled in sports, Brit excelled in academics. She had her eyes set on attending Harvard, MIT, or Stanford.

Marjorie looked up. "She's having a sleepover at a friend's house." She turned to her husband. "We have to let her know."

"I'll call her right now," Dennis said and left the room.

Marjorie faced Holt. She held out her arms and he embraced her. There were many times he had gone to her when he needed a shoulder to cry on. She was more of a mother to him than a sister.

"Oh, Greg," she said.

Holt's eyes were moist as he stared into hers. Until he met Nancy, he always thought Marjorie was the most beautiful woman in the world. With age, wrinkles had started to appear on her face. Gray strands were visible in her hair, but her eyes were still vibrant and youthful.

That day, however, they were filled with pain and anguish.

He wanted to tell her everything would be all right, but he knew it would never be. Holt had lost a child he barely knew, and it continued to haunt him. Isaiah was the first-born, and he had become the pride and joy of the family. Holt's only wish now was that Marjorie did not fall apart like their mother. Marjorie had been the one constant thing in his life. She was the rock that held him together. If something happened to her, Holt did not know how he would keep going.

EIGHTEEN

The Callaway Private Investigation Office was on top of a soup and noodle restaurant. In order to get to the office, potential clients had to walk to the back of the building, go up the narrow metal stairs, and knock on a black metal door with no sign. There was only a telephone number taped to the door. If someone was eager to find him, they could always call him. Or better yet, they could visit his website and contact him there.

There were several reasons for not having a sign displayed outside. Over the years, Callaway had gotten himself into too many difficult situations. This had caused him to borrow money from unsavory people. These people did not take too kindly when their money was not paid back on time. Even if Callaway was only a few hours late with the money, he would have thugs on his tail in no time. Callaway preferred not to deal with them in his office, where there was only one way in and out. It would be easy for someone to corner him in the office and do harm to him.

Then there were the husbands and wives of his clients. Callaway had caught them in compromising positions, and as such, they acted like cornered wild animals. They would do anything to prevent their misdeeds from reaching their spouses. If confronted, some clients' spouses even offered to double his fee, just as long as he handed over the incriminating evidence.

Callaway never did.

Once he made an agreement with a client, it was set in stone. Callaway would not break it, no matter how much money was thrown his way. If word got out that his loyalty was not to his client but to the highest bidder, no one would hire him. Catching cheaters in action required a great deal of delicacy and trust. That trust was irreparable if broken, and he took winning and keeping the trust of his clients seriously.

He unlocked his office and entered. The space was small and windowless, lacked air conditioning, and the heating barely worked, making the winter months unbearable at times.

He could always close the office. It was not vital to his profession, but he liked the idea of having a place to go to. He could not imagine waiting at home for the phone to ring. Instead, he preferred waiting in his office for the phone to ring. Another factor for keeping the office was the low rent. It was perhaps the cheapest in the city.

He shut the door and pulled up a chair behind a small desk. A sofa was in the corner, which Callaway sometimes used as a bed. There were springs poking out from certain spots, but the sofa was not entirely uncomfortable. After an exhausting day, with nowhere else to go, the sofa was far better than sleeping on a park bench. If his office had a shower and bathroom, he would consider living there permanently just to save money.

On the wall across from the sofa was a flat-screen TV, courtesy of a generous client. He grabbed the remote and turned the TV on. It was always on the twenty-four-hour news channel. Callaway always wanted to know what was going on in the city. There was no telling where he would find his next client.

He then turned on the laptop on the desk. He hoped someone had contacted him about a job. After what happened the night before, he could use some good news.

NINETEEN

The members of the crime scene unit went over the crime scene diligently. They found three shell casings—one near the front right tire, one underneath the Chrysler, and one on the passenger's side floor mat. The evidence further supported the theory that Isaiah was ambushed. The key was still in the ignition, and his seatbelt was still on, which indicated he did not even have a chance to react.

Fisher pondered these facts over and over as she surveyed the crime scene. The press had gathered in full force. A star athlete had been murdered, and the press never failed to pander to public interest in such crimes. Were it not for Officer McConnell; the gathered press would be all over the scene. They could care less if they contaminated the evidence. They had stories to file.

Fisher found herself glancing over at McConnell. She was not sure why. Maybe it was because he was tall and handsome. And she also caught him staring in her direction a few times.

She blushed whenever their eyes met. He merely smiled back. There was something happening between them, but she did not want to get distracted. She had a huge task in front of her, one that was tragic and personal.

Holt was a wreck when he had driven away. He did not want to leave, but he trusted her. She would not miss any details that could help them find the person who had brutally killed Isaiah.

Isaiah did not even see his attacker coming. His arms and hands had no defensive wounds, which further showed how his killer had snuck up on him.

Fisher shook her head. *No person should die like this*, she thought.

There was something else that troubled her about the scene. A six-foot-high wooden wall covered the back of the furniture store. There was no way the shooter could have driven up from behind, parked his car, fired into the Chrysler, and sped away.

There was only one way in and out at the furniture store, and the Chrysler was parked in such a way that it faced the door. Isaiah would have seen the killer approach.

What if he did, but he did nothing about it? What if he was waiting for his killer? That would explain why the keys were in the ignition, his seatbelt was secured, but the Chrysler was not running.

What if Isaiah came here to meet someone, but then an argument broke out and he was killed because of it?

This was a possibility, a very strong one.

But there was another possibility. What if the shooter came on foot? That would explain the ambush theory, and a shooter fleeing on foot could have been seen by someone. Maybe the person who called 9-1-1 had seen the killer. At the moment, though, they had no idea who he was or where he was.

Fisher rubbed her eyes. This was supposed to be her day off. With Isaiah being Holt's nephew, Fisher was now the lead investigator on the case. The police department had guidelines for detectives working on cases involving loved ones. They were not entirely prohibited from participating, but it was frowned upon. There was fear that the personal nature of the investigation could affect the detective's ability to do his or her job. But Fisher was now in charge, and Holt would assist her. She was not going to let him down.

Isaiah's body had already been taken to the morgue, and the CSU would be on the scene for the next couple of hours. There was nothing more she could do here. She decided to survey the area. She wanted to know why Isaiah was here in the first place.

TWENTY

Fisher ducked under the yellow police tape. Immediately, the press converged on her. They snapped photos of her, aimed video cameras in her direction, and hurled questions at her. She suddenly felt overwhelmed.

It's a good thing Holt's not here, she thought. *He would have punched some reporters.*

She was trying to push her way through when Officer McConnell appeared next to her. He held the press back as she made her way across the road. She gave him an appreciative nod. He tapped the brim of his cap in return.

The furniture store was surrounded by apartment buildings and retail stores. On the opposite side was a motel. Fisher hoped their security cameras caught something.

As she got closer to the motel, her hopes were quickly dashed. The motel looked to be in far worse shape up close than from afar. The exterior paint was peeling or chipped, the cracked windows were held together by duct tape, and the front door handle was rusted and had turned brown.

She went inside. A pungent smell hit her nose—a combination of mold and body odors.

The lobby carpet was damp and stained. The interior walls were painted an ugly color, and the paint bubbled here and there. As she passed the elevators, a sign posted next to them made her pause: CHILDREN UNDER 18 NOT ACCOMPANIED BY AN ADULT ARE NOT PERMITTED TO USE THE ELEVATORS. STAIRS ONLY. She thought the rule was odd but continued ahead.

She found the owner in a cramped office. He gave her a gap-toothed smile. He was wearing an old shirt, jeans, and a large buckled belt.

"Morning, ma'am," he said.

She flashed her badge. "What's with the sign at the elevators?" she asked out of curiosity.

"Oh, that," the owner replied with a short laugh. "The elevators don't always work properly. We once had a kid get stuck in them. It took the firefighters two hours to get him out. The kid was traumatized by the ordeal. I figured I'd raise the age limit for elevator users in case something like that ever happened again."

"Didn't the kid's parents sue you?"

"They wanted to, but once they realized this place was worth less than the cost of hiring a lawyer, they decided not to."

"What about liability insurance? They could have gotten something from that."

"I got no insurance," the owner replied.

Fisher was surprised.

"I got a license, though," the owner said. "It's probably forty years old. I got it here somewhere if you want to take a look."

"No, thanks," Fisher replied. "Are you aware there was a murder across the road from your motel?"

His eyes widened. "There was?"

"You didn't know?"

"No. I rarely leave the motel. I have to be here in case a guest arrives."

Right, Fisher thought.

"And do you get a lot of guests?" she asked.

"Absolutely."

"You do?" she said, not believing him.

"We charge by the hour, so we see people at all times of the day… and night."

She understood. He was referring to hookers and their clients. His motel was used as a rendezvous spot.

"Do you have security cameras?" she asked.

He shook his head. "Never needed them. Can't afford them either. Plus, my guests would prefer not to be recorded entering and leaving the establishment." The owner made it sound like it was a five-star hotel. *It's more like a dump*, Fisher thought. *The people who visit are nothing but unsavory characters.*

What was Isaiah doing in a neighborhood like this?

TWENTY-ONE

After going through his emails, Callaway leaned back in his chair, feeling completely dejected. He could not believe no one was reaching out to hire him. There was not a single message about a job. Just to make sure everything was working properly, he went on to his website and used the Contact page to send himself a message. It came through without a hitch.

How can I have no queries? he thought. The city was brimming with cheaters and philanderers. Surely, they could use his services.

After the Paul Gardener case, Callaway figured he would hit it big. People would be contacting him in droves. And they were.

Unfortunately, all these people wanted him to do something he was not qualified for. Relatives wrote to him, seeking help in exonerating their loved ones. Even convicted criminals were sending him information on their cases with the hope that Callaway would somehow be able to get them out of prison. They thought he was some kind of "miracle man" who would find the missing evidence that could lead them to their freedom.

Most, though perhaps not all, were guilty of the crimes they were punished for. A jury of their peers had gone through the evidence and given a verdict against them. There was nothing Callaway could really do to change that. He was not a lawyer, and he was no longer a law enforcement member. True, he had contacts both in high and low places—mostly low places—and he was dogged and determined to complete any job he had agreed to take on. Apart from that, he was no different than other civilians.

There were cases of unsolved murders or missing persons going back decades that broke his heart. The people who contacted him about such cases were barely clinging onto hope, and they felt Callaway was their last resort.

He could always take their money and "try" to look into those cold cases, but he knew he would only be toying with his clients' emotions. He did not have the time or the resources to take on cases that dated back many years. If the police could not do anything, how could a guy like him do it?

Losing a loved one to crime and never being able to see them again was not something Callaway took lightly. The people who reached out to him were looking for answers, or they simply wanted justice or closure. He knew full well he could never give that to them, so he always politely turned them away. Better to disappoint them now than take their money and disappoint them later when he came up empty. The latter would be like pouring salt on their wounds. He would not take advantage of the desperate, which is exactly what these people were. Callaway was not the savior they were looking for.

He sighed and rubbed his face. His hand inadvertently touched his nose. Bolts of pain shot up into his brain. He grimaced. He had placed a bandage over his nose, but even then, it was still sensitive.

He would need more painkillers.

TWENTY-TWO

Fisher was at the Milton PD seated behind her desk when she spotted Holt stepping out of the elevator.

She got up and approached him. His face was drawn, and he looked like he had been through hell.

"How's Marjorie doing?" she asked.

"Not well."

"And your brother-in-law?"

"Dennis is not talking much. I think it hit him harder than Marjorie. He's grieving in his own way, I guess."

"Did you take them to the morgue?" Fisher asked.

"I did," Holt said. "I knew it was Isaiah already, but Marjorie and Dennis wanted to see him with their own eyes. They wanted to confirm their worst fear."

Holt's jaw tightened.

"How are *you* doing?" Fisher gently asked him. She could see he was trying to put up a stalwart front, but she could also see the turmoil in his bloodshot eyes.

"I'm good."

Fisher looked around. There was no one around them. "You can talk to me, Greg. I'm your partner."

"I said I'm good."

His eyes moistened.

Fisher sighed. "If you don't talk to me, I'm going to report you to OAP."

The Officer Assistance Program was set up to help officers with professional or personal matters. If they were under mental stress, going through difficulties at home, or having financial troubles, they were required to speak to an OAP staff member. The department believed officers under some form of duress would not be able to perform their duties as required. Worse, they could do something that could harm their career, or more importantly, affect the department negatively. The latter was the real reason for the OAP. A vast majority of the officers believed the department could care less about what they were going through. The only thing that mattered was the budget and the performance of the department as a whole.

Holt grimaced at the thought of going to the OAP for help. He sighed, sounding heartbroken. "I never thought losing Isaiah would affect me so much," he said slowly. "Nancy and I have been through our share of hardships, and I always figured because of that, I would be able to handle anything life threw my way. I'm not so sure of that anymore."

"A loss is a loss," Fisher said. "No matter who it is and when it happens, it affects us all in powerful ways."

Holt let her words of wisdom sink in.

"How is Nancy?" she asked.

"She did not take the news well," he replied. "I sent her to her mother's. I thought it would be good for her." He cleared his throat and wiped his eyes. "What's going on with the case?"

The determination was back in his voice.

"I still have not been able to contact the furniture store owner."

"Do you have his address? We should go knock on his door," Holt said, eager to do something.

"I think we should focus on the owner of the Chrysler."

"Do you have a name?"

"I ran the license plate through the motor vehicle database and found it's registered to a Jay Bledson."

Holt's eyes widened.

"I know who that is," he said.

TWENTY-THREE

Callaway was browsing news articles on his laptop when he heard a noise that made him pause.

Someone was walking up to his office.

He was not expecting anyone. He glanced at the desk drawer, where he now kept his gun.

He reached for the drawer, but a gut feeling made him pull his hand back.

I'm being paranoid, he thought, shaking his head. *I don't owe money to anyone, nor have I done anything wrong.*

The footsteps came to a halt. The door opened, and a woman poked her head in. Callaway relaxed. His landlady was short, slim, and Asian. Her hair was tied into a ponytail, and she had on a floral-pattern dress and flat heels.

His landlady never showed up unless he was behind on rent, or he did something that warranted her speaking to him. On a number of occasions, he had forgotten to turn off the lights before leaving or left the TV on at full volume all night. Once during the winter, he did not shut the door properly, and strong winds blew it open. The heaters worked on overdrive to warm up the room, and the heating bill skyrocketed.

The landlady was a stickler for money, and Callaway could not fault her for that. His rent barely covered any expenses, and she also had the soup and noodle restaurant to run. He had heard the restaurant was struggling as of late.

He raised his arms up high. "Ms. Chen, I didn't do it. I swear."

She ignored his comment and looked around the office. She did not step inside. The office was his property, after all, just as long as his rent was up to date.

"I'm good for this month and next," he added. With the fee from the Gardener case, he was able to cover his unpaid rent and also pay in advance for the upcoming months.

"I'm not here about that," she said with a wave of her hand. Her eyes narrowed. "What happened to your face?"

"It's not important."

"You look like a guy who got beat up by a woman."

"Not a woman, but her husband," he said, correcting her.

"You look like a sad pig," Ms. Chen said before she burst out laughing.

He sighed. *I better get used to the jokes until my face heals*, he thought. "What can I do for you, Ms. Chen?"

She turned serious again. "There is a lady in the restaurant who wants to talk to you."

"Why doesn't she come to my office? I'm right upstairs."

"She can't."

"Why not?"

"You'll see for yourself."

She turned around and descended the metal stairs.

What the hell just happened? he thought.

He locked his office and went down to the restaurant. It was small, with enough space for eight tables and chairs. He quickly spotted a woman seated at one of the tables by the windows.

She had dark, cropped hair, and she wore an oversized sweater. Her eyes were covered by large sunglasses, which Callaway recognized as those worn by people with sight impairment. The walking cane next to the table further confirmed this. She also wore black leather gloves.

He approached her table. She smiled. "You're Lee Callaway, right?" she said.

"How'd you know?" he asked, surprised.

"When I asked the lady for you, I heard her leave the restaurant. The door chimes whenever someone enters and leaves. The lady's shoes also make a very distinctive sound when they hit the floor, so I could tell when she was back. Right after that, I heard the door chime again, along with footsteps approaching me, so I can only assume you are Lee Callaway."

The smile did not fade from her face.

"Amazing," he said. "Do you mind if I sit down?"

"Please do," she replied. "It would make for an awkward conversation if I'm sitting and you're standing."

He pulled up a chair. He was almost grateful she could not see the heavy bandage covering his nose. "What can I do for you, Ms.…?"

"Elle Pearson, but please call me Elle."

"Okay, what can I do for you, Elle?"

"I need your help finding my sister."

TWENTY-FOUR

Milton College boasted over five thousand undergraduates and close to three thousand graduate students. The school specialized in arts and sciences and had a separate school of engineering.

Isaiah was not a top prospect in high school. He only blossomed once he got to college. As a result, top basketball programs in the country were not knocking on his door. North Carolina, Louisville, Duke, Kentucky, had all passed on him.

Holt remembered that Isaiah was crushed. He believed he had what it took to make it in the top-tier schools. Dennis, on the other hand, was grateful his son had not been accepted in any of those programs. He worried Isaiah would get lost in the limelight. He also wanted Isaiah to get an education. Dennis was an alumnus of Milton College. He wanted his son to follow in his footsteps. But he was not ignorant of Isaiah's potential.

In recent years, Milton College had risen from being known as an academic school to one, which also had a thriving basketball program. They had the funding needed to push the program forward, and they had a young coach who knew how to connect with the players. Some of the top high school prospects in the state had joined the team. They saw the Milton Cougars as an opportunity to play big minutes and thus showcase their talent for professional scouts.

Isaiah was just looking for the opportunity to step onto the court. He knew the moment he did. The world would see what he could do.

When the college offered Isaiah a scholarship, Marjorie and Dennis were beyond elated. Their son would go to a respectable college, and he would not be far away from them. But it came with a caveat: Isaiah would have to prove he could make it onto the team.

Over the summer, Isaiah was on campus every day. He worked harder for the upcoming season than all the prospects combined. Holt had driven him back and forth for practice on a number of occasions. He had seen the focus and determination on Isaiah's face. He tried to tell him to enjoy his time as a student, as these could be the best years of his youth. But Isaiah would have none of it. He wanted to succeed, and he was not going to let anything stop him.

Holt could not fault Isaiah for wanting the best for himself. Holt also had the same sense of determination when he was focused on a case. He thought of nothing else but catching the perpetrator.

Holt and Nancy were in the stands for Isaiah's first game. Holt was overcome with pride when he saw Isaiah in the Milton Cougars uniform. Isaiah was subbed into the game in the middle of the first half, with his team trailing behind by ten points. Isaiah's infectious energy, his hounding of the other team's best players, and his ability to hustle and do all the dirty work resulted in his team squeaking out a win. Isaiah tallied eight points, twelve rebounds, two steals, and three blocked shots in that game.

The joy on Nancy's face that night was something Holt would never forget.

TWENTY-FIVE

The five-thousand-seat gymnasium was located in the middle of the campus. During home games, the crowds were loud and boisterous, sending a vibrant surge of energy into the arena. But now the gym was eerily quiet. The news of Isaiah's death had reached the college.

Holt and Fisher entered the gym and spotted two people at the other end of the court.

An older man was consoling a student. The student was in tears as the man spoke gently and reassuringly to him.

Holt had never spoken to Assistant Coach Jay Bledson before, but he had seen him on the sidelines during the games. Bledson was short in comparison to the players he coached. He was slim, and he was wearing a maroon t-shirt—the Cougars team color—and he had on black shorts.

Holt introduced himself and Fisher, after which Bledson took them further away from the weeping student. He did not want the student to overhear their conversation.

"Isaiah's death has hit the team hard," Bledson said with sadness in his eyes. "We have a road game tonight. I don't think anyone on the team is thinking about that right now."

"Where's Coach Loughton?" Holt asked. Earl Loughton was the Cougars' head coach.

"He's meeting with faculty right now. And I believe afterward he'll visit Isaiah's parents."

"Isaiah was my nephew," Holt said.

"I'm sorry for your loss," Bledson said.

"Thank you."

"Isaiah mentioned that someone in his family worked for the Milton Police. I guess he was talking about you."

Holt felt a pang of sadness. *Isaiah talked about me?* he thought.

"You're here about the Chrysler, aren't you?" Bledson asked, getting right to the point.

"Yes. It is registered to you," Holt replied. "Why was Isaiah driving it?"

"He said he needed it to run an errand."

"And you let him take it?"

"Sure, why not? Most of these kids come from poor families. They don't have much money, so forget being able to own a car."

Holt felt a spark of irritation. "Isaiah's parents have money," he said.

Bledson stared at him. "Listen. I try to help out these kids as best as I can. If they need to go somewhere, I'll give them a ride. If they want to borrow my car while I'm on campus, I'll let them. Just so long as they don't damage it."

"What time did Isaiah borrow your car?" Holt asked.

Bledson pondered the question. "I came to campus around six…"

"This morning?"

"Yes. I try to come in early. It gives me time to work out, and if any of the players want to run drills, I'm available to them."

"What happened after you came in?" Holt asked.

"The moment Isaiah saw me, he asked to borrow the car."

"What was his demeanor like? Was he stressed or upset?"

Bledson thought for a moment. "He looked like he hadn't slept the entire night. I asked if everything was okay, and he gave me a noncommittal answer. I could tell he had a lot on his mind. I did not want to push it, though. He was in a hurry, and he had to be somewhere quick."

Was the furniture store where he had to be? Holt thought.

Bledson said, "I let him take the car on one condition: He had to be back for the eleven a.m. practice. Coach Loughton would be furious if he wasn't. I remember Isaiah grinned and said he'd be back before any of the guys broke a sweat."

Holt remembered that grin. It could be mischievous and reassuring. He often grinned when he was about to do something he should not.

"The next thing I heard was that something terrible had happened to him." Bledson shook his head, his eyes full of disbelief.

Something terrible did happen, Holt thought. *A promising young man's life was brutally taken away.*

TWENTY-SIX

Callaway looked at Elle. "What's your sister's name?" he asked.

"Katie," Elle replied. "Katie Pearson."

"Okay. What happened to her?"

"I don't know. The last time I spoke to her was over three months ago."

Callaway blinked. "Three months?!" he said a little too loudly.

"I contacted the police shortly after our last conversation."

"And?"

"They first told me it's not illegal for a person to disappear, especially if it's an adult."

"How old is your sister?" Callaway asked.

"She turned twenty-two a month ago."

"And what have the police done so far?"

"After I filed a missing persons report, I've not heard back from them."

Callaway knew that was not unusual in cases like these. There were thousands of stories of people who were never found or seen again. The police departments were already backlogged with unsolved murder cases, so a lot of times, the less violent crimes were pushed to the back burner. Unless there was suspicion of foul play, these cases were rarely investigated thoroughly.

"Where does your sister live?" Callaway asked.

"In Milton."

"And you?"

"I live in Mayview."

That's just an hour from here, Callaway thought.

"What was your sister doing in Milton?" he asked.

"She was working and studying."

"Do you have a photo of your sister?"

She unzipped her purse, searched inside, and placed a Polaroid on the table. Callaway picked up the photo.

Katie was smiling. She had blonde hair, dark eyes, and perfect teeth.

"Do you have another photo? Perhaps one with her standing?" Callaway asked. In his experience, a full-body shot was more helpful than the one of a profile.

"Sorry, this is the only one I have," Elle replied.

"What about on your cell phone?"

She smiled. "Why would I have them on my phone when I can't even see them?"

Callaway felt flustered. "Right, sorry. Do you have the police report that you filed?"

Elle again reached into her purse and pulled out a folded document. She slid it across the table.

Callaway scanned the report. It had the missing person's name, age, height, weight, hair color, eye color, build, nicknames, known allergies, medical condition, articles of clothing they were last seen wearing, and so on. The report was dated three months earlier.

"Have you been to Milton before?" Callaway asked.

"This is my first time."

Callaway figured that. The police report was filed in Mayview.

"Have you spoken to the Milton PD? Your sister was in Milton at the time of her disappearance, you know," he said.

"I did speak to them, and they told me another missing persons report was not necessary as one had already been filed in Mayview."

"Really?" Callaway was surprised by this.

"My sister's information was already logged in NamUS."

The National Missing and Unidentified Persons System was operated by the Department of Justice. The information in the system was used by law enforcement officials, agencies, and even individuals in searching for missing persons.

"And you are certain your sister was in Milton?" Callaway had to be sure before he proceeded.

"Yes, I'm sure."

"How?"

"She told me."

"She texted you?"

"No, we spoke on the phone."

"Why didn't she text you?"

"I don't know how to text."

"Why not?"

"I can't see."

Callaway's face turned beet red. *Second time I put my foot in my mouth*, he thought.

"Don't be embarrassed," Elle said, sensing his embarrassment. "I've had people say far worse things to me before."

"I did not mean to offend you with my questioning," he said. "I've taken on cases before where a person has gone missing, and after weeks of searching, I've found them in another state, sometimes living under a different name. There is nothing I nor the police can do to compel them to return to their family. If they are an adult, they are free to leave the country, state, or city whenever they want."

"My sister has not left the country, nor the state, nor the city."

"How do you know?"

Elle fell silent. "I can't be certain, of course, but what I can tell you is my sister and I spoke regularly. Three months ago, she stopped answering my calls. I've waited patiently for the police to tell me they've found her. I have now taken it upon myself to do something about it. Are you going to help me or not?" Her voice was gentle but determined.

"I'm not sure what I can do," Callaway replied. Missing persons cases often did not result in positive outcomes, and Callaway did not want to give Elle false hope. Since she was blind, Callaway would feel like he had abused Elle's trust in him if he searched for Katie and failed.

She reached into her purse for the third time and pulled out an envelope. She laid it on the table. The envelope was thick and heavy.

"It's five thousand dollars. All upfront," Elle said.

Callaway's mouth nearly hit the table. He needed a moment to compose himself. "That's a lot of money, Elle, and believe me when I say this, it is money I could desperately use right now. But you'd be throwing it away. It might be better if the police looked into it."

"They are not doing anything."

"You should have a case number from your missing persons report. You could contact the person in charge of your case and get an update."

"I already did."

"And?"

"I get the standard answer that they are investigating this matter and they will let me know the moment they find something."

Callaway sighed, "That's no surprise, given how the Milton PD is stretched thin right now."

"Please," Elle said. "I need someone whose sole job is to find my sister."

"What if I'm not able to find her?" he asked.

"Katie was my younger sister. She was also my best friend. I don't know where she is, and it is eating away at me. There are times I go to bed crying. There are also times I can barely function. I am willing to do whatever it takes to find out what happened to her, even if it means I may never see her again."

Callaway was silent for a moment. "Fine. I'll look into it and get back to you."

He reached for the envelope.

Elle blocked his hand with hers.

"I want to come with you wherever you go."

Callaway frowned. "It might be better if I did this on my own. I don't want to inconvenience you, or worse, put you in any danger."

"It's my sister, and it's my money," Elle said.

Callaway stared at her.

"Forgive me if I don't trust you just yet. I can't see with my eyes, which means I don't know if you will do what you say you will."

That seems logical, he thought. "Okay, fine."

She smiled once again.

He thought of something. "How did you find me?"

"I heard about the Paul Gardener case."

"Right, of course," Callaway said.

That case finally got me a client, he thought.

TWENTY-SEVEN

Holt and Fisher were inside a room with glass walls at Milton College. A security officer was seated behind a set of computer monitors. The security cameras, located in every corner of the campus, had recently been installed due to a string of sexual assaults that had rocked the college.

A masked man dressed in dark clothing had attacked female students as they walked to and from class. All the attacks had taken place at night, and the victims were unable to identify their attackers. The college hired extra security officers and placed restrictions on students walking alone. The attacks would've continued had someone not come forward with information.

The roommate of a law student told campus police that on the night of the attacks, the law student would disappear for hours. The authorities were going to bring the law student in for questioning, but then they learned the man's roommate had previously been reprimanded for cheating on his exams. The whistle-blower in that situation happened to be the law student, and the authorities worried the tip could be a false lead given out of spite. They also worried the real attacker could disappear for good if they caught the wrong person. Instead, they took no action against the law student and continued their investigation in secrecy. Several months went by without an incident. The extra campus security was reduced, and restrictions were lifted on students walking on campus after dark.

One night, the law student was seen leaving his room. He was dressed in black, and he had a mask in his pocket. The law student hid behind a set of trees, shielded in darkness, as a female student left her class. She was on her phone, unaware that someone was watching her as she walked back to her dorm.

The law student waited for the right moment to pounce. What no one was told at the time was that an undercover officer had been placed across the hall from the law student. For several months, the officer never let the law student out of his sight. Now the officer was tailing the law student. When he made his move, so did the undercover officer. Before the law student could reach the female student, he was on the ground and handcuffed.

Holt knew all the details because Isaiah had told him. Isaiah had wanted Holt's opinion on what to do to keep his female friends safe on campus. Isaiah was big and strong, and he was a protector for those he cared for.

As Holt stared at the monitors, he could not help but wonder if he could have protected Isaiah had he known what he was up to that morning.

The security officer played with the keyboard until he found what he was looking for. He pointed to a monitor on the left.

The image showed the parking lot next to the gymnasium. The clock at the bottom indicated the time was a little after six a.m. They watched as the doors opened and Isaiah came out of the building.

Holt's back arched, and his hands tightened into balls. He clenched his jaw, feeling emotions rush through him. Only a few hours later, his nephew's bullet-riddled body would be found.

Fisher placed her hand over his fist to calm him. Her gesture helped, but not that much. Holt could not tear his eyes away from the screen.

Isaiah rushed to a car parked in the corner of the lot. They recognized it as the Chrysler. He shoved the key into the door, unlocked it, and got behind the wheel.

He raced out of the lot a moment later.

Bledson was telling the truth, Holt thought. *He did let Isaiah borrow his car.*

But something troubled him. Why was Isaiah in such a hurry to leave? Was he meeting someone at the furniture store? And was this person responsible for Isaiah's death?

He wished he had the answer.

TWENTY-EIGHT

The house looked run-down from afar and looked no better up close. The grass had not been mowed in months, and discarded appliances and furniture were scattered on the lawn. The window shutters were broken or missing, and the exterior paint was peeling and faded.

Callaway read the address to Elle to make sure they were at the right place.

"Yes," Elle replied. "That's the address Katie told me."

Why would Katie live in a dump like this? Callaway thought as he knocked on the front door.

A moment later, a large woman appeared from behind the screen mesh. "If you're selling something, I'm not buying," she said in a hoarse voice.

"We are looking for someone," he said. "Her name is Katie Pearson. We believe she lives at this address."

"No one by that name lives here," the woman replied.

"Are you sure?"

"Of course, I'm sure. It's my damn house."

Callaway held up the Polaroid. "Can you take a look?"

The woman squinted. "Never seen her before. Listen, I'm missing my favorite show. You got the wrong house."

Elle spoke up. "Do you have tenants in your basement?"

The woman's eyes narrowed. "Yeah, I do. So?"

Callaway understood where Elle was going. "Do you mind if we spoke to your tenant?" he asked the woman.

"Yeah, I do mind. Now get off my property before I call the cops."

"Please," Elle said. "I'm looking for my sister. She's missing."

The woman stared at her. "Fine. Go around the back and knock on the door. He's probably sleeping, so you're gonna have to bang on the door to wake him up."

The woman slammed her door shut.

Callaway shook his head and proceeded to the back of the house. Elle followed behind, tapping her stick as she did. Callaway wondered if he should hold her hand to assist her, but she looked like she did not need his help.

Callaway pounded on the basement door with his fist. A man stuck his head out a minute later. His eyes were slits, and he blinked like he was lost in a daze. "Who are you?" he asked.

Callaway smelled marijuana on him. "We are looking for this person." Callaway held up the Polaroid again. "Her name is Katie Pearson. Do you know her?"

The tenant came out to get a better look. He was wearing a stained t-shirt and shorts. "Nah, man. I've never seen her before, but I kinda wish I had."

He grinned.

Callaway ignored the comment. "How long have you been staying here?"

"I moved in two months ago."

That's after Katie went missing, Callaway thought.

"And do you know who lived here before you?"

The tenant shook his head. "No idea. You can ask the landlord upstairs."

"She's not very friendly," Callaway said. He had no desire to knock on her door again.

The tenant nodded. "She's one mean lady," he said.

Callaway turned to Elle. "Maybe Katie might not have told you the right address." He knew it was common for people to be untruthful about where they lived if they did not want their families to find out.

"Katie would never lie to me," Elle said. Callaway opened his mouth to speak, but Elle surprised him by asking the tenant, "Sir, is your rent four hundred plus electricity?"

"Yeah, it is," the tenant replied.

"That's what my sister paid too. And is your apartment covered with sunflower wallpaper?"

The tenant's mouth dropped. "Yeah, how did you know?"

"My sister told me."

"Do you mind if I confirm this?" Callaway asked, feeling curious.

The tenant hesitated. "I don't know," he said.

"I know you got weed in there, and I don't care," Callaway said. "I just want to take a quick look."

The tenant held the door for him. Callaway went down the steps. The smell of marijuana was strong, almost unbearable. The basement was cramped and dark, but Callaway easily spotted the wallpaper. It was ugly and covered in sunflowers.

He hurried back outside, grateful to breathe fresh air again.

"You were right," he said to Elle.

"Katie always complained that the yellow wallpaper made her want to throw up," Elle said.

TWENTY-NINE

Coach Earl Loughton had a boyish face, sharp eyes, and salt-and-pepper hair. Even though he was still in his early thirties, the premature gray hairs were a result of the stress and pressures of being a head coach. Loughton was wearing a white polo shirt, black shorts, and white basketball shoes. He had a whistle hanging around his neck.

Holt and Fisher were in Loughton's office. The walls were adorned with photos of all the teams Loughton had coached over the years. Loughton was a rising star in college basketball, and Milton College had just given him a multi-year contract worth millions of dollars, including bonuses.

Loughton was a hard-nosed coach who demanded a lot from his players, but he also cared about the young men under his watch. Isaiah had nothing but positive things to say about him.

Holt had met Loughton once before, during a practice scrimmage the team was having. Holt decided to drop by and see Isaiah play. When he saw Isaiah hold his own against older, bigger, and more experienced players, he knew the kid had a bright future ahead of him.

Holt was also able to exchange a few words with Loughton. He came away agreeing with Isaiah's sentiments about the man.

"I'm sorry for your loss," Loughton said. "I know Isaiah meant a lot to you."

"Thank you," Holt said, but Loughton's condolences did little to ease his grief.

"I spoke to his parents, and I can't imagine what they must be going through," Loughton continued. "We are all devastated by this tragedy. I offered to cancel tonight's game out of respect, but his parents were adamant that the team play. It was what Isaiah would have wanted."

Holt knew it was typical of Isaiah to put others before himself. He never wanted anyone to go out of their way to do something for him. He was a humble person.

"Isaiah was the heart and soul of the team," Loughton said. "He was one helluva player and a great kid. We had great hopes for him."

"We did too," Holt said.

Loughton nodded. "Thanks for letting me talk to my guys first. I know you want to question them."

"No problem," Holt said. "We saw the footage of Isaiah leaving campus this morning. He left pretty quickly. Any reason why he'd be in such a hurry?"

"I wish I knew," Loughton replied. "I really do. We try to keep an eye on them. They are still kids, and we don't want them getting into anything that might reflect badly on them, the team, or the college. We pay extra attention during road games. We try to keep all the players on the same floors of the hotel, and we position coaches in rooms on each end of the hall, so we know if someone's leaving the property. We once had a hotel mess up our booking, and we had players all over the hotel. The next morning, we found our two point guards, our starting center, and a couple of bench players heavily intoxicated. One of them had snuck out, purchased alcohol, and brought it back to the hotel. Later that day, we lost the game by almost thirty points. Isaiah wasn't like that. He took the game seriously. He never drank, he ate well, and he worked hard. A role model for the other players."

"Was there anyone on the team he was particularly close to?" Holt asked.

"Sure. Our point guard."

THIRTY

Byron Fox choked back tears as he sat across from Holt and Fisher. They were in the campus cafeteria. Byron sported an afro, a goatee, and a stud earring in his left ear. He took a sip of his juice. Holt and Fisher had coffee and tea, respectively.

"I can't believe Isaiah's dead," Byron said, shaking his head. "Who would do something like that to him?"

"We are trying to find out," Fisher replied.

Byron looked at her and nodded.

"Your coach said you and Isaiah were close," Fisher said.

"Yeah, we were."

Fisher wanted to ease into the questioning, so she started with the soft questions. "How'd you two meet?"

"On the court, of course. If you were on his team, Isaiah had your back. As a point guard, it was my job to dribble the ball up. The opposing team would send bigger players on me. They would try to trap me so I would give up the ball. Sometimes they'd get rough to mess up my game. Isaiah would have none of that. If a player shoved me, the next time they had the ball and they were going around a screen, Isaiah would give him an elbow to the face. He wouldn't get away with it all the time. The refs would whistle him. But it would send a message to the opposing team that if they tried anything, they'd have to deal with him."

"But, your friendship was off the court as well, right?" Fisher asked.

"Yeah, for sure. When we weren't practicing or working out or playing, we listened to music. We both liked R&B and rap. We argued nonstop on who the best band was or who the best singer was. We were planning to record our own songs."

Holt remembered how Isaiah knew all the lyrics to the songs that came on the radio. He would sing along whenever he was in the car. If Isaiah had not gotten into sports, he definitely would have done something in music.

"Do you know why Isaiah left in such a hurry this morning?" Fisher asked, getting to the point.

"I had no idea he was even gone. I was sleeping when someone woke me up and told me."

"When did you last see him?" Fisher asked.

Byron thought for a moment. "We hung around last night."

"And how was his demeanor?"

Byron stared at her. "Demeanor?"

"I mean, was he upset, angry, calm, anxious…?"

"Oh, right. He was calm, I guess." Byron sat up straight. "What I'm saying is that with Isaiah, you could never really tell. He never wore his emotions on his sleeve, you know. In my case, if I was excited, everyone knew I was, and if I was down, then you knew to stay away from me."

"So, there was nothing out of the ordinary with Isaiah last night?" Fisher prodded.

"I mean, he was on the phone most of the time."

"Who was he talking to?" Holt asked.

"I'm not sure, but I think it was a girl," Byron replied.

"What's her name?" Holt asked.

"I don't know. We talked about everything, but certain things he kept to himself. I didn't push him on it. It was none of my business. I had to respect his privacy, you know. He never asked me questions about my personal life. I never told him my dad was in and out of prison for dealing drugs, or that my mom was caught for shoplifting because we had no money." Byron shook his head. "I can't believe I'm telling you guys this stuff. You are the police. My head's been really messed up ever since I found out about Isaiah."

Fisher was not interested in Byron's personal life. "How did you know it was a girl Isaiah was talking to?" she asked.

"He would leave the room whenever he would get a call. A couple of times, I heard him say the word 'baby.'"

"Baby?" Fisher asked, confused.

"Yeah, like '*baby* I'll take care of you,' '*baby* I love you,' like what you'd call your girlfriend, you know," Byron replied.

THIRTY-ONE

The fast-food restaurant already had a line at its counter when Callaway and Elle arrived. Callaway asked Elle to take a seat at a table while he stood in line behind a large man.

Elle said her sister worked at this location. She and Callaway hoped someone at the restaurant might have information on Katie.

Callaway glanced over at Elle. She was sitting upright with her cane in her hand. He could not imagine what she must be going through. Not being able to see and not knowing where her sister was.

After the large man had ordered his super-sized combo, Callaway approached the counter and asked the girl on duty for the manager.

She waved a man over. He was young, with pimples all over his face and whiskers on his chin. His name tag read *Gary*.

"What can I do for you?" Gary asked.

Callaway pulled out the Polaroid. "I'm looking for this woman. Her name is Katie Pearson. She was an employee here."

Gary stared at the photo. He shook his head. "I've never seen her before."

Callaway blinked. "Are you sure?"

"Yeah, I would remember someone who worked for me."

"How long have you worked here?"

"Four years, and a year and a half of those as a manager."

Callaway frowned. "Can you show the photo to your employees? Maybe someone might remember seeing her."

"I don't know. We're kind of busy right now."

"Please. It's important." Callaway pointed at Elle. "Her sister hasn't spoken to her in months."

"Okay, sure," Gary said. "Give me a minute."

Callaway walked over to Elle. As if sensing him or perhaps smelling him, her back straightened and she turned to him. "What did they say?" she asked.

"The manager has never seen Katie, but he'll ask his employees," Callaway replied.

"How can that be?" Elle asked, surprised.

"Are you sure it's the right address?" Callaway asked.

"Of course, it is."

Elle thought for a moment. "Across the street, is there a record store?"

Callaway looked out the window. The sign had two vinyl records at the beginning and end of the name. "Yes, there is."

Elle smiled. "On her breaks, Katie would go to the store and browse through the records in their catalog. She loved jazz and classical music."

The manager returned. "I'm sorry, but none of my employees have seen this person."

"That's not possible," Elle said sternly. "My sister works here."

"If she did, we would have some record of her employment. No one by the name of Katie Pearson ever worked here, ma'am."

There was silence when Elle said, "Is your name Gary Nelson?"

"Yes, it is."

"And you live with your parents in Lafferty?"

Gary's mouth dropped. "Yeah, I do."

"I also know you have an employee who hurt his arm while surfing in Miami. You have another employee who broke off her engagement when she caught her fiancé with her best friend."

"How do you know all that?" Gary asked.

Callaway was thinking the same thing.

"I know because my sister told me," Elle said.

Gary swallowed and adjusted his cap.

Callaway turned to him. "How do you explain this?" he asked.

"I can't," Gary replied, still bewildered. "You can check what I just told you with my employees if you like."

"I intend to," Callaway said. He was not leaving until he got to the bottom of this.

THIRTY-TWO

Holt was seated at the dining table. Marjorie was at the stove making tea. Fisher was upstairs in Isaiah's bedroom.

Holt was not ready to go through Isaiah's stuff. He feared he would break down if he did.

He looked out the window at the backyard. Dennis had set up a basketball net so Isaiah could practice. Holt remembered many nights when he would drop by and see Isaiah shooting baskets in total darkness. Holt once asked him why he did not just turn on the floodlights Dennis had installed. Isaiah told Holt he wanted to see if he could make a basket blind.

Holt was reminded of his time in high school. He was tall with big hands, and his high school coach encouraged him to try out for the basketball team. He made it on the team, but he was relegated to the bench for most of the games. What he never forgot was how his coach would make his players shut their eyes and practice shooting without a ball. The coach believed mental visualization was just as important as physically shooting the ball.

Marjorie came over and placed a steaming cup before him. "I'm not sure how your partner takes it, so I didn't put any milk or sugar in her cup."

"Fisher likes it black," he said.

"Should I go upstairs and call her? It'll get cold," Marjorie asked.

"No. Let her do her job," Holt replied. "Plus, she prefers her tea lukewarm anyway."

Marjorie nodded and sat down. Holt could not help but feel like his sister had aged since he broke the news to her.

"How's Dennis doing?" he asked.

"He's withdrawn into himself. When his mother passed away, he drew into himself for weeks. It's his way of grieving. But I am worried. I need him now more than ever, and if he shuts himself off from *me,* I don't know how I'm going to get through this."

Holt placed his hand over hers. "I'm *always* going to be here for you," he said. He meant every word of it. Marjorie gave him hope and courage at times when he had none. If it were not for her, he would not have become a police detective. He would have gotten himself into trouble with the law and would be rotting in jail.

Growing up, Holt was always getting into fights. Kids picked on him because of his size. They felt like if they could take him down, then no one would mess with them in school. He was no gentle giant, though. He had a mean streak in him. He once knocked out a kid's two front teeth with a single punch.

Holt hated bullies, but after years of fending them off, he became one himself. He started picking on kids much smaller than him. He was also going through teen angst, which made him a horrible person to deal with. When Marjorie found out, she broke down crying. She told him to leave the house and never come back. She was much older than him, and she was working during the day and studying at night to put a roof over their heads. Holt remembered feeling worse than trash. He had let down the one person who meant more to him than anyone in the world. He vowed he would never do anything to hurt her again. And he never did.

"Where's Brit?" he asked. He still had not spoken to his niece.

"She's really upset," Marjorie replied. "She's still at her friend's house. It might be better for her to be with someone her age right now. Later I'll take her someplace to talk."

Holt nodded and took a sip from his cup.

Fisher appeared in the kitchen. She was holding a large plastic bag. She had tagged items that could be useful in their investigation.

Marjorie said, "Your tea is ready."

Fisher grabbed the cup, took a sip, and then gulped it down in one breath. "Thanks," she said.

Outside the house, Holt asked, "Did you find anything in Isaiah's room?"

"His laptop is password-protected," she replied. "I'm hoping someone in IT can access it. But I didn't find his cell phone."

Holt frowned. "We didn't find it on him either."

"He wouldn't have left it at home," Fisher said. "Kids nowadays can't live with a minute away from their phones."

"They sure can't," Holt said.

"Maybe the shooter took it," Fisher suggested.

Holt pondered the possibility. "But why?" he asked.

"Maybe it had something the shooter didn't want anyone to see."

"We need to see his phone logs," Holt said.

"I'll contact his service provider."

THIRTY-THREE

Callaway spoke to each employee at the fast-food restaurant, and they all said the same thing: they had never heard of or seen Katie Pearson.

Callaway knew someone was not telling the truth. His instincts were saying Elle was leading him on a wild goose chase, but he could not find a single reason why the woman would fabricate a story about a missing sister. She knew intimate details about each of the employees, and those could only have come from someone who had worked there.

On average, people spent more time with their co-workers than their family members. They shared just about everything with each other. The camaraderie was especially strong in the service industries. The hours were long, the work was hard, and the pay was often very low. The people an employee relied upon to get through the day were those who were with them in the trenches. They knew what each other was going through, and they could sympathize with their plight because they, too, were going through the same thing. Callaway missed being a deputy sheriff for that reason alone. The rapport he had with the other members of the sheriff's department was something he never forgot. As a private eye, he worked mostly on his own. He had no one to gripe to. Not that anyone would listen. He gave up a stable and secure job for something with no benefits and no respect. Most people did not know what private investigators really did, so there was no way for them to truly value the service provided. Whatever they knew came from detective novels and movies, which always depicted tough-guy sleuths taking on cases involving damsels in distress. Callaway wished his life was as exciting as that, but in reality, his was boring and uneventful.

Elle's case had intrigued him. She had put up five thousand dollars, and Callaway would scour every inch of the city to find her sister.

He had visited all the hospitals in Milton. Even though her sister had been missing for three months, there was still the possibility a Jane Doe had been admitted to one of them.

What if her sister had gotten in an accident and was so badly hurt she was unable to communicate? What if something terrible had happened and the authorities were unable to identify who she was? The what-ifs were endless, and Callaway had to make sure something worse had not befallen her sister.

At each hospital, Callaway provided Katie's name, her photo, and a detailed description of her in case her appearance had changed from the time the photo was taken. The person at the information desk would go through all the records dating back three months. Whenever the answer was no, Callaway could sense both relief and disappointment in Elle's voice. On the one hand, she was relieved nothing had happened to her sister, but on the other, she was disappointed they had not found Katie yet.

As they drove, Callaway said, "There is one more place we still have to check."

He wished they did not have to go there, but he saw no other option.

THIRTY-FOUR

Fisher glanced at her watch. She was at the Milton PD, and the time was getting late. She had hoped to run some things through the police database before she headed home.

Isaiah's death had hit close to home, and both she and Holt were making sure nothing was overlooked. The first few hours of an investigation were crucial. If any evidence was missed at the crime scene, there was still a chance to go back and retrieve it. Later, there was a strong possibility people or the elements—if the crime scene was outside—could taint or destroy the evidence. If witnesses were not interviewed immediately, their memories of the events could fade, or they could suddenly change their stories.

Fisher grabbed her coat and headed for the elevator.

She saw that Holt was at his desk.

"You should go home and get some rest," Fisher said.

"I just had coffee. I'm good," he said, not looking up from his computer.

When Holt put his mind to something, he became obsessive. He could work all night to satisfy whatever was bothering him.

Fisher had a feeling there was more to his late work than just tenacity. Nancy was at her mother's house, and Holt would be going home to an empty house. He did not want to be alone. Fisher did not want him to be either.

"All right," she said. "If you're not leaving, then I'm not leaving either."

He finally looked up. "You need sleep, Fisher."

She smiled. "I'm making fresh coffee."

He stared at her. "Today was your day off, you know."

"It was, but this is more important."

He suddenly looked unsure. He wanted to keep working, but he did not want Fisher to work late because of him.

Fisher said, "Why don't I buy you a drink? We've had a long day, and I think we need something to unwind with."

"I have a lot of things to do," Holt said.

"Just one drink, that's all."

He stared at her for a moment. "Fine, but only one," he said.

The bar was just around the block from the police department. The place was frequented mostly by off-duty cops.

They ordered beers and found a table in the corner. Holt took a sip and said, "After finishing this, I'm heading back to my desk, just so you know."

"I know," Fisher said with a smile.

They drank in silence. Every once in a while, someone from the department would come over and give their condolences to Holt. They all knew who Isaiah was. It was not hard to miss a large framed photo of Isaiah on Holt's desk. The young man meant a great deal to him. She knew that when Holt's adopted son died, it was Isaiah who had moved in with him and Nancy because Holt was overcome with grief.

Isaiah would sit and talk with him for hours. They would talk about sports, school, life, anything but the loss he had suffered. Isaiah was open with his emotions, and he was also communicative, something neither Holt nor Dennis were particularly very good at. This was a trait that made him a leader on his team.

Fisher was grateful for what Isaiah had done. She hated to see her partner suffer. She feared after the loss of his adopted son, Holt might never return to work. He did, and he was a better detective than before.

They emptied their bottles. "Thanks for the drink," Holt said and stood up.

"Why don't you call it a night?" Fisher suggested. "It's been an emotionally draining day. Go home and get some rest. Tomorrow I promise we'll leave no stones unturned to find who did this to Isaiah."

Holt stared at her.

His shoulders drooped, and he nodded.

THIRTY-FIVE

The city morgue was located in an old government building. The exterior was ugly and uninviting, and the interior was no different. The walls were painted in dark colors, and the floor tiles looked like they had not been changed in decades.

Callaway did not come to the morgue often—there was never really much need in his line of work—but when he did, he always found himself depressed afterward.

What did I expect? he thought. *A celebration of someone's death?*

There was only one person on duty this late at night. The morgue attendant was young and pale, with bushy hair and thick round glasses. He did not look far removed from some of the dead in the morgue.

Callaway introduced himself and Elle. He hated to bring her here, but he had to make sure of something.

"Do you have any unidentified bodies?" Callaway asked.

"Loads," the attendant answered.

Callaway did not like the sound of that.

"We do our best to ID them so we can contact their next of kin, but sometimes it's just not possible," the attendant said.

Callaway understood. The bodies were in the worst shape imaginable.

Callaway held the Polaroid out for the morgue attendant. "Any chance someone resembling her was brought in?"

The attendant pushed his glasses up his nose and squinted. "I think we may have someone who looks like her."

Callaway's heart dropped. He turned to look at Elle. She was tightly gripping her walking cane.

"Can we see her?" Callaway asked.

"Sure, you can, but…"

Callaway smiled, shoved his hand in his pocket, and pulled out a twenty-dollar bill. "That's for you, my man," he said.

The attendant shook his head. "I was saying, you can see the body, but you're going to have to sign the register over there."

He pointed to a ledger on the counter.

"Oh," Callaway said, placing the bill back in his pocket. *Jumping to conclusions, Lee?* he thought.

They followed the attendant down the hall. The lights were fluorescent, and they flickered above their heads. Callaway felt like he was in some gory horror movie. A shiver went up his spine at the thought of a crazed maniac waiting for them with a chainsaw in the next room. He glanced at Elle. She was walking calmly next to him.

They entered a room that was slightly cold. Several gurneys lay side by side. The attendant approached one and said, "She was brought in this morning."

"This morning?" Callaway said.

"Yeah, that's what I said."

Elle's sister has been missing for three months, he thought. *Maybe someone discovered her body just now.*

A long white sheet was placed over the body. Callaway was almost glad that Elle would not be able to see whatever gruesome image lay underneath the sheet.

The attendant paused to give Callaway a moment to brace himself. He then pulled the sheet cloth away, revealing the face of a young woman. Her skin had turned gray. Her lips were blue, and her eyes were closed.

"Can you describe her, please?" Elle said.

"Um, sure," the attendant said. "The victim looks to be around the age of twenty to twenty-four, she is five-two, and she has blonde hair."

Elle was silent.

Callaway said, "Her sister was turning twenty-two, she was five-two to five-three, and she also had blonde hair."

"Oh," the attendant said.

"Where did they find her?" Elle asked.

The attendant grabbed a clipboard and flipped a page. "She was found overdosed behind a dance club. She had a combination of recreational drugs and alcohol in her system."

"My sister did *not* do drugs," Elle said.

"Right, sure. Anyway, they tried to revive her, but it was too late," the attendant said.

Callaway said, "Who was she with?"

The attendant checked the clipboard. "Doesn't say, but sometimes the clubs don't want the responsibility, or they don't want to deal with the police, so they'll leave the body outside. They'll argue the person walked out on their own accord and then dropped dead. It did not happen on their property, so it's not their problem."

"She had no ID on her?" Callaway asked.

"None that the paramedics could find. It could have been in her purse, which she wasn't carrying when they found her."

"You check for fingerprints?"

"Sure, but it'll take some time to get a match. As I said, they brought her in this morning."

Callaway rubbed his chin, thinking.

"Does your sister have any birthmarks or any distinguishing marks on her body?" the attendant asked Elle.

"Yes," Elle replied. "She has a mole on the side of her neck."

The attendant turned the head to the side. He lifted the hair up. The skin on the neck was clear of any blemishes or spots that might look like a mole.

Callaway leaned in to make sure.

"No," the attendant said.

"She also has a dark spot on her upper right shoulder. It's the size of my palm." Elle held up her gloved hand. "Katie called it her good luck charm."

The attendant flipped the body over. He grabbed a flashlight and moved the light over the skin. It was white and pale. "No dark spot of any kind."

Elle turned and left the room.

THIRTY-SIX

Out in the hall, Callaway found Elle crying.

"You didn't have to come here," he said, feeling concerned.

"No, I wanted to," she said.

"It's not Katie."

"I know, but that girl in there, she's someone's sister, someone's daughter. I couldn't help but think of her family and how they must be worried sick about her."

"I'm sure they are looking for her just like you are looking for your sister," Callaway said.

"Are they?" she asked.

Callaway had no answer. If he had not heard back from a loved one, he would be on the phone or knocking on doors to find out what happened.

Elle said, "When we were young, my parents took my sister and me on a camping trip. While my parents were getting dinner ready, Katie decided we should go check out the woods nearby. I thought it was a bad idea. It was getting dark, and I worried we might get lost. Katie was more adventurous than me. She always had been. She wanted to experience life to the fullest. She wanted to go skydiving, cliff jumping, bungee jumping—you name it, she wanted to do it. I never talked her out of it. It almost felt like she was living her life for the both of us. Anyway, it got dark really quickly, and we got separated in the woods. She was running ahead of me, and I couldn't keep up. I yelled her name as I frantically searched for her. When I found her, she was huddled under a tree, crying hysterically. I promised her that I would not let anything happen to her and…"

Her voice trailed off. There was a long moment of silence before she adjusted her dark glasses and said, "I have to find her. I *will* find her." There was conviction in her voice Callaway had not heard before.

He said, "I promise we won't stop until we know what happened to her."

"Thank you," she said with a weak smile.

THIRTY-SEVEN

Fisher opened the door to her apartment and entered. She placed her keys in the bowl in the hall and headed to the kitchen. On top of the fridge was a lockbox. She placed her weapon inside and shut the box. The box was strategically placed. The kitchen was next to the hall and the front door. If there was any threat, Fisher could swiftly get to the box and her weapon without being in the line of fire. Her training kept her on high alert even when she was off duty.

She pulled off her boots and rubbed her soles. She was used to being on her feet, but that day had an added strain. The adrenaline had worn off a long time ago. She had been pushing herself with caffeine, but now she was lethargic. Maybe it was the beer she had.

She checked her voicemail, and there was one from her best friend. She was wondering when they could schedule lunch next.

Fisher suddenly felt a headache coming on. She massaged her temples and exhaled. She was not sure when her next day off would be. Holt would not stop until he found Isaiah's killer, and as his partner, Fisher could not let him go at it alone.

Holt's obsession knew no limits. He was still actively looking into cases dating back ten years. He would not classify them as cold cases. He genuinely believed he would solve them before he retired.

Fisher did not have the heart to tell him that might not happen. Unsolved cases were part of the profession. She only hoped Isaiah's did not turn into one. If that happened, she feared Holt would quit the force to focus solely on finding the person who ended his nephew's life.

She spotted the romance novel on the coffee table. She was supposed to catch up on her reading that day. At the moment, though, her mind was all over the place. She would not be able to focus on a book.

She dropped on the sofa and turned on the TV. She hoped a light romantic comedy would help alleviate the stress she was under. On the screen, the leading man was trying his best to woo the girl of his dreams. Fisher, however, was not paying attention. She was thinking about Isaiah.

THIRTY-EIGHT

Holt and Fisher had already listened to the 9-1-1 call and found it had come from a blocked number. The caller had not left a name, nor did he stay at the scene of the crime. If they were going to make any progress on the case, they needed to find who this person was. They believed he must live in the vicinity of where Isaiah was killed. How else would he have found Isaiah's body? This narrowed their search down, but it was still labor-intensive.

They knocked on all doors within walking distance of the furniture store. People clammed up the moment they found out they were speaking to cops. The neighborhood had seen its share of tragedies, and people were suspicious of the police. Drugs and violence had become an everyday part of people's lives. They feared retribution from local gangs if they spoke up.

Fisher was glad she did not go for her morning run. Her feet were still sore from the day before. *I should have worn flats instead of heels*, she thought as she moved to the next door.

Holt was breathing hard next to her. His forehead glistened with sweat as he adjusted his shirt collar and tie.

An hour later, Fisher was beat, and she could tell Holt was too. But the look of determination on his face told her he was not about to stop.

"We should head back to the station," she said. "We can make more progress at our desks than pounding the pavement."

"Someone had to have seen something," Holt said with a scowl.

Holt was like a pit bull who had taken a bite and was not willing to let go. Unfortunately, he had not bitten into anything that was useful to them.

Fisher blinked as something flashed in her eyes. She squinted and realized she was seeing light reflecting off the lens of a camera. It was next to a window on the third floor of an apartment building.

"I think we may have found something," she said.

When Holt saw what she was pointing at, a smile crossed his face.

They hurried into the building and took the elevator up to the third floor. Fisher had counted the windows from outside, and if her math was correct, the apartment with the camera was three units down from the end of the building.

They located the apartment. Fisher knocked. When they did not get a response, Holt banged on the door with his fist.

"I'm coming! I'm coming! Hold your horses!" an old man shouted.

They saw a shadow through the peephole. Holt and Fisher held up their badges.

The door opened slightly. A small man wearing a purple robe stuck his head out. He had silver hair, wrinkled skin, and tiny eyes.

"Can I help you?" he asked hesitantly.

Fisher spoke before Holt did. She worried he was too pumped up and might scare the man. "Is that your camera pointed down to the street?"

"Yes, it is. But I'm not a voyeur," he said, suddenly defensive.

"We're not concerned about that," Fisher said. "Can we take a look at your footage?"

"Um…"

The old man hesitated. "Do you have a warrant…?"

Holt said, "It's very important, sir. A young man was shot two blocks from here, and we want to make sure your camera didn't catch anything vital to our investigation."

The old man's eyes narrowed. "Is it the basketball player they are talking about on the news?"

"Yes, it is."

"Oh, ok." The old man held the door open for them. They entered and found the apartment crammed with every knickknack imaginable. The man did not look like a hoarder, but he was getting close to becoming one.

He took them to a corner where a laptop was placed on a table.

"If you don't mind me asking," Fisher said, "why do you have a camera rigged up?"

"This building is old and falling apart, but for the past couple of months, management has started fixing it up. The basement garage is under construction, which means I have to park on the street in the meantime." He pointed at a row of cars parked next to the sidewalk. "That blue Mustang over there, that's mine. I've had it for over thirty years. It's my constant companion. I won't let anything happen to it. But ever since I had to move it outside, I've had kids scratch it with keys, leave garbage on it. I've even had someone spray-paint male genitals across the side door. So to stop these kids from messing with my Mustang, I installed the camera, and I put up a sign on the windshield stating that if anyone tries anything, the camera will record them, and I will report them to the police."

"Has it worked?" Fisher asked.

The old man sighed and shook his head. "Not really. These kids cover their faces when they vandalize my car, but I figure I gotta try something to deter them, you know?"

Holt was getting impatient. "Can we see the footage from yesterday?"

"Do you have the exact time you want to look at? Or else you'll be sitting here all day."

Holt turned to Fisher. "When did the 9-1-1 call come, do you remember?"

Fisher did.

The man sat down behind the laptop and quickly began to tap the keys. He then hit the last key a little too dramatically. "Voila!" he said, leaning back in his chair.

Holt and Fisher strained their eyes to get a better look. The image was of the street next to the building. They could see the row of cars.

Fisher found herself shifting her feet in anticipation. She was not sure if they would see anything, but they desperately needed some sort of miracle.

A man appeared down the street. He had on a hoodie, and he was riding a bicycle. He had a backpack slung over his right shoulder.

He suddenly stopped. He was two cars away from the Mustang. The man pulled out what looked like a cell phone. He looked around and dialed a number.

"It's the exact time the 9-1-1 call was made," Fisher said, pointing to the time at the bottom of the screen.

Holt grunted.

When the man ended the call, Fisher said, "Pause it."

The old man did.

Fisher said, "The call to the 9-1-1 command center was less than a minute." She then pointed to the time again. "The call he just made was also less than a minute."

Holt's face was dark.

Fisher knew exactly what was going through his mind.

The man on the bicycle knows what happened to Isaiah.

THIRTY-NINE

Callaway took a bite of the egg sandwich, chewed it, and swallowed it down with hot coffee. Joely had topped his cup with a fresh brew. Callaway now had enough money to pay for breakfast, lunch, and dinner.

Elle's five-thousand-dollar retainer had come at the most opportune time. He could now even pay Julio for the repairs on the Charger, but he would have to catch him later on those oil changes. He was refreshing the loose change in Julio's Impala, though.

Callaway casually glanced at the newspaper on the table. The front page was all about the Isaiah Whitcomb murder. Callaway knew Whitcomb was related to Holt. He had had a few run-ins with Holt, and he could not say they were pleasant. The man was a good detective, he had to give him that. But according to Callaway, Holt sometimes did not see the forest for the trees. His strong desire to apprehend the perpetrator could almost blind him from looking at other scenarios or suspects.

The door chimed, and Elle walked in. Callaway waved at her, but then he turned beet red when he realized his gesture was useless.

He got up and escorted her to his table.

Once seated, Joely came over with a coffee pot in her hand. "What can I get you guys?" she asked.

"I'm good," Callaway said, putting his hand over his cup. He already had two cups, and he worried he would have to run to the bathroom again if he had any more.

"What about the lady?" Joely asked with a smile. Callaway could tell there was something behind her smile.

"I've already had breakfast," Elle replied politely. "Thank you."

"No problem. I'll be over there if you need anything."

Joely winked at Callaway and walked away.

He rolled his eyes and turned to Elle. "How are you feeling?" Their visit to the morgue had shaken her up badly.

"I'm doing much better," she said.

He leaned closer and said, "I can look for your sister on my own. I do it all the time. It's my job, you know."

"No, I want to go with you," she said.

Callaway stared at her. "The morgue was just the beginning," he said. "We might have to go places a lady shouldn't go."

"If it leads me to find my sister, then I want to be there," Elle said with the same conviction Callaway had heard before.

"There is something that's been nagging me all morning," Callaway said a moment later.

"Okay."

"I hope you don't take it the wrong way."

She smiled. "You can ask me whatever you like, Mr. Callaway."

"Call me, Lee."

"Okay, Lee."

He leaned in close again. "I'm curious… how did you know about your sister's birthmark? Also, that story about your sister getting lost in the woods… how is that possible when you are…"

He let his words trail off.

"You mean blind?"

He swallowed. "Yes."

"I wasn't always blind. I had some sight when I was younger. I could make out shapes and colors and even people. I could read a book in large print. I also did math in bold fonts. I watched TV and did things most children my age could do. I had to be extra careful, though, as I was prone to tripping, falling, and running into things. I didn't mind it. In fact, I accepted it as a part of my life, because I guess I really didn't know any different. But when I was fourteen, I contracted chickenpox, and after that, I lost all my sight. Since then, I've had to get by with what I have."

They were silent for a moment.

"I'm sorry. I shouldn't have asked," Callaway said.

"Don't be. I'm not sorry. What I lack in vision, I make up in other ways."

"Like what?"

"I've learned to listen more carefully. I can sense just by hearing someone's voice what they are feeling."

He raised an eyebrow. "You can do that?"

"Yes. I know when you said you are sorry, you truly meant it."

"I did," he said.

Elle's smile widened. Then her face turned serious. "Lee, how do we find my sister?"

FORTY

Holt and Fisher stood at the front of the room while the twenty or so uniformed officers spread themselves out in the open space.

Projected on the wall behind Holt and Fisher was an enlarged photo of a man on a bicycle. Even with the extrapolated pixels, it was easy to make out the man's features. He had dark skin, short hair—which was shaved at the sides—and a thick bush of hair under his chin.

Fisher was grateful the apartment owner had invested in a high-resolution camera, or else they would be looking at a blurred image.

Fisher said, "This man on the screen is a person of interest in Isaiah Whitcomb's murder. He was seen in the area where the victim's body was discovered. We also believe he was the one who made the 9-1-1 call. At the moment, he is not a suspect, but he may know something that could shed light on our investigation." She looked over at Holt, who promptly handed out to each of the officers a 6x9 photo of the man. "It is imperative we speak to this man," Fisher added. "Canvas the neighborhoods and find out if anyone recognizes him."

A hand shot up. "If we see him, do we apprehend?"

Fisher shook her head. "No. Right now, we have no probable cause to arrest him. He hasn't done anything wrong. If you find his whereabouts, you call us immediately."

Another hand shot up. "Is he armed?"

"We don't know, and for that reason, take every precaution necessary."

When there were no more questions, Fisher dismissed the officers. She watched as they quickly left the room. She had wanted to run the photo through the department's facial recognition software, but getting any matches could take time. Holt was already eager to get back on the streets. He was ready to knock on a thousand doors if it came down to it. Fisher's feet were not looking forward to that. She had done enough canvassing, so she thought of getting some patrol officers involved.

With the room almost empty, an officer came over. He had silver in his hair, a slight pouch of a belly, and big meaty hands.

He shook Holt's hand and offered his condolences.

"Thank you," Holt said. The officer shared a story of a loss he once had suffered. Holt just nodded. Fisher could tell Holt was not comfortable discussing grief with a fellow officer. He was a private person, but Isaiah's death had put a spotlight on him.

"My son plays football for Milton College," the officer said.

Holt's eyes focused. "Did he know Isaiah?"

"I asked him when I heard the news, and he didn't. They were in different sports programs, and with classes, practice, and games, they barely got any time to fraternize. But my son did speak highly of your nephew's athletic abilities. He said he was going to be a big star one day."

Holt sighed, feeling a fresh wave of grief. "Yes, he would have."

The officer nodded. "Although, my son did mention their recruiting tactics were quite unconventional." Before Holt could ask further, the officer's partner appeared in the door. They were running late for their shift. The officer shook Holt's hand again, said a few words of encouragement, and left the room.

FORTY-ONE

The Supreme Fashion Academy was located on the top floor of a structure that had five floors and was supported by a series of colored pillars that were at different angles.

To Callaway, the building looked like a tabletop on tilted legs. He never understood architecture or art. Both were subjective and required an appreciative eye. *Look at all that wasted space*, he thought while looking at the area underneath the structure. The area's sole use was as a walking path.

Real estate prices had skyrocketed in the city the last couple of years, and rent had risen with them. *No wonder so many kids in their twenties are still living with their parents*, Callaway thought.

The day Callaway turned eighteen, he was out of his parents' house as if it was on fire. He could not wait to get a place of his own and be his own boss. But in hindsight, that might have been a rash decision. At the time, he had no money and no job. Even now, there were times he had not a single penny to his name, and no cases. In desperate times, he would take on part-time work. Fortunately, he had been spared the likes of having to wear a giant mattress and wave to passing cars for some time.

Elle walked next to him as they made their way underneath the building. The fancy structure was attached to an older building, which, if his memory was correct, was built in the 1920s.

"Is it magnificent up close?" Elle asked.

He glanced at her. "Sorry?"

"The building. Is it wonderful to look at?"

"I'm not sure what you mean?"

"Katie used to say it was like a piece of art."

Elle's sister had come to Milton to enroll in the Supreme Fashion Academy. Callaway had glanced at their website and found out the academy provided programs in fashion modeling, fashion styling, fashion photography, fashion design, and fashion makeup. Katie was specializing in makeup. She had hoped to work as a makeup artist for all the top models in the world.

"I wouldn't call the building a piece of art," he said. *It looks more like a piece of furniture*, he thought. "But, it does leave a strong impression on you."

They spoke to the admissions officer. "No one by that name was ever enrolled here," she politely told them.

Callaway showed her the Polaroid. "This is Katie Pearson, ma'am. Are you sure she was not here?"

The woman shook her head.

"You liar," Elle said angrily.

Shocked, Callaway glanced at Elle.

She proceeded to describe the program down to the last detail.

The admissions officer looked perplexed.

"Are you absolutely positive my sister was never here?" Elle asked.

The woman showed Callaway an alphabetical list of students who had attended the academy. Callaway scanned the list carefully, but he failed to find Katie's name.

Damn odd, he thought.

"I know what you're thinking," Elle said as they left the admissions office. "My sister is real. She is not a figment of my imagination."

"I never said she was," Callaway said. "It's just that…"

"No one's heard of her," she said, finishing his sentence.

"Yes."

She abruptly stopped. Her grip tightened on her cane. She lowered her head and said, "I spent most of last night thinking the same thing. How is it possible that no one has seen or met my sister? You've probably noticed by now that I'm not very talkative, but my sister was the opposite. When she got excited about something, she would talk nonstop. And because I couldn't see, she would describe things in detail for me so I could visualize them in my mind."

Callaway realized that as a sighted person, he took many things for granted. They said a picture was worth a thousand words, and that number was probably required to create a mental image for someone like Elle.

"I wanted to ask you something," he said.

"Go ahead," she said.

"I noticed that you wear gloves all the time. Why is that?"

"I take them off when I need to touch or feel something. It helps to form an image in my mind."

"Wouldn't it be easier not to wear them?"

Elle blushed. "I should have mentioned this earlier, but I'm also a germophobe. Maybe that's why I'm still single."

Callaway felt guilty for asking her personal questions. What she did or how she dressed was none of his business.

"Let's go back to the office," he said. "Hopefully, we'll catch a break soon."

FORTY-TWO

They were headed for the Impala when a woman's voice called out from behind them.

"Wait!"

Callaway turned and saw a young woman running toward them. She was dressed in a light red sweater, black pants, and high heels. Her hair was pulled back in a bun. Her skin was smooth, with not a blemish in sight. Her lips were painted a dark color, and her eyes were covered in black mascara.

"Can I help you?" Callaway asked, staring at her.

She paused to catch her breath. "You're looking for Linda Eustace, right?"

Callaway blinked. "Who?"

"Linda Eustace," she repeated.

"I'm not sure who that is."

"I'm a student at the academy," the woman said.

I could tell that from a mile away, Callaway thought.

"I work part-time at the admissions office. I was there when you came in to speak to the admissions officer," she explained.

"Okay," Callaway said. He was not sure where this was going, but he was willing to indulge her. *She's attractive, so that helps*, he admitted to himself.

"I saw you show that photo to her," the student said.

Callaway pulled out the Polaroid. "You mean this one?"

"Yes."

"And?"

"I know her."

Callaway turned to Elle. She looked as surprised as him.

"You know Katie Pearson?" Callaway asked the student.

"I don't know that name, but I do know the woman in the photo, and her name is Linda Eustace."

Callaway turned to Elle again. Now she looked utterly confused.

"Are you sure?" Callaway asked the student, holding the photo closer to her.

She stared at the Polaroid. "I'm one hundred percent positive. She was in one of my makeup classes. She never spoke to anyone. She pretty much kept to herself, but she was great with cosmetics. She could make a homeless person look like a celebrity. She had the talent."

Callaway's brow furrowed. "Do you have any idea where we can find her?"

The woman shook her head. "As I said, I never spoke to her. Then one day, she stopped coming to class."

"Do you know when that was?"

The woman pondered Callaway's question. "If I had to take a guess, the last time I saw her was probably a couple of months ago."

"Could it have been three months ago?" Callaway asked.

The woman thought some more. "It could have."

That's how long Elle's sister has been missing, he thought.

Another thought occurred to him. *If that woman in the Polaroid is not Katie Pearson, then who is Linda Eustace?*

FORTY-THREE

When Holt received the call from Marjorie, he rushed over as quickly as possible. He drove around Marjorie's neighborhood in a panic. Marjorie told him Dennis had not come home the night before, and he was not picking up his phone. He was known to take his boat onto Milton Lake and not return until the crack of dawn. Marjorie went to look for him, but no one at the marina had seen Dennis. She had called his work, his friends, and his co-workers, but no one had spoken to him since they had extended their condolences.

Worried sick that something might have happened, she contacted Holt. He assured her he would find him.

Dennis had always been odd, as most computer engineers were. He preferred being left alone to tinker with his gadgets, spend hours glued to his computer screen, or sit in a small boat all day waiting for fish to bite.

Holt was never bothered by Dennis's peculiar behavior. He was an educated man who was also deeply devoted to his family. Holt was beyond ecstatic when Marjorie married Dennis. He saw the love he had for her.

Dennis always made sure Marjorie was not without anything. He showered her with gifts, dinners, and vacations. He helped out around the house and with the kids as well. Even though Marjorie worked as a physical therapist, it was Dennis's income that provided them a comfortable lifestyle.

Dennis's story was not unlike many in America. He grew up in a poor black neighborhood to a single mother and an absent father. He and his four siblings lived in a cramped one-bedroom apartment, with Dennis sharing a bunk bed in the living room with his brother. His two sisters slept with their mother in her room.

Dennis had seen his mother's struggles and had vowed his life would be different. He would get an education, take care of his soul mate, and be there for his children. Dennis was proud he had accomplished all that and much more.

As Holt drove around, he felt a sharp pain in the pit of his stomach. He knew how close Dennis and Isaiah were. When Isaiah was younger, father and son were inseparable. Dennis would take him fishing. He would spend hours playing video games with him. They even shared a love for comic books. Still, the two could not have been more opposite from one another. While Dennis was shy, reserved, and introverted, Isaiah was gregarious, loud, and was the life of the party.

Holt felt that Dennis saw in Isaiah what he wished he could be. Isaiah had an inner fire that could not be banked. He was going to do something that only a select few ever got the chance to do: make it to the pros and earn millions of dollars in the process. But now, Dennis's hopes for his only son were shattered.

FORTY-FOUR

Holt was about to turn the car around and head back to Marjorie's house when he spotted a man sitting on a bench across from a basketball court.

Holt parked and approached him.

Dennis was wearing a sweatshirt and track pants. He had a day-old growth of beard on his face, and his eyes were bloodshot. Holt took a seat next to him. He saw a case of beer underneath the bench, and a half-empty beer bottle next to Dennis's foot.

"How're you doing, Dennis?" Holt asked.

Dennis did not turn to him. He was staring directly at the empty basketball court.

Holt smelled alcohol on him, and he wondered how many bottles he had drunk.

Dennis was fortunate no one had reported him to the police. He would be charged with public consumption of alcohol, which was a state felony.

After a brief pause, Dennis replied, "I used to bring Isaiah here when he was a boy. I would let him play with the bigger kids. I used to push him hard." Dennis's eyes welled up. "I wanted him to get better and make a name for himself. Now I don't care for any of that. I just want my son back."

He covered his face with his hands and broke down.

Holt wanted to comfort his brother-in-law, but he didn't know how. He was fighting back the tears as well.

"I already miss him so much," Dennis said.

"I do, too," Holt said.

Dennis abruptly lifted his head and wiped his face with the back of his sweatshirt sleeve. He inhaled deeply and reached for the beer bottle.

Holt stopped him. "Why don't you let me take that," he said. "I think you've had enough for one day."

Dennis stared at him and then nodded.

Holt drove him back to the house.

Marjorie was waiting by the front door. She looked relieved when she saw that her husband was with her brother. She hugged Dennis and mouthed, "Thank you," to Holt.

They disappeared inside.

Holt was about to drive off when a girl came running out of the house. Holt rolled down the window as she approached.

His niece had golden curly hair, emerald eyes, and freckles on her cheeks. As a child of an interracial couple, she had features from both her parents. But Brit had her mother's smile, which always warmed his heart.

But at the moment, Brit was frowning.

"Do you mind if I sit with you, Uncle Greg?" she asked.

He unlocked the doors. She got in the passenger seat.

"How are you?" he asked.

She shrugged and then hugged herself.

Holt suddenly felt a pang of guilt. Ever since the murder, Holt's thoughts were preoccupied with Isaiah and Marjorie and Dennis. He had forgotten that Brit had lost a brother.

Unlike his connection with Isaiah, Holt did not have much of a relationship with Brit. Maybe that had to do with the fact that she was a girl. He was never interested in all the girly stuff she was into, so they had nothing to talk about. But he still loved her and cared for her. She was a sweet girl who was receptive to other people's feelings. She had what some would call "emotional intelligence" on top of being academically intelligent.

Holt always hoped that as she got older, they would find something they were both passionate about.

Brit said, "Mom and Dad are really messed up after what happened. I'm worried about them."

"They're grieving, so things won't be normal for some time."

Brit pondered her uncle's words and then nodded. "I can't believe he's gone," she said.

"I know," Holt said.

She turned and faced the open window. The cool air blew into the car. He thought about rolling up the window, but he did not. He was not sure if she was cold or hot.

"Was Isaiah seeing anyone?" he asked. He wondered if Brit might be able to confirm Byron Fox's claim that Isaiah was talking to a woman the night he died.

"I don't know," Brit replied. "I've been busy with my studies, and ever since Isaiah went to college, I barely got to see him."

Brit was only at the Cougars' season-opening game. She was not a sports fan.

They were silent for a moment before Brit turned to Holt and said, "Uncle Greg, why would someone hurt Isaiah?"

Her eyes were brimming with tears.

Holt had been thinking the same thing. Isaiah was the type of person who would never hurt a fly. *What had he done to deserve this fate?* he thought.

"I promise, I will find who took Isaiah from us," he said.

Brit leaned over and hugged him. A strong emotion rose inside him, and he put his arms around her. He wanted to tell her everything would be all right and everything would go back to normal. But he knew they would never be the same and that they would never fully recover from the loss of Isaiah.

FORTY-FIVE

Elle and Callaway were back at his office. Elle was seated on the sofa bed, and Callaway was seated at his small desk. He had to escort Elle up the narrow stairs. He stayed behind her in case she missed a step and tumbled backward. She was much shorter than him. Even in her oversized sweater, he could tell she did not weigh much. He would have no problem catching her if she fell.

The office was crammed, and now that he paid attention, he realized the office also reeked of stale body odors and rotted food. Callaway had slept in the office whenever he was evicted from his apartment, which resulted in him not showering for days or weeks. He did not cook, so takeout was his form of getting a meal. There were empty Styrofoam boxes piled up in the corner.

He should have cleaned out the office, but he never expected to bring a client here. He normally met them at their place of residence, at a coffee shop or bar, or sometimes in a park where the client did not want anyone finding out he or she had hired a private investigator. It was mostly paranoia, Callaway believed. He was not a spy who had information that could threaten national security. He was a PI who caught people who were a threat to their marriages and nothing more.

On his laptop, he typed the name given to them by the student at the fashion academy. To his surprise, the search resulted in a dozen hits. Linda Eustace was active on several social networking sites. He clicked on them. There were photos of her lounging on a beach, drinking colorful umbrella drinks, and posing in front of well-known monuments around the world.

He figured the student might have been mistaken, but as he stared at the montage of photos, he could not help but see that Linda Eustace was indeed Katie Pearson.

"What did you find?" Elle asked.

He was not sure how to break his discovery to her.

"Unfortunately," Callaway replied gently, "Linda Eustace is your sister. There are dozens of photos of her on the internet."

He was met with silence. "Are you sure?" she finally said.

"The resemblance is uncanny, I'm afraid."

Callaway thought of something. "The Polaroid you gave me, are you sure it's Katie's."

Elle scowled. "Are you asking me this because I'm blind?"

Callaway winced, but he had to ask. *What if the photo was of someone else?* "You said you had lost your eyesight when you were fourteen," Callaway said. "The Polaroid looks like it was taken when your sister was in her early twenties, so how would you know it's her?"

"She gave it to me only a year ago."

"Why?"

"I asked her for it."

He frowned. *Something doesn't add up*, he thought.

Elle said, "She was leaving for Milton, and it was the first time she would be away from me. I wasn't emotionally ready to let go. I actually tried to talk her out of going, but I knew I could only keep her with me for so long. Eventually, she would have to find her way into the world. She gave me the Polaroid so that I would always have a piece of her with me." She laughed. "It sounds so absurd now that I think about it. People normally keep a memento like a necklace, or a ring, maybe even a scarf with their loved one's perfume on it. I chose to keep a photo that I can't even tell is hers."

Callaway was silent again. What she was saying made sense, but he had a nagging feeling he could not push away.

Elle said, "When I'd not had any contact with Katie, I would take out the photo and hold it. It felt like she was right there with me. Once, though, I spilled coffee over the photo, and I thought I'd ruined it completely. I asked a neighbor if it was destroyed. He told me the photo was not damaged, but there was a brown stain on the back. Is there?"

Callaway flipped the Polaroid over. There was indeed a dark smudge on the back. "Yes."

She smiled. "Then, that is Katie's photo you are holding." Her smile faded when she said,

"This Linda Eustace… how can you be sure it's Katie? What if it's someone who looks like her?"

Callaway again wanted to tell her they were the same person. He scrolled through the social networking site and said, "The last photo was posted exactly three months ago. It was around the time your sister disappeared."

147

Elle's face darkened. She reached for her walking cane and stood up. He feared she would leave the office.

"Why would she lie to me?" Elle said. "Why would she not tell me about this other life she was living as Linda Eustace?"

"Maybe she thought you'd be hurt if you knew she was having a great time traveling around the world without you."

"I would never be jealous of my little sister. Her happiness means everything to me."

Callaway suddenly understood what was nagging him. Maybe Elle's sister was living a double life that she did not want her to find out about.

"When we first spoke, you said this was your first time visiting Milton," he said. "I never asked you then, but why had you not visited before?"

"I offered to come," Elle said. "Each time I did, Katie would make some excuse. She'd say she was too busy with work or school. One time I told her I had packed my bags and I wanted her to pick me up from the bus stop. I was hoping she would take me to where she was staying, but she said she'd caught a viral infection and was bedridden. She did not want me to catch it." Elle frowned. "She knew of my phobia about germs, so it was convenient for her to use it to talk me out of coming to Milton." She shook her head. "How stupid I was not to realize she was keeping me at a distance."

FORTY-SIX

They parked next to a police cruiser and got out. Holt and Fisher approached the uniformed officer. He was tall and slim with long sideburns and a heavy mustache. He looked like he had stepped out of a 1980s cop show.

"Erik Wilcox," he said.

"Officer Wilcox, what have you got for us?" Holt asked.

"I've patrolled this neighborhood for a couple of years now, and I've come to know some of the residents pretty well. One of them said they recognized him." Wilcox held up the photo of the bicyclist. "His name is Bo Smith. He is a small-time drug dealer. They say he's been in and out of prison for fraud and theft." Wilcox pointed at a nearby apartment building. The exterior was painted gray, and the building had rail balconies and large windows. Most were either shaded or were too high to see inside. "The resident said he'd seen Smith riding his bike up and down the neighborhood, and that he lives in one of the units in that building."

"Is he armed and dangerous?" Holt asked.

"I don't know."

Fisher said, "Should we call for backup?"

She could tell Holt was itching to go in and get Bo Smith. If he could do it himself, he would. But he turned to her and said, "What do you think?"

Fisher ran the scenarios through her mind.

Holt was not known for his tact. If there was crucial information he needed, he would use his size and his position on the force to intimidate the witness. Fisher did not agree with him, but she understood why he did that. The bad guys did not play by the rules, so why should they not be allowed to bend them once in a while? Unfortunately, the defense team would have a field day in court should their client lodge a complaint about Holt's behavior.

Technically, they did not have an arrest warrant for Smith. He was not a suspect in Isaiah's death. He was a person of interest. They only wanted to know what he knew. The defense would ask, *Was a SWAT team necessary when you merely wanted to speak to Smith? Was a group of armed officers required to gather such information?* Worst of all, the defense would argue that their client only provided the information out of fear for his safety. He was outnumbered and outgunned. He had no choice but to cooperate with the police. The defense would then ask the judge to rule Smith's information as inadmissible.

They were not going to go in heavy, not when Smith had given no indication he was a threat. He had made the 9-1-1 call, after all. If he was responsible for Isaiah's death, he surely would not have done so.

Then there was the matter of their security. What if Smith *was* dangerous? What if he had a cache of weapons on his premises? This was something she could not take lightly. She would never forgive herself if anything happened to those under her command.

"It's your call, Detective Fisher," Holt said, knowing full well she was mulling over all her options. "Whatever you decide, we'll go with that." He wanted her to know he was not going to hold her decision against her.

Fisher turned to Wilcox. "Which floor is Smith on?"

"Fourth. Apartment 407."

"We go in right now in case someone alerts Smith that we are looking for him," Fisher said.

Holt smiled. She was basically saying, *We don't have time to wait for backup because Smith could disappear.*

She unlocked her trunk and pulled out two Kevlar vests. "But we go in with protection."

"Yes, ma'am," Holt said, grabbing a vest from her. He was grinning from ear to ear.

She just hoped they would not need them.

FORTY-SEVEN

After checking their weapons, they moved toward the front of the building. An older man with grocery bags had just scanned his key fob when they caught up to him. They held the door for him, but the look on his face said he would rather not go inside.

"I think I forgot something in my car," he said as he hurried away.

They moved into the lobby and saw a group of people waiting by the elevators. The moment they saw them, they scattered.

They sense something bad is about to go down, Fisher thought. *I hope not.*

Instead of taking the elevator, which could box them in and allow their target to escape, they took the stairs. It was only four flights up, and Fisher was grateful for that. Her feet were now beginning to feel less sore, and she did not want to make them ache again.

Holt took the front, Fisher was in the middle, and Wilcox was behind her. Wilcox looked like he could handle himself in a shoot-out. The hard look on his face showed he meant business. Fisher tightened her grip on her weapon. She was a good shot. She could hit a target a hundred feet away.

They reached the fourth floor. Holt stuck his head out into the hallway. He looked around and said, "It's clear."

They entered the dingy hallway.

A strong odor hit their nostrils, a combination of spices, marijuana, and body odor.

They gathered around the door to apartment 407. Fisher placed her ear to the door and listened. Loud rap music was playing inside.

She looked at Holt and Wilcox and nodded, silently telling them Smith was home.

She banged on the door and yelled, "Bo Smith! It's the police! Open the door!"

She moved to the side in case Smith decided to fire through the door.

There was no response.

She repeated the command again.

When there was still no response, she gave Holt the signal. Holt faced the door, took one step back, and then kicked the door with his right foot. The side panel cracked and snapped as the door swung in.

They moved inside. There was a narrow hall in front, a kitchen on the right, a door leading into the bathroom, and a living room straight ahead.

Holt continued down the hall. Fisher turned into the kitchen. It was empty. There were dirty dishes in the sink. Flies were swirling over a half-eaten piece of meat pie.

She spotted a bedroom door across from the kitchen and moved ahead.

She reached for the handle and threw the bedroom door open. There was a mattress on the floor, and clothes were strewn around the bed.

After checking the closet, she went back out. She found Holt and Wilcox staring at something on the sofa.

When she got closer, she realized they were standing before a man. Smith's eyes were closed, and his head was tilted back. His mouth was open, and there was drool flowing down his chin.

A black belt was strapped around his arm, and a syringe was stuck in his skin beneath the belt.

On the table before him was a backpack. *Is it the same one we'd seen him wearing in the security camera footage?* Fisher thought. Next to the table was a BMX bicycle, which further confirmed they were in the right apartment.

The TV was playing a loud rap video.

"Is he dead?" Wilcox asked.

"Let's find out," Fisher replied. She leaned in, yelled his name, and shook his shoulder. Smith was unresponsive.

She leaned closer and saw there was a bluish tint to his lips. She placed two fingers on the side of his neck.

"There's a pulse," she said.

Smith had the telltale signs of an overdose. If he did not get immediate medical attention, he would soon be dead.

FORTY-EIGHT

The ride was quiet as they drove to Mayview. After Callaway broke the news to Elle that her sister was living a different life in Milton, she had gotten eerily silent.

She'd sat on his office sofa, staring ahead while gripping her cane. She hardly spoke two sentences to Callaway, and this concerned him.

He did not know her that well, apart from the fact that she was blind, had phobias, and was peculiar at times. He had once caught her smiling about something. When he checked, it was a group of children laughing and giggling while playing at the playground in the distance. He was certain she was focused on them. Maybe her hearing had become more acute, like that blind superhero from the comic books he used to read as a kid.

He did not ask her why she was smiling. A part of him was happy for her. She had been robbed of sight and was now compensating with other senses. Callaway could not imagine what he would do if that were to ever happen to him. He would likely spend the remainder of his life drinking it away thinking, *What's the point when I can't have any fun*?

Sure, people with disabilities lived a full life, but Callaway functioned on stimulation. He rarely contemplated his actions. If he did, he would still be a deputy sheriff, married, and seeing his little girl grow up. Maybe a sudden illness might curb his reckless behavior? Maybe then he would focus on what was more important: his daughter and her happiness.

When Elle finally stood up to leave his office, he offered to drive her wherever she wanted to go. She was so shocked by her sister's betrayal, he felt an obligation not to leave her alone.

She told him she wanted to go home, and he was grateful that she agreed to let him drive her.

They drove for another ten minutes in silence before Elle finally spoke. "It's my fault."

He gave no reply. He did not want to interrupt her.

"I've always been hard on my sister. I've wanted the best for her. Katie could do whatever she wanted in her life. She had nothing that would hold her back. She was free to follow her dreams, something I could never do. I loved her dearly, but maybe I was too harsh with her at times. It felt like if she did not do everything, she was wasting the gifts she had been given. In a way, if she made something of herself, then I made something of myself too. She was going to succeed for the both of us. Now I realize I was pinning my dreams on her."

Makes sense, Callaway thought. Her sister did not want Elle to know what she was up to because she worried she might disappoint her. Then this led to a bigger question: *What was Katie Pearson up to that she had to change her name to Linda Eustace?*

Callaway said, "If you don't mind me asking, what was your dream in life?"

She blushed. "You don't want to know."

"I do."

After a pause, she said, "I wanted to be a professional skater."

"Ice skater?"

She smiled. "Yes. I loved the way they glided on the ice like they were flying. They looked like they were free with not a care in the world."

"Did you skate before?"

"I did until I lost my sight."

"When did you start skating?"

"When I was five."

"You can still skate. You know how to do it. There is nothing stopping you from getting back on the ice."

She turned back to the window and said nothing for the remainder of the ride.

FORTY-NINE

Once they arrived in Mayview, Callaway pulled in front of an apartment building built of brown-stone. Elle got out, turned around, and said, "Thank you."

"You're welcome," Callaway replied.

She moved toward the entrance but then turned back. "Do you want to come upstairs for a cup of tea?" she said.

Callaway considered her offer. He had an hour's drive back to Milton, and he could use some caffeine in his system.

"Sure, that'll be nice," he said.

He parked the Impala in the visitors' parking lot and found her waiting by the front door. She removed a string from around her neck that had a key fob attached.

"I tend to lose things easily," she said with a smile.

"I'm sure," he said.

She scanned the fob and the door opened. She tapped her cane and moved to the elevator. She felt along the walls, found the button, and pressed Up.

Callaway thought of offering to help Elle, but he did not want to offend her. This was her home, after all, and she knew it better than he did.

The elevator doors opened, and they entered. The buttons had braille next to the numbers. She quickly found the floor she was looking for.

They got off on the seventh floor. Elle tapped her cane along the edges of the hallway to guide her. She stopped at a door and moved her fingers over the apartment number.

"This is my place," she said, unlocking the door with her key. "Please come in."

The apartment was pitch-dark when he entered. She came in behind him and closed the door. She moved past him and said, "Have a seat."

Callaway could not tell where the chair was. All he saw was black. "Um… do you know where the light switch is?"

"Oh, dear," she said. "I can function without lights, but I forgot you can't. It's on the right."

He pressed the switch, and the apartment lights came on. Elle's home was small, but it looked spacious. There were minimal furnishings, and the walls were bare, with no photos or paintings.

"Unfortunately, I don't have a TV," Elle said. "Alfred, please turn on the radio!"

Classical music filled the room.

"How'd you do that?" he asked, startled.

Elle smiled. "I have a smart device."

Callaway saw a black cylindrical device next to the sofa.

"It operates on voice command," Elle explained. "It tells me the news, plays music, plays audiobooks, and even orders pizza. When I bought it, the people at the store were kind enough to set it up for me."

"Cool," he said, clearly amazed. "But who's Alfred?"

"It's from my favorite comic book," she replied. "I configured the device to answer to that name. It makes me feel rich and important. Why don't you sit down while I make tea?"

Callaway took a seat. Elle disappeared into the kitchen. He scanned the interior and realized everything was carefully placed, so Elle was safe from bumping into things and could easily find anything she misplaced.

She returned with a tray that held two steaming cups of tea and a plate of cookies. "I hope chocolate chip is okay with you," she said.

"My favorite," Callaway said with a smile.

She placed the tray before him, grabbed a cup, and gently sat on a chair across from him. He noticed she was not wearing her gloves. He also noticed a band on her ring finger.

"You're married?" he asked, feeling surprised.

"Oh, this," she said, holding up her ring. "It's a friendship ring. Katie and I used to give each other bracelets with our names on them. But as we got older, we gave each other rings with our names engraved in them. We vowed that until we found that special someone, we would always wear these rings as a sign of devotion to each other."

Callaway took a big bite of his cookie and a sip from his cup. The cookie was soft and chewy, just perfect with the hot tea. "I was thinking," he said, "if you get yourself a guide dog, it'd be much easier for you to get around, you know."

"I used to have one. After he died, I didn't have the heart to replace him."

"Oh, sorry to hear that." Callaway stifled a grimace. He was trying to make small talk, but he was horrible at it.

"Do you have family, Lee?" Elle asked.

He thought about telling her that his personal life was perfect, but he had a feeling she would somehow catch him lying.

"I used to be married," he replied.

"I'm sorry," she said.

"Don't be. It was my fault."

"Children?"

"A little girl."

Callaway suddenly realized he had been so busy helping Elle look for her sister that he had forgotten to make time to see a special person he had not seen in a while.

FIFTY

Bo Smith was cuffed to the hospital bed. He was confused and disoriented but sedated. A blood sample had been taken, and Fisher was certain the toxicology report would show heroin in his system.

The black backpack contained a bag of heroin. Smith had injected way more heroin than his body could handle. *Even drug dealers get a little too greedy sometimes*, Fisher thought.

Holt had called 9-1-1 the moment Fisher found Smith still had a pulse, but his skin had turned cold to the touch. Emergency responders would need time to arrive on the scene and give him medical attention.

He was not going to make it until the EMT showed up.

With the opioid crisis raging through the city, each law enforcement officer was given training and equipment to treat an overdose. Fisher had rushed down to her car and retrieved a small medical kit from the trunk. Inside was an injection with the drug naloxone. Naloxone had the same receptors as heroin. Once administered, the drug could displace the heroin in a person's brain, stopping an overdose. But naloxone's effect was shorter than heroin, serving as a stopgap until medical attention could be given.

Fisher had administered the drug, and Smith had held on.

When the emergency responders arrived, they placed him on IV fluids to stabilize him, monitoring his breathing all the while. Then they had taken Smith to the hospital.

Fisher and Holt watched Smith from a window outside his room. Smith's heart rate and breathing were normal, and the bluish tint on his lips had faded.

Holt fidgeted next to her. He was eager to go inside and grill Smith about what he knew of Isaiah's death. But Fisher held him back. Smith had come close to death, and if they pushed him too soon, he might not be as responsive as they would like.

The doctors were not appreciative of the detectives' presence either. Their main concern was their patient's well-being, while Holt and Fisher's main concern was the information he had.

Fisher knew Smith could not be questioned under the influence of medication. At the moment, he was not a suspect in Isaiah's death, but that could quickly change during their interview with him. If that happened, they had to be certain he was aware of the questions and his answers. A judge could throw out his statement if there was any indication Smith was not of sound mind. Fisher could not allow that to happen, not when Smith's recollections were vital in finding out what happened to Isaiah.

FIFTY-ONE

Almost an hour later, Holt and Fisher were allowed into the room. Bo Smith's eyes were watery, but while he had been confused upon first awakening, he was lucid by now.

They flashed their badges when he said, "Hey, why did you put me in cuffs?" He moved his wrist, rattling the metal rail on the side of the bed.

Fisher said, "Mr. Smith, you were found unconscious in your apartment from an overdose. We also found a small bag of heroin, which we believe you had injected."

"I'm not a junkie, okay?" he said, pointing his finger at her. "That was the first time I tried it. I swear."

They did not believe him, but they also knew he was not entirely untruthful. Unlike most addicts, there were no additional puncture marks on his arms or legs.

Holt spoke. "We don't care about the drugs. You made the 9-1-1 call regarding Isaiah Whitcomb's body. Isn't that right?"

Fisher could see Holt was trying hard to be calm, but he looked like he was ready to explode.

Smith blinked. "Yeah, I called 9-1-1. Why? Did I do something wrong?"

Before Holt could grill Smith, Fisher quickly asked, "Please explain how you found Mr. Whitcomb."

"I was riding my bike when I spotted the car. It looked like someone had gone crazy on the car. There was glass everywhere, and I even saw blood. I mean, I've seen people get shot before, but this brother's car was covered in blood, you know."

Holt clenched his jaw.

"And what did you do?" Fisher asked.

"I went to check who it was—I thought it could be someone I rolled with, you know—but when I looked, I knew it was Isaiah Whitcomb."

"How did you know him?" Fisher asked.

He looked at her like she was dumb. "The brother was gonna make it to the pros. He was a stud, man. When I saw him like that, all bloody and dead, I had to call 9-1-1."

Fisher could see the veins throbbing in Holt's neck.

"After you called it in, why didn't you stay at the scene?" Fisher asked.

"I didn't want the police to start asking me questions, you know what I'm saying? I've got a bit of a reputation," Smith replied.

"We know. You're a drug dealer and user."

"I'm not a drug dealer or user," he said, feeling offended. "I sometimes hustle to earn some extra cash, but I don't do drugs."

"We found a bag of heroin in your apartment."

"I found it that morning."

"Where did you find it?"

Smith looked away.

"Bo," Fisher said, "you better start being honest with us, or else we won't be able to help you." She was using a tactic used by every officer during an interview or interrogation: make the interviewee feel like the authorities are on their side and get them to confess.

"I found it in the car," Smith said.

Fisher blinked. "What car?"

"The car Isaiah Whitcomb was in. Aren't you listening?"

"That's a lie!" Holt yelled.

Smith almost jumped off the bed. The cuffs held him in place. "I'm not lying. I found the bag in the glove box."

"Isaiah did not do drugs!" Holt growled.

He moved toward Smith.

Fortunately, an officer at the door heard the commotion. He was bigger than Holt. He came in and helped Fisher restrain her partner. Then they escorted him to the hall.

Fisher returned to the room and said, "Bo, if you don't come clean with me, I will make your life a living hell."

"Listen, lady, I swear to you. I took the bag of heroin from the car. I also took his wallet."

"Whose wallet?"

"Isaiah Whitcomb's."

Fisher paused. They had searched Isaiah at the scene and found his wallet was missing. This had troubled her. Why would Isaiah leave the campus without his wallet? The only reasonable answer was that someone had taken it from him after he died.

Bo Smith took the wallet.

"What did you do with it?" Fisher asked.

"There was some cash in it. I took it and then dumped the wallet."

"Where?"

"In a garbage bin."

"Which garbage bin?"

Smith searched his mind frantically. "In front of a tattoo parlor."

"What's the name?"

"I don't know, but it was only a block from where I found Isaiah Whitcomb."

FIFTY-TWO

Fisher found Holt pacing the hallway. The officer who had assisted her in removing Holt from the room was standing not too far from him.

She walked up to Holt.

"He's lying to save his ass," he said. "He knows who killed Isaiah. Or he did it himself."

"If he did, then why did he call it in?" Fisher asked.

"I don't know. Maybe he regretted it once he realized what he had done."

"We listened to the call. Smith knew the victim was Isaiah, a basketball star. He even said so in the recording. And by the sound of it, he came across as a fan of his."

Holt only grunted.

"Whoever shot Isaiah ambushed him," Fisher continued. "When we were in Smith's apartment, we searched it and found no weapons."

"Maybe he dumped the weapon," Holt said.

"And kept the heroin?" she asked with a raised eyebrow.

Holt opened his mouth but then shut it.

"He is lying, though," Fisher said.

"About what?"

"That he's no junkie. Even though we found no drugs apart from the heroin, the apartment reeked of cannabis and crack."

"That's why I don't believe a single word he is saying," Holt said. "Smith did not find heroin in the Chrysler."

Fisher crossed her arms over her chest. "Okay, let's say you are right about that."

"I am," Holt shot back.

"If that's the case, then what was Isaiah doing in a neighborhood like that so early in the morning?"

Holt blinked. She could tell he was mulling this over.

Holt cursed and began pacing again.

She followed him. "Something doesn't add up, I agree," she said. "But right now, we don't know much. So I am more inclined to give Smith the benefit of the doubt."

Holt faced her. "I know Isaiah. He grew up right before my eyes. If there was any indication he was into something illegal, I would have sensed it."

"Would you have?" Fisher asked.

"What do you mean?"

"You loved Isaiah—everyone who got to know him did—and it's that love that blinds people from the truth. How many times have you read about someone who, by all accounts, was a good, decent, hardworking family man who ended up committing horrific crimes?"

Holt thought for a moment. "What if the drugs belonged to Jay Bledson?" he suggested.

Fisher had considered this. Isaiah was found dead in the assistant coach's car, but there were gaping holes in Holt's theory. "We can ask him, but I don't think it will lead us anywhere," she said.

"Why not?"

"A few reasons. One: Bledson would not be stupid enough to let a student take his car with drugs stashed in it. Two: Isaiah had told Bledson he needed to borrow the car for personal reasons. We saw him on the security footage rushing out of the practice facility, so it is obvious he was going somewhere to meet someone. Three: When we interviewed him, Bledson did not give off any indication that he was concerned the police had found drugs in the Chrysler. It is only now, after we spoke to Smith, that we are aware of the heroin. My guess is that Bledson had no idea and still doesn't know about the drugs in his vehicle."

Holt shook his head and continued pacing. She knew it was his way of working through the information he had just been handed.

A uniformed officer walked up the hall. He spotted Fisher and approached her. In his hand was a clear plastic bag. Inside was a black leather wallet.

When Smith had told her where he had dumped the wallet, Fisher had made a call for a patrol officer to go check it out.

"Where did you find it?" she asked him.

"Outside a tattoo parlor," the officer replied. "Fortunately, the garbage truck was not scheduled to pass by until later today."

Fisher pulled a pair of latex gloves from her pocket. She removed the wallet and flipped it open.

Isaiah's driver's license was in the inside flap.

Fisher turned to Holt. His eyes were narrow and his expression was serious. She could tell what he was thinking.

Bo Smith is telling the truth.

FIFTY-THREE

After leaving Elle's apartment, Callaway drove back to Milton. During the drive, he could not help but think about all the mistakes he had made in his life. There were too many, and by the end of his journey, he was utterly depressed. He had begun the day feeling sorry for Elle. Now he was feeling sorry for himself.

Instead of heading home, he took a detour.

He pulled into a house's driveway and smiled. The home's lights were on, which meant the occupants were home.

He checked himself in the rearview mirror and frowned. He had forgotten about the bandage on his nose. He considered ripping it off, but the thought of pain made him reconsider.

Guess I need to rely on my charm instead of my good looks, he thought.

He got out and approached the front door. He practiced his smile. When he was ready, he knocked.

A moment later, the door swung open. The smile on his face instantly disappeared when he saw who it was *not*.

"Can I help you?" the woman said. She was short and plump with rosy cheeks, and she wore thick glasses.

"Um… where's Patti?" he asked.

"And you are…?" the woman replied.

"I'm Lee."

The woman crossed her arms. "Oh, so you're Lee. Patti told me stories about you."

And they are all true, he wanted to say, but didn't.

"Who are you?" he asked.

"I live down the street."

"So, what're you doing in Patti's house?"

"I should ask you the same question."

Why is this woman giving me a hard time?

"I'm here to see Nina. Can you go tell her that her father is here?"

"Sorry, no can do."

"Why not?"

"I have specific instructions from Patti. Nina is supposed to do her homework, watch a little bit of TV, and then go straight to bed."

Callaway was beginning to fume. "Maybe you did not hear me. I'm Nina's father and Patti's ex-husband. Please go and get my daughter so I can speak to her."

"Maybe you did not hear me," she said, raising her voice and getting closer to him. He took a step back. She looked like she could beat him up. "Nina is not supposed to have any visitors."

He swallowed. *Maybe I should come back another time*, he thought.

A little girl appeared behind the woman. "Daddy," she squealed.

She rushed out and gave him a big hug.

Sabrina "Nina" Callaway was nine years old. She had dark hair, emerald green eyes, and a smile that could melt even a Russian gangster's heart.

"Hey, sweetheart," he said.

She frowned. "What happened to your face?"

His hand moved toward his nose. "It's a long story. Where's your mom?"

"She has a late shift tonight."

Patti was a nurse, and she worked long shifts at a local hospital. She worked hard to put food on the table and keep a roof over Nina's head. On top of that, she had done an exceptional job raising her. Unfortunately, Callaway could take no credit for how bright his daughter was. Nina got Patti's beauty and her brains. He just prayed she did not get any of his bad habits to balance everything out.

"Come inside," Nina said with excitement.

"I don't think it's a good idea," the woman said. "I was told not to let strangers in."

"I'm not a stranger," Callaway said, feeling offended. "As I told you, I'm Patti's ex-husband and Nina's father."

"Then why aren't you babysitting her?" the woman asked.

She has a point.

"Call Patti," Callaway said. "Ask her if I can spend time with Nina. If she says no, I'll leave."

Nina turned to him. "Dad, I don't want you to go."

"Baby, we have to do what your mom says. She's earned it." Callaway meant every word. Patti had sacrificed so much for their daughter, and he had done diddlysquat. If he tried to undermine her authority, his behavior would negatively affect Nina. He did not want to be one of those parents who tried to sway their child against the other parent. He was grateful that Patti wanted him to be a part of Nina's life. It was up to him to make the time to be there. Patti believed a girl's development was strongly tied to her relationship with her father. Callaway hoped that one day he would make up for all the time he had lost.

The woman saw how happy Nina was and said, "All right, I'll call your mom and ask."

She went inside. Callaway held his only child. "So, how's Grumpy Neighbor treating you?" he asked.

"She's nice. She's teaching me how to bake cookies, cupcakes, and muffins."

I bet she likes eating them too, he thought.

"I like her," Nina said.

He smiled. "If you like her, then I guess I can tolerate her too."

The woman returned. "Patti said you can come inside."

Nina jumped with joy and said, "Yay!"

Callaway jumped with joy too, clapping his hands as he did.

Nina rolled her eyes. "Mom's right. You need to grow up."

He laughed and followed her in.

FIFTY-FOUR

The Chrysler had been taken to the police impound for testing. The vehicle would be stripped apart, and any evidence found would be photographed and tagged in case it needed to be presented at a trial.

Once Holt and Fisher heard Bo Smith's statement, they immediately requested a drug analysis on the Chrysler. The Milton Police Department now had access to quick testing methods, the same ones used at airports and border crossings.

A swab test was conducted on the car's glove compartment, and the test came back purple.

The color was an indicator of heroin.

Thorough testing would be conducted for the courts later, but the discovery was enough for Holt to pay a visit to his sister.

With a heavy heart, he broke the news to Marjorie. She yelled and called him names he had heard his father call him when he did something wrong as a kid. He did not take her words personally. He had told her what no mother wanted to hear.

Her beloved son may have died due to a drug deal gone wrong.

"How dare you tell me Isaiah was selling... selling…"

Marjorie could not get herself to say *heroin*. She cupped her hand over her mouth and fell on the sofa. She let out an anguished wail as she wrestled with her feelings.

Holt's eyes were moist as he watched her slump down in agony. He wanted to reach out and hold her, but he knew she would not let him. At that moment, he was the enemy. He had accused Isaiah of something unfathomable, and by extension, he had accused her of being a bad parent, someone who had raised a drug dealer.

He turned to Brit, who was standing across from him in the living room. When his eyes met hers, he saw the same pain as in her mother's. She burst into tears and rushed up the stairs. He heard her bedroom door slam shut a moment later.

Dennis stood near the fireplace. He had not moved an inch. Holt looked to him for help, but Dennis refused to make eye contact.

Holt was alone. He felt like the walls were closing in on him. He began to feel suffocated as if someone was strangling him. Holt had suffered severe asthma as a child, and he began to feel like his condition was returning.

He shut his eyes as hot tears streamed down his cheeks. He could not breathe. He was choking. He was going to die.

He felt a hand on his shoulder. He opened his eyes. It was Marjorie. The venom she had for him a moment ago was replaced by concern.

She wrapped her arms around him. He let her hug him. He needed her more than she could ever imagine.

Dennis came over. He opened his mouth, but no words came out. He stood there for a moment. He then placed his hand on Holt's shoulder, held it there briefly, and then left the room.

Holt was not sure how long Marjorie hugged him, but he was grateful for her gesture. She then looked him in the eye. "Isaiah was not into drugs, no matter what anyone says. He just wasn't, Greg."

He stared at her. "How can you be so sure?" he slowly asked.

"I'm his mother. I know it. And you know it too."

I thought I did, he thought, *but right now, I do not know what to believe.*

FIFTY-FIVE

Callaway was on the sofa. Nina was curled up next to him with her head resting on his lap. They had been watching a movie when she fell asleep. He was worried she would want to watch a girly movie, but she surprised him by wanting to see a science fiction one. Even though he was relatively uninvolved in her daily life, she still shared some of his interests.

As a kid, Callaway loved reading stories about robots, aliens, and spaceships. He dreamed of one day voyaging with the crew of the starship *Enterprise*. When he learned they were not real, he was heartbroken. But even then, the feeling of traveling through galaxies looking for adventure and discovering new life and new civilizations had not left him. Maybe that was why he was so restless, always looking for the next exciting opportunity to get involved in.

The neighbor was in the kitchen. She only came out to see if Nina needed anything. Callaway had a feeling she would rather stare at the stove than spend a minute in the same proximity as him. He was perfectly fine with that. He would rather read an encyclopedia than have a conversation with her.

He brushed the hair off Nina's face. His little girl was growing up fast. Soon she would be a teenager and then an adult. She would start dating and maybe even get married.

He always swore to be a bigger part of her life, but something prevented him from doing so. He knew the answer, whether he admitted it or not. Callaway did not know how to be a parent. He always found a way to mess it up.

Nina was the most precious thing in the world, and he was afraid he would do something that could affect her development. He was known to get drunk whenever the opportunity arose. He risked his life savings on sure bets, which turned out not to be on many occasions. He rushed into relationships with women, and just as quickly ended them.

All in all, he was not the role model he wanted to be for his girl.

The best thing he did, and the hardest, was to get out of the way of Nina's growth. She was coming into her own as a person, and he did not want his influence to negatively affect her.

Some could argue his way of thinking was a copout. He was avoiding the responsibility and sacrifice millions of parents made each day for their children. But Callaway would argue that not all people were made to be parents. There was no course, certificate, or test that told a person they could do the job and do it well. It was a learn-on-the-fly kind of thing, and Callaway did not trust himself enough to do a half-decent job.

He worried he could damage Nina for the rest of her life by leaving her with emotional scars.

He shuddered at the thought.

He was an absent father—there was no doubt about that—but if his little girl found herself in some kind of trouble, he would drop everything and be there for her. He would lie, cheat, and steal to make the problem go away. He would even put himself in harm's way to protect her.

FIFTY-SIX

Callaway heard a car approach the driveway and then come to a halt. A minute later, the front door opened, and he could hear footsteps in the hall.

Patti's home, he thought.

The neighbor appeared from the kitchen and rushed to her. Callaway could not see them because his back was to the hall, but he could hear them.

"Thanks so much for looking after Nina," Patti said.

"It's no problem. Nina was a good girl."

"What about him?" she asked. "Was he a good boy?"

He smiled. Patti had a great sense of humor. Even better than his.

"I'm surprised you married a guy like him," the neighbor replied.

"We all make mistakes when we are young."

The smile on his face fell.

Ouch, he thought.

"Thanks again for taking care of Nina."

"No problem. Anytime."

He heard the front door close.

Patricia "Patti" Callaway entered the room, and he immediately found himself breathless. Even after all these years, he could not believe he let her get away. She had short dark hair and brown eyes that were amazing lie detectors. Her lips were always curled into a smile, no matter how bad things were in her life.

She was wearing a coat over her green scrubs. *She must be exhausted after a twelve-hour shift*, he thought, but he still found her stunning.

"You wanna grab your jaw off the floor, or do you want me to do it?" she said.

He did not realize his mouth was open. He shut it and realized his tongue was suddenly dry.

She placed her purse on the floor, pulled off her coat, and sat across from him. She rubbed her feet and said, "What're you doing here, Lee?"

"I came to see Nina."

"Okay, sure," she said, not believing him.

"I missed her."

She stared at him and went back to rubbing her feet.

"You're not going to ask what happened to my face?" he asked, pointing at his bandaged nose.

"I'm sure you deserved it."

Damn, he thought. *She's good.*

"Tiring day?" he asked.

"Always is when you work at a hospital."

"Someone died on your watch?"

She went silent.

"Oh, sorry, that was insensitive."

"So, where's the Charger?" she asked.

"There's a bucket of metal parked in my driveway." She was referring to the Impala. Patti knew how much he loved his car. He would never go anywhere without it.

"The Charger is in the shop."

"What happened to it?"

"It needs a bit of work."

"I bet the same person who did that to your face also smashed up the Charger."

She is very good.

"You can say that."

He looked around. "The house looks great. I'm glad you fixed it." Patti had been saving up to renovate the house, but that was not easy while being a single parent. The roof had been leaking, the basement was flooding, and some of the windows needed to be replaced.

"Thanks to you," she said. "I even managed to upgrade the kitchen cabinets."

"I'm glad I could help." He looked down at Nina and smiled. Her eyes were closed and she was breathing softly. She looked like an angel.

"Do you mind putting her to bed?" Patti asked. "I was on my feet all day. I can't carry her upstairs."

"I would love to," he replied, overjoyed by the opportunity.

He gently lifted her up in his arms. She was much heavier than he remembered, but she was older now, so this was to be expected.

He carefully took each step so as not to wake her.

He placed her head on the pillow and covered her body with a blanket covered in hearts. He then watched her sleep for a couple of minutes. He had made a lot of mistakes in his life, but Nina was not one of them.

He went downstairs.

Patti said, "You hungry?"

He stared at her.

"I got takeout on the way home. You're welcome to share some."

He smiled. "Yeah, that would be nice."

FIFTY-SEVEN

Fisher found Holt behind his desk, typing away on his computer. Even this early in the morning, she was not surprised to see him at the station.

"How's Nancy?" she asked.

"She's still at her mother's," he replied without looking up. "I'm inclined to leave her there until this case is resolved."

"You mean, Isaiah's?"

"Yes."

"We don't catch them all, you know."

"We *will* find the person who killed him," Holt said with conviction.

She wished she could believe that too. In her experience, the odds of solving a crime was very low. An investigation was a combination of grunt work and pure luck.

If an investigation was like a mystery-room puzzle, where all pieces were scattered about and the players had to just find them, all investigations would be solved within hours.

"What are you working on?" she asked.

"I'm catching up on paperwork."

She spotted a newspaper on his desk. The front-page headline read FALL FROM GRACE, BASKETBALL STAR'S SORDID LIFE WITH DRUGS.

Isaiah's high school graduation photo was next to the headline.

Fisher scowled. *How did the media get wind of the drugs so fast? Did somebody at the hospital blab, or was it somebody here? I hope it was the hospital, but if somebody here with a press connection talked, they better keep mum, or Greg is going to tear into them.*

She knew it was not unusual for reporters to cozy up to officers. The reporters got a scoop, and the officers got their names in print. In Isaiah's case, no officer would dare say anything on the record. They preferred anonymity over finding themselves at the end of Holt's fury. The reporters did not care either way. They got the story they wanted, and when the time was right, they would make it up to the officer by giving them a positive profile in the next story that involved them.

"Does your sister know?" she asked.

"I broke it to her last night."

"And?"

"She doesn't believe it."

"What about you?"

Holt stopped typing and shrugged.

"You can't be serious," Fisher said, surprised by his reaction. "You actually believe that headline there?"

Holt finally looked at her. "I don't believe it. I believe the evidence found at the scene." He slid a document to her. "The lab report came back. There were traces of heroin in the Chrysler's glove compartment. The result is one hundred percent conclusive."

"That still doesn't prove Isaiah was involved in drugs," she said.

"What if he was?" Holt said. "There's a lot we don't know about the people we love. Isn't that what you said to me back at the hospital?"

She fell silent.

"After our discovery, I remembered an incident I had forgotten about—or maybe chose to forget about. When Isaiah was sixteen, I caught him smoking pot behind his school. He was with other kids, and I happened to drive by when I saw him. He said it was his first time, but the way he inhaled the stuff told me it was not something new to him."

Fisher was quiet for a moment.

"He was still a good kid," she said.

"He was," Holt agreed.

"And it still doesn't change the fact that we have to find the person responsible for his death."

"It doesn't," Holt said firmly.

FIFTY-EIGHT

Callaway was behind his desk when he heard someone climbing the steps to his office. He stood up to check and saw Elle by the door.

"You should not have come up on your own," he said. "It's not safe for you." It had rained earlier, and the metal steps were wet and slippery.

"I managed fine, don't you think?" she said with a brief smile.

He guided her to the sofa. "How're you feeling?" he asked. When he had left her apartment the night before, she was pretty down.

"I'm feeling better, thank you," she replied.

Callaway looked at her face. Due to her blindness, he was unable to gauge her emotions. He could usually tell if someone was sad, angry, or confused just by looking them in the eye. The sociopaths or habitual liars were the hardest people to read. They were able to suppress their emotions deep inside them. But the eyes of average folks were a key to knowing what was going on with them. But with Elle, Callaway had to look for other indicators as to her mood.

Elle gave him another brief smile. Callaway could tell it was forced.

"I was going through the social networking sites for Linda Eustace," Callaway said, "and I was wondering… is your family wealthy?"

Elle shook her head. "No, my father worked in a cubicle his entire life. And my mother worked mostly in administrative jobs."

"According to the posts by Linda—I mean, Katie—she's traveled extensively in the past year."

"Ever since she came to Milton, you mean?" Elle asked.

"I'm guessing, yes. The photos of her are tagged for countries like Spain, Barbados, and Jamaica. There are others of her in Miami and Las Vegas, but it's the countries that I'm curious about. How could a student working at a fast-food restaurant afford to go to these places?"

"I don't know. I wish I did."

Elle was quiet for a moment. "I now realize I did not know my sister as well as I thought I did," she said. "Everything she told me over the phone was a lie. She never lived at the address she gave me, she did not work at the place she told me she did, and she enrolled at the fashion academy under a different name. I think she was creating a new life for herself. A life that did not involve *me*. I held her back, and the moment she arrived in Milton, she was free to be whoever she wanted."

She took a deep breath.

A thought occurred to Callaway. "Was Katie seeing someone? Was a rich boyfriend perhaps funding her trips?"

Elle placed her finger on her chin as she thought. "When Katie moved to Milton, she mentioned she had met someone," she replied.

"Who?" Callaway asked, almost jumping off his chair.

"I believe she told me his name was… Bruno Rocco."

"Bruno Rocco?" he repeated.

"Yes, that's what I think she said."

He turned to the laptop and typed the name in. He frowned. "There are no Bruno Roccos living in Milton. Perhaps it was a false name she gave you."

Elle sighed. "I can't believe I did not mention this to you earlier. I never made much of it. Do you think this Bruno Rocco knows what happened to my sister?"

"Could be, but how long ago did your sister tell you she had met him?"

"When she moved to Milton."

Callaway frowned again. "That's over a year ago, and I don't see any photos of her with any man. He could just be an acquaintance or a friend. I'll ask around to see if anyone knows someone with that name. In the meantime, we know Katie was living a double life as Linda Eustace. This gives us something to work with. And I know just where to start."

FIFTY-NINE

Fisher spotted a manila envelope on her desk chair. She grabbed it and realized it contained Isaiah's cell phone records.

She ripped the envelope open and pulled out the call sheet. She scanned the sheet and then rushed to Holt's desk. He was still working away on his computer.

"On the morning Isaiah was killed, he had made several calls to one number," she said.

"Give me the number," he said.

She read the digits, and he punched them in. "It's registered to a Cassandra Stevens," he said.

Fisher flipped through the documents in her hand. "There are also several text messages between Isaiah and Cassandra Stevens."

She let Holt see them.

Isaiah: HEY GIRL, I'M STILL WAITING FOR YOUR CALL.

Isaiah: HOW'D THE MEETING GO?

Isaiah: ARE YOU OKAY? I'M WORRIED ABOUT YOU.

Isaiah: CALL ME. PLEASE.

"All these messages were sent in the early morning," Holt said, scanning the phone log. "She then called him back close to two hours after his last message. They spoke for one minute and twenty-seven seconds."

"He texted her again soon after that," Fisher said.

Isaiah: YOU GOT CUT OFF.

Isaiah: WHAT HAPPENED?

Isaiah: IF YOU DON'T CALL ME BACK, I WILL CALL THE POLICE.

"She then sent him a reply," Fisher said, pointing to a message.

Cassandra: I'M OK. EVERYTHING IS FINE NOW. MEET ME AT THE FURNITURE STORE PARKING LOT AND WAIT FOR ME.

"That's where he was found," Holt said, looking up.

"He then sent her another text," Fisher said.

Isaiah: I'M ON MY WAY.

"And there is one final text from Isaiah to her."

Isaiah: I'M HERE. LET ME KNOW WHERE YOU ARE AND I'LL COME GET YOU.

Soon after that text, Isaiah was murdered.

Holt and Fisher pondered what they had just read.

"Now we know why Isaiah was in that neighborhood," Holt said. "He went to meet this woman."

"Could she be the woman Byron Fox was talking about?" Fisher asked.

Holt stood up and grabbed his coat. "We need to speak to her. She may know what happened to Isaiah."

SIXTY

The red neon silhouette of a woman flashed brightly above the black exterior of the Gentlemen's Hideout.

"This can't be the right address," Holt said, staring at the listing for Cassandra Stevens he had pulled from the online phone directory.

"I'm not surprised," Fisher said.

"Why not?"

"Just look at the name. It's one a lot of strippers use."

"How would you know?"

"I've worked undercover before," she replied. "Cherry, Candy, Charity, Chastity, Cassandra—they all have the same ring to it."

"I don't know. Cassandra sounds different than the others."

Fisher rolled her eyes. "Would Cassie work better for you?"

He opened his mouth but then closed it. "What was Isaiah doing with a stripper?" he said a second later.

"I'm not sure, but let's find out."

Fisher pulled the door handle, but the door was locked. She checked the schedule on the front window and saw the club did not open until after lunch. It was still mid-morning.

"Maybe we should come back later," Holt said.

"Wait." She pointed to a piece of paper stuck next to the club's hours. The club was looking for girls, and there was a number to call if they were interested. Fisher dialed the number and got a man on the line. He told her he was the club's owner.

When she told him who she was and why she needed to speak to him, he said, "Give me twenty minutes and I'll be right over."

Exactly twenty minutes later, a black Mercedes pulled into the parking lot. A man in his fifties with gray hair, a slight pouch, and a double chin got out and approached them.

"Derek Kuzminskas," he said.

Fisher and Holt introduced themselves. "We are looking for a woman who may work in your establishment," Fisher said. "Cassandra Stevens."

"Yeah, Cassie is one of my dancers," he said.

Fisher smiled at Holt. *Cassie.*

"You mean she's a stripper," Fisher said.

"They prefer to be called dancers," he said, correcting her. "Cassie is a regular and one of my main attractions."

"Is she working today?"

"I'm not sure. She hasn't come to work for the past two days."

Fisher shot a glance at Holt. He was thinking what she was. *That's how long Isaiah's been dead.*

"Is it normal for girls not to show up for work?" Fisher asked.

"It is, and it is not," Kuzminskas replied.

Holt and Fisher looked puzzled.

"Okay, this is how it works," Kuzminskas said. "If a girl is a good dancer and customers keep coming back to see her, she gets the best time slot, which is usually when the club is super busy. If a girl shows up on time and on the days she is supposed to, she gets the other preferred time slots. If a girl misses her time to go on stage or she isn't very good at it—you gotta realize, not every woman is cut out for this kind of work—then we let her go, or if she's desperate, we'll give her a slot when there's hardly anyone at the club. The girls call it 'purgatory.' So, to answer your question, this isn't a nine-to-five job where if you don't show up, your boss will call you at home to ask why, you know what I mean?"

"But Cassandra was a regular, you said. Isn't it unusual for her not to show up when she is scheduled to?" Fisher asked

"It is, but I don't run after these girls. If one stops showing up, then there are many more to take her place. It's the way the business works."

Fisher thought this over. "Can you give us her home address?"

"I can't confirm what she gave me is her real address. I bet Cassie's not even her real name."

"I suppose you don't ask your dancers for their Social Security numbers then," Fisher said. Thanks to her undercover work, she knew strip club owners did not follow normal employment practices.

Kuzminskas chuckled. "Listen, I pay these girls in cash. They want it that way. They got family troubles, or they are running away from some kind of trouble. They don't want anyone finding them, especially not the government. Also, some of them do this to earn enough for school. You wouldn't believe how many student doctors or lawyers work here. Plus, they don't want their family or friends finding out what they do when they are not studying."

"Okay, give us the address you have on file," Fisher said. "We'll confirm if it's real or not."

"Sure, I've got it in my office."

"Oh, and we're going to need a photo of her," Holt added.

SIXTY-ONE

The house was in a nice neighborhood. The home had a stucco exterior, a flat roof, and bay windows.

Callaway pulled up behind a Porsche Cayenne. The Impala stuck out in the row of fancy parked cars that lined the street.

His online search for Linda Eustace had led to this house. Callaway hoped the moment they knocked on the door, they would find Katie. The reunion would be odd, for sure. Katie had done everything to hide her other identity from Elle.

"Are you sure you want to go in?" he asked Elle. "It might not go as you would like it to."

"If my sister is in there, then I want to meet her," Elle replied. "I want her to tell me why she has kept me in the dark the entire year."

"Okay, sure, let's go," Callaway said.

They walked up to the house. Callaway rang the doorbell. A moment later, a woman answered the door. She was wearing a blue dress, earrings, and high heels.

"Can I help you?" she asked.

"Sorry to bother you, but we're looking for Linda Eustace."

"And you are?"

"I'm Lee, and this is Linda's sister, Elle."

"Oh, I didn't know Linda had a sister," the woman said. "She never once mentioned it."

Why would she? Callaway thought. *It would lead people to ask more questions.*

"Do you know where Linda is?" Elle asked, eager to finally be face-to-face with her sister.

The woman let out a short laugh. "I know this may sound strange, but Linda's not been seen for almost three months."

That's how long Elle's not had any contact with her, Callaway thought.

"And who are you?" he asked.

"I'm Linda's landlord. I own this house. Linda was renting my guesthouse. She used to give me a check at the end of each month, but then she just disappeared. After two months, I had to empty the guesthouse to rent it out again. I sold most of her furniture to recoup the unpaid rent. If I had known she had family, I would have contacted you instead. I'm really sorry about that."

Elle was silent. Callaway could feel her disappointment. He, too, was looking forward to some sort of resolution to the case.

"I kept a box of her personal stuff," the woman said. "I didn't have the heart to throw it out. You can go through it. It's in the garage."

"That would be nice. Thank you," Elle said.

Three cardboard boxes were piled up next to some gardening equipment in the corner. "It's the one on the top," the woman said, pointing. She then left to give them space to sift through the items.

Callaway pulled the box down and opened it. At the top were trophies and medals. "Your sister was a swimmer?" he asked.

Elle was surprised by the question. "Why do you ask?"

"Never mind," he said, and moved on. He found framed pictures under the trophies. He lifted the first one. Katie was smiling next to a diving board.

"What did you find?" Elle asked anxiously.

"Photos of Katie when she was younger."

"Do you mind?" Elle asked, removing the glove on her right hand.

Callaway gave the picture to her. She moved her fingers over the photo. Callaway sensed she wanted to touch something that belonged to her sister, maybe allowing Elle to feel Katie in some way.

Callaway lifted the next picture. Katie was posing with another woman. The woman had dark curly hair, a brown complexion, and hazel eyes.

"Did Katie have any friends in Milton?" he asked.

"She never mentioned anyone to me."

The way Katie and the woman were smiling and making peace signs at the camera told him they were good friends.

He did not see any other photos. He was sad Katie had cut Elle out of her new life, but her behavior made sense. The more people she had from her past life, the more questions they would raise.

What was Katie afraid of that made her change her identity? he thought.

He pulled out a binder. On the front were the words *Fashion Academy* printed in neat shorthand.

"This must be Katie's stuff from when she was going to school," he said.

He shoved his hand deeper into the box and pulled out a small leather satchel. He unzipped the bag and realized it held women's hygiene products.

"What's that?" Elle asked.

Callaway handed the bag to her. He returned to the box. So far, he had not found anything that could be useful to them. He sifted through more items and realized there was nothing more to see.

He turned to Elle.

He noticed something lying next to her foot. *It wasn't there before*, he thought.

"Did you drop something?" he asked.

"Did I?"

"Oh, right," he said, feeling sheepish. He leaned down and picked the item up. It was a wallet-size black-and-white photo of a man. The picture looked like a mug shot. The man's features were rough and hard. The back bore the initials *BR*.

"Who's BR?" Callaway asked.

Elle thought for a moment. "Could it be Bruno Rocco?"

"It might well be," Callaway replied, staring at the photo.

SIXTY-TWO

Why was Isaiah calling a stripper on the morning of his death? Holt wondered.

Fisher was right that Cassandra Stevens was not her real name. He was unable to find her in the police department's database. He even tried "Cassie Stevens" and came up empty.

The only thing they had was the address the strip club owner had given them. They were on their way to check.

Fisher was in the passenger seat, and he could tell she had a lot on her mind.

"I know what you're thinking," he said. "First it's the heroin, and now it's a stripper. What did Isaiah get himself into?"

"Yeah, I was thinking that," she admitted. "But I was also thinking that something doesn't add up now that we know Cassandra Stevens is involved."

"What do you mean?" he asked.

"I don't think Isaiah's death had anything to do with drugs."

"But heroin residue was found in the Chrysler's glove compartment."

"I think someone planted that there."

"Bo Smith?"

"No. He wouldn't risk putting it there and then get caught taking it. He nearly overdosed on the stuff."

"Okay, but I don't see how the heroin doesn't play a role in what happened."

"If you examine Isaiah's text messages to Cassandra, you will see that she was in some sort of trouble and that he was worried about her. He even mentioned going to the police. Why would someone who was carrying heroin on him offer to contact the police? It doesn't make sense."

"A lot doesn't make sense at the moment," Holt said.

"Right. And then in her text back to Isaiah, Cassandra told him to meet her at the furniture store's parking lot. This tells us Isaiah's visit to that neighborhood had nothing to do with a drug deal. He was just following her instructions. Also, Cassandra never once mentioned any drugs in her messages to him."

"But they did speak for one minute and twenty-seven seconds. That's enough time for her to tell him to bring the drugs to that location."

Fisher gave him a hard look. "It sounds like you believe Isaiah was a drug dealer who died during a deal gone bad."

Holt shook his head. "No. As a detective, I follow the evidence, not what's in my heart. Isaiah was found dead in a vehicle that had traces of an illegal drug. Whether it's his or not is still to be determined. He was in contact with a woman who was not involved in a respectable profession. Whether she was his girlfriend or not, I am not sure. What I am sure of is that he had no business being where he was two days ago. He was supposed to be in class, which he had skipped to meet this woman. Isaiah made a choice—a terrible one—that resulted in him getting killed."

Holt's knuckles were white as he gripped the steering wheel. He was preparing himself for the worst. In case the truth of Isaiah's death turned out to be unpleasant, he wanted to be ready.

They were now on a deserted open road. There was nothing but farmland on either side of them.

"Where are we?" Fisher asked.

"I don't know, but I punched in the right address in the GPS."

The screen was indicating they were less than a mile away from their destination. Fisher had a sinking feeling they were not going to find what they were looking for.

Her instincts were proved correct when the GPS alerted them that they had passed their stop. There was no sign of any residence as far as their eyes could see.

The address Cassandra Stevens had given the strip club owner was false.

SIXTY-THREE

Callaway and Elle were back at the restaurant. Joely had already served them. Callaway had ordered coffee and a cherry-filled Danish while Elle requested plain tea.

The box containing Katie's personal items was in the Impala's trunk. He did not want to leave the box behind. They would be put out to the curb as garbage otherwise.

"I would like to take the box with me," Elle said.

"Of course, it's your sister's, and that makes it yours."

She took a sip from her cup. "I have a terrible feeling something bad has happened to Katie."

Callaway knew the feeling. Creating a new life was one thing, but it was entirely another to suddenly leave that life behind. Katie would have at least taken the trophies with her. They looked like they meant a great deal to her.

"What about Bruno Rocco?" Elle asked. "Did you find anything on him?"

"I made calls to my contacts in various law enforcement departments. What they told me doesn't make sense."

Elle was about to take a sip from her cup, but she stopped, holding her drink close to her lips. "What do you mean?"

"There is a Bruno Rocco, but he's serving twelve years in Mainsville Penitentiary. He was connected to some big-time mobster whose name escapes me at the moment, but even the mobster is behind bars."

"So what does Rocco have to do with Katie?" Elle asked.

"I wish I knew," Callaway replied. "I have a feeling your sister was not entirely truthful to you. She may have given you the name 'Bruno Rocco' so you would not ask any questions."

"What about the photo we found in the garage? It had the initials *BR* on it."

"It could be someone else," he said. "But, I'll keep checking my sources to see what comes up."

Callaway munched on his pastry. Elle sipped her tea.

"I wanted to ask you something," she said.

"Go ahead," he replied.

"Back at my apartment, you mentioned your ex-wife and daughter, but you never talked about your parents."

"They are dead."

"I'm sorry to hear that. Any siblings?"

"I have a brother."

"Older or younger?"

"Older, much older."

"What does he do?"

"He's a captain in Harlow County. It was because of him that I joined the sheriff's department."

"Where?"

"Spokem County. It's not far from Harlow. They are almost neighbors if you ask me. I was raised in Harlow. I did not want to work under my brother, so I applied to the sheriff's department in the next county over."

"When was the last time you spoke to your brother?" she asked.

Callaway was silent. He had not spoken to his brother in years. They never saw eye to eye. Their last conversation was when Callaway told him he was quitting being a sheriff's deputy. The disappointment was palpable in his brother's voice.

Callaway came from a long line of law enforcement officers. His uncle and father were state troopers, and his grandfather was a prison warden. His father never pushed him to follow the family tradition. He had Callaway's older brother for that. But he was proud when Callaway told him he would become a member of the sheriff's department. Callaway was grateful his father never lived to see the day he walked away from the profession. He would have been grief-stricken.

"It's been a while," he said solemnly.

"I'm sorry I asked," she said. "I just wanted to know how far you would go to search for your brother if he was missing."

Callaway gave Elle a firm look. "I would move heaven and earth to find him," he said.

SIXTY-FOUR

Even with Cassandra Stevens's address leading them nowhere, Holt was determined to push ahead. Isaiah may not have been the Boy Scout; some thought he was, but he was still his nephew. He would never forgive himself if his nephew's death turned into a cold case.

Cassandra was a big piece in this mystery. She was the one who had *lured* Isaiah to his demise.

Holt wanted to find out why.

They were back at Milton College. Holt and Fisher found Byron Fox on the basketball court. He was practicing his free throws when they approached him.

Byron had already worked up a sweat. He spotted them and asked, "You find out who killed my boy, Isaiah?"

"We're working on it," Holt replied. "But first, we need to ask you a few questions."

Byron stopped bouncing the ball. "Okay."

Holt held up a poster from the strip club. He pointed to a girl dressed in revealing clothing, extra makeup, and high heels. She had the girl-next-door kind of look. "That's Cassandra Stevens. Isaiah was sending her messages on the morning he died. I want to know where he met her," Holt said.

Byron made a face. "How would I know?"

"You were close to him," Holt said. "He must have told you something."

"He didn't. That's the honest-to-God truth. I was suspicious he was talking to a girl, but I never got her name."

Holt pointed at Cassandra's picture again. "So, you've never seen this woman before?"

Byron glanced at the photo, but he quickly averted his eyes. "I gotta go," he said.

He began to move away from them.

Holt moved in front of Byron. "You know who she is," Holt said. His eyes were hard as rocks.

Byron, who was six-three, could have grappled with Holt if he wanted to, but he knew to assault a cop was not a good idea.

Fisher came up next to Holt. "If you know anything, please tell us," she said. "Isaiah was your best friend, and someone murdered him in cold blood. We want to find out why."

Byron stared at her for a moment.

His shoulders drooped, and he let out a deep sigh. "I shouldn't tell you this, but I do remember seeing her before."

"Where?" Fisher asked.

"On campus."

"When?"

"During a recruitment session."

Fisher was confused. "Recruitment session?"

"Yeah, all the high school basketball prospects were invited to this session. It was supposed to help us get to know the school better, but it turned into a party instead. There was music, food, and even girls."

"Why was Cassandra Stevens there?"

"I don't know, but she and a couple of other girls danced for us."

"You mean they stripped for you," Fisher said, correcting him.

"Yeah, you can say that."

"And Isaiah was at this party?"

"Sure, most of the freshmen on the team were."

"Who organized the party?" Holt asked.

Byron bit his bottom lip, looking unsure if he should say more.

"You can tell us," Fisher assured him. "We want to find Isaiah's killer."

Byron sighed. "It was organized by Assistant Coach Bledson."

SIXTY-FIVE

Holt and Fisher confronted Jay Bledson in his office. Bledson was not surprised they had finally uncovered his dirty little secret.

"Why would you invite strippers to a party where some kids are under eighteen?" Holt growled.

Bledson lowered his head. "It's not something I'm proud of, believe me, but I had no choice."

"What do you mean, you had no choice?" Holt shot back.

Bledson sighed. "It's not easy getting the best prospects to sign up with your school when there are bigger and better programs out there. The schools that make it to the NCAA tournament each year get money from the tournament—and we are talking millions of dollars here. You should see their arenas and practice facilities. Even their equipment centers are world-class. Milton College doesn't have the money nor the reputation for competing with other schools for talent. We are not known for having the best athletics programs. We are better known for our educational departments."

Holt knew this was true. Dennis was an alumnus, and he had graduated as a computer engineer.

"I was hired to scout young players," Bledson said. "I visited many high schools in the state, and no one wanted to come to Milton for even a tour of the campus. I was desperate, so I started studying the recruiting tactics of small colleges and universities. I could not promise the kids money or financial incentives. That would be impossible to do discreetly. You hear stories of players from poor neighborhoods who get to college, and suddenly their families are driving brand-new cars or moving into a bigger house. It reeks of bribery, and people can smell it a mile away."

"So you thought it was better to hire strippers?" Holt asked.

"It sounds lurid, but that's not how it started. I wanted to hold a party on campus with live music, dancing, lots of food…"

"Alcohol?" Fisher asked.

Bledson shrugged. "Yeah, sure. Don't think these kids weren't already drinking in high school, though."

"But it's still illegal to serve them liquor," Holt scolded him.

"Of course, I know that, but it was all monitored."

"By whom?"

"Me."

"Forgive me if I don't trust you to watch these kids," Holt shot back.

"That's fine, but even then, none of the sought-after recruits were showing up at these events. I just wanted to show these kids that Milton College was a fun place, and I couldn't even do that. Then I got the idea to…"

He let his words trail off.

"To bring these girls in to strip for them?" Fisher said.

"I've been to the Gentlemen's Hideout before, and I asked the owner to send over a couple of his best girls. They were only there to entertain them. I never encouraged or paid the girls to sleep with the players. Never. But word got out, and more and more talented kids started showing up at these parties. Once they saw what Milton College could offer, they signed up."

"And Isaiah met Cassandra Stevens at this party?" Holt asked.

Bledson shrugged. "He must have. I don't know."

"Does Coach Loughton know about these parties?" Holt inquired.

"No, I set it up on my own."

Holt did not believe him. A college coach was the second most powerful person after the college president. *It's highly unlikely he would not be aware of what's going on behind his back*, he thought.

Bledson saw the skepticism on Holt's face. "Coach Loughton thinks the students are coming to Milton because of our focus on academics. We encourage and guide these students to complete their degrees. Most of them know they will never make it to the pros, so they are keen on getting a higher education."

He paused for a moment to collect his thoughts. "Isaiah was special, though," he said. "He would have been the first Milton College graduate to jump to the professionals."

Holt stood up. "You're right. Isaiah was special, and he was going to go to Milton College regardless of these parties or not. He wanted to be closer to his family, and he wanted to make his father proud." He pointed a finger at Bledson. "Because of *you*, he met this woman at one of your parties, and she directed him to a place where he ended up dead."

Bledson covered his face with his hands and broke down.

SIXTY-SIX

Elle protested, but Callaway left her behind at the restaurant. He was not about to take a lady where even he hated going. His destination was not a safe place, and the people there were known to be involved in unfriendly situations.

He knocked on a steel door and waited. He was behind a strip club called the Gentlemen's Hideout. The establishment had just opened its doors, but Callaway was in no mood to watch women undress.

He had a task that was becoming more and more bizarre as the days went by. What was supposed to have been a straightforward search for a missing person had now become more complicated. Katie Pearson had disappeared three months ago. Then he discovered she was living her life as Linda Eustace. When he and Elle went out looking for Linda, they found she too had disappeared.

A small window in the door slid open. Two eyes peered out at Callaway.

"Who is it?"

"It's your uncle," Callaway replied, annoyed.

"Uncle Moe? Is that you?"

"Baxter, open the door!"

"Name please?"

Why do I have to do this each time I come here? Callaway thought. "It's Lee Callaway."

"Do you have an appointment?" Baxter asked.

Callaway narrowed his eyes. "I do, actually."

"What time?"

Callaway checked his watch and rattled off the current time. "I'm actually running late. If you let me in, I'll be able to make it to my appointment."

"You're not trying to trick me, are you?" Baxter asked.

Callaway smiled. "How can I do that? You're the smartest guy I know."

Callaway could see Baxter was smiling. The door was unlocked and it slid open.

Baxter came out. He was six-foot-four, weighing close to two hundred and fifty pounds, and he sported a buzz haircut. He always wore a tight t-shirt, even when the weather was chilly. The shirt exposed his well-defined biceps.

"Follow me," he said.

They went up a flight of narrow stairs. The sounds from the strip club boomed through the walls.

They stopped at another door.

Baxter paused and then rapped his knuckles on the door. Callaway rolled his eyes. Baxter had a screw loose in his head, which made him juvenile and dangerous.

"Come in," a voice bellowed from inside.

The door opened, and Callaway was escorted into a small, narrow office. A wide desk took up most of the space.

Mason was seated in a leather chair. He was short, rail-thin, and had a sleeve of tattoos on both of his arms. He sported a small goatee, and he wore prescription glasses.

"Your appointment has arrived," Baxter said proudly.

"I didn't have any appointments today," Mason said.

Baxter turned to Callaway. His eyes suddenly filled with rage.

"Well, I might not have been entirely truthful, but I did try to call to make an appointment," Callaway said. "It's not my fault your phone's not working."

Mason sighed and looked at the spot on his desk where his phone usually sat. "The phone had an unfortunate accident."

Mason looked over at the wall behind Callaway. There was a large dent in the drywall.

*Mason must have flung the phone across the roo*m, Callaway thought. *I bet the thing is now in the dumpster.*

Mason was a loan shark and a very ruthless one at that. If you borrowed money from him and were late in repaying, he would send Baxter to get the money. Not only would he make sure you paid up, but he would also make sure you never delayed paying Mason again. He would make an example out of you.

In desperate times, Callaway had come knocking on Mason's door. He hated himself for that, but sometimes he was left with little or no choice.

I'm stupid that way, Callaway thought.

"What can I do for you, Lee?" Mason asked.

"I'm looking for someone, and I need your help," Callaway replied.

Mason blinked and looked over at Baxter. "Did he just ask me for help?"

Baxter was smiling. "I think he did."

Mason looked at Callaway. "I don't find people. That's your thing."

"I'm kind of stuck, and I figured someone like you would know people in low places."

"I'm offended."

"Don't be. It was a compliment."

Mason stared at him. "Why would I go looking for this person?"

"It would mean a lot to me."

Mason laughed so hard, he almost fell off his chair. Even Baxter was chortling.

Callaway shook his head.

Once Mason and his goon had their laugh, Mason wiped tears from his eyes and said, "That was the funniest thing I *ever* heard." He turned to Baxter. "Isn't that right?"

"My stomach hurts from laughing," Baxter replied.

Dimwits, Callaway thought.

He pulled out a wad of hundred-dollar bills.

Mason and Baxter suddenly looked like they had been hit by falling anvils.

"What's that for?" Mason asked.

"I wouldn't ask you for help assuming you would simply do me a favor, would I?"

Mason glared at Callaway. "Quit screwing around, Lee. Seriously, why would I waste my time looking for someone for you?"

"I'll *pay* you to look for this person, genius," Callaway replied. "You think I'm holding toy money here?"

Mason's eyes narrowed. "You're offering *me* money?"

"Yep. I know the world is ending, right?" Callaway quipped.

"That's never happened before," Mason said, clearly dumbfounded.

Callaway chuckled. "There's always a first for everything, right?"

"How much is it worth to you?" Mason asked, revealing his stained teeth. He looked like a hyena circling his prey.

"Five hundred."

Mason frowned. "That's *not* a lot of money."

Callaway shrugged. "It's not a lot of work. All you have to do is make some calls. That's it." He glanced at the bare spot on Mason's desk. "Unless you can't get a new phone, I mean."

Mason snorted. "I don't live in the Stone Age. Of course, I can get a new phone."

Callaway smiled. "Then it won't be too much work for you."

"Who am I looking for?" Mason asked.

Callaway held up a photo of Katie. He had made a copy on his way over.

"Who's she?" Mason asked.

"Someone I'm looking for, smart guy. She may have gotten herself involved with the wrong people. I need you to find out if anyone's seen her. She may be calling herself Linda Eustace." He pulled out a copy of the man's photo. "She may be hanging out with this guy. I can't be certain, but he might be going by the name of Bruno Rocco."

"That's two people you want me to look for."

"Okay, then I'll double it and make it a grand." The money was coming from the five thousand Elle had given him. He had thought about asking her for more, but the girl was already going through so much. He felt wrong to get more out of her.

Mason considered Callaway's offer. "I can make some calls, but it'll cost you two grand."

Callaway put the money back in his pocket. "Sorry, not interested," he said. "Have a nice day, Mason."

Callaway moved to the door.

Baxter blocked him.

Callaway glared at him. "You're not going to hit a paying customer, are you, Baxter?" He was in no mood to let Baxter threaten him. "Imagine if the word got out. No one would come here, knowing how you operate your business."

"Relax," Mason said, putting his arms up. "Baxter would never do anything unless I say so. He just did not want you to leave without finalizing the deal. That's all."

Callaway stared at Baxter.

Baxter smiled back.

Callaway turned to Mason. "So, we got a deal?"

Mason smiled. "Of course, we do."

Callaway pulled out the bundle of money. "I want this information as soon as possible, and by that, I mean yesterday."

"No problem," Mason said. He was salivating as Callaway counted out the bills.

SIXTY-SEVEN

Nikos Papadopoulos had short graying hair, a potbelly, and a tanned, wrinkled face. His brown eyes had seen much in his sixty years. He had arrived in the United States with his family when he was eight years old. His father opened up a furniture store where he and his siblings spent most of their youth helping him out. Nikos watched how his father handled manufacturers and how he managed customers. He was tough with the former and kind with the latter. The furniture store was so successful that his father opened up two more locations. He gave one store to two of his older children to manage, and the flagship store was going to be run by his youngest son when he was old enough.

But Nikos had other plans. He did not want to be in the furniture business. His heart was set on opening a restaurant. He loved to eat, and he figured he could parlay that interest into creating dishes for others. His father was dismayed that he did not want to continue the family business, but he still lent money to Nikos so he could follow his dream.

After three years of blood, sweat, and all his savings, the restaurant was an utter failure. Nikos had no idea how the restaurant business worked. His prices were too low when he first opened, resulting in massive losses, and when he raised prices, customers stopped coming. His servers kept quitting, and so did his cooks. The staff turnover would set him back weeks because he would need to retrain his new hires. Then there was the rat infestation that nearly derailed the restaurant's launch. Somehow they had found a way in through a hole in a wall. That should have been a sign of things to come, but he had poured in all his money to renovate the place. He could not turn back. But things kept going wrong. If it was not the city licenses he had to maintain, it was the appliances that kept breaking down. When all was said and done, Nikos shut the doors and was left with debts he could not repay. He soon declared bankruptcy.

The furniture business, however, had thrived during the time Nikos was gone. The business's success had caught the attention of a retail giant. They made an offer to his father he could not refuse. He sold the business, split the proceeds with his older children, and returned to Greece to retire.

Nikos was given nothing. He had turned his back on the family, and he still owed the money he had borrowed from his father. The loan was forgiven, but no additional funds were given to him after the family business was sold.

Bitter, he joined a large company that supplied frozen pastries, croissants, biscuits, and other delicacies to restaurants, coffee shops, and grocery stores. Nikos started off on the factory line and worked his way up to line manager. He got married during this time and had two children, but he never lost the desire to prove to his family and his father that he was not a failure for trying to start a restaurant. He was young and naïve at the time, but with age, he gained a lot of experience.

The moment he reached thirty years of service at the company, Nikos cashed out his pension, much to the dismay of his wife and children, and invested the money in his own furniture store.

Unfortunately, things did not go the way he had hoped after all the years of waiting. The location was ill-suited for a high-end furniture store. The clientele were bargain hunters looking for cheap and affordable items. The products Nikos had imported from Italy, Germany, and Denmark sat in his store for months. And with the economy turning sour, things went from bad to worse. He had two burglaries that cost him thousands in losses.

He soon liquidated the remaining inventory, paid back the suppliers, and was now looking for a buyer to take the building off his hands.

His father had died the year before, but Nikos was not invited to the funeral. When the family decided to sell his father's properties in Greece, however, Nikos flew over to fight for his rights. His father never made a will, and as his offspring, Nikos was entitled to his share.

After a long and protracted battle with his siblings, Nikos was given a house his father once lived in. Nikos immediately sold the place so he had the capital to start a business again.

He then received a call from his wife, who told him something terrible had occurred on his property.

Nikos took the first available flight to Milton.

He unlocked the furniture store's front door and scowled at the vile graffiti spray-painted on the front window. The vulgar street art reminded him of the mistake he made in opening a business in a rough neighborhood rife with drugs, violence, and crime.

He heard a beep and hurried to the back of the store. He punched in his access code and disabled the alarm. Even though the outside security camera was not functioning—some punk kids had smashed it—Nikos had installed a second camera inside, just behind the front windows.

He headed to his office in the back of the store. He placed his bag on a table and then pulled out a laptop. While the machine loaded, he left the office and surveyed the open space that was once the showroom. He sighed as he thought about how he had managed to mess up another business. Most people were never given a second chance, and he somehow threw his away.

He would be extra vigilant with the money he had just inherited. Third chances were rare, and he was not going to squander his.

He went back into the office. An external hard drive was hooked up to a small black box that was connected to the camera by the front window. The camera only turned on when there was movement. Nikos did not expect the camera to do anything but act as a deterrent for vandals, recording nothing of consequence. When he was told someone was shot and killed outside the store, he had to come and check.

He hooked up the hard drive to his laptop and played the video files.

What he saw made his eyes go wide with horror.

SIXTY-EIGHT

Holt was with Nancy at her mother's house when he received the call. He dropped everything and rushed over. He did not even kiss Nancy goodbye as he left, something he always did. The hour drive felt like it was two hours.

He pulled into the parking lot and spotted Fisher by the front door. He got out when she approached him.

"Have you seen it?" Holt asked, getting straight to the point.

"No. I was waiting for you," she replied. "The owner's name is Nikos Papadopoulos, and he is quite shaken up."

"Where is he?" Holt said.

"Inside."

They entered the store. Papadopoulos was hunched over on a chair. His face was pale, and he reeked of vomit.

"Mr. Papadopoulos, this is my partner, Detective Holt," Fisher said to him.

Nikos nodded in his direction, but he looked like he was on the verge of tears.

"Can you show it to us?" Fisher asked.

He nodded again and took them to his office. Holt winced. The smell of vomit was strong in the confined space, emanating from a wastebasket by the desk.

Nikos tapped the keyboard on his laptop, picked up the wastebasket, and left the room. He did not have the stomach to watch the footage a second time, but he was courteous enough to get the worst of the foul reek out of the room.

The image was black and white, and the camera was aimed at the parking lot across from the store entrance.

The image flickered whenever the camera came alive upon sensing movement. The two detectives waited with bated breath as a car pulled into the parking lot.

Holt's back tensed.

It's the Chrysler! he thought. *Isaiah's behind the wheel!*

His nephew drove around the lot until he pulled into a spot. The car's trunk was facing the camera. The rear lights turned off a moment later. Isaiah's large silhouette was visible from the back windshield.

The image then went blank.

Holt and Fisher were not sure how much time had passed before the camera flickered on again.

A man appeared on the screen. He was dressed in black from head to toe, and he wore a motorcycle helmet.

He came up behind the Chrysler on the right. There was no way for Isaiah to see him coming.

Holt clenched his jaw and balled his fists. He knew what was about to happen.

The man was holding a gun. He aimed at the passenger side window and fired three shots.

Holt could see the silhouette in the driver's seat shake violently before slumping and going still.

Tears filled Holt's eyes. He had just witnessed the cold-blooded murder of his nephew.

The shooter waited a few seconds. He lowered his gun and removed something from his jacket pocket. The object looked white. He opened the passenger door and leaned inside.

Holt could only surmise the killer was placing the packet of heroin in the glove compartment.

He emerged, pocketing something in his jacket.

It could be Isaiah's cell phone, Holt thought. *We never found it.*

The killer rushed out of view.

The screen went blank.

Holt sighed and got ready to leave the office. Fisher stopped him.

"What?" he asked her.

"It's not done."

More footage started. A man riding a bicycle appeared on the screen. It was Bo Smith.

He rode past the Chrysler and stopped. He turned around and then circled the vehicle. He stopped by the driver's side window and put his hands over his head as he recognized who it was.

Smith circled the vehicle one more time and stopped at the passenger side door. He jumped off the bicycle and began to search inside. He stuffed something inside his pants pocket. Holt guessed the object was Isaiah's wallet. Smith then opened his backpack and placed something else inside: the heroin he would later nearly overdose on.

The screen went black.

The two detectives now knew Smith was not the killer, but finding the black-clad man who had committed the brutal crime was going to be a challenge.

SIXTY-NINE

After speaking to Mason, Callaway returned to the restaurant.

The booth where he had left Elle was empty.

"Your friend left right after you did," Joely said.

"Did she say where she was going?" he asked.

"She didn't say anything. And I didn't bother to ask."

He scratched his chin and nodded. Elle was not particularly excited that he had gone without her. She felt like they were a team. She was also his employer, and she wanted to keep a tab on what he was up to.

He thought about calling her but decided against it. Back at her apartment, she had told him she worked for a nonprofit organization that helped visually impaired people. She still had a life in Mayview that required her attention.

"What's her deal, anyway?" Joely asked, snapping him out of his thoughts.

"Who?"

"The woman you were with earlier."

"Her sister's gone missing, and I am trying to help find her."

"How's your search coming along?"

He shrugged. "We're making progress," he said with little conviction.

"She's got that quiet intensity to her," Joely said.

Callaway raised an eyebrow. "How would you know that?"

"I'm a woman. I can sense these things. Don't be fooled by her shy, introverted exterior. I bet if you put her in a corner, she'd fight her way out."

Elle is highly motivated to find her sister, Callaway thought. *She will do just about anything to know where Katie is.*

"She's also kind of cute, you know," Joely said with a wink. "Have you…?"

Callaway shook his head. "She's a client."

"Hasn't stopped you before."

Callaway sighed. "You got me there."

"Is it because she's blind?" Joely asked.

Callaway was horrified at that thought. Would he be interested in someone who had some form of handicap? Of course, he would. The reason he never thought of Elle in that way was because of what she was going through. She was not just a client who wanted to get money out of a cheating spouse; she was desperate to find a loved one whom she had not heard from in months.

A thought occurred to him, which he was not proud of. Her blindness had made him more attentive towards her, almost in a protective way. She never asked for special treatment. He just took it upon himself to tread carefully whenever he was around her.

He caught something playing on the TV behind Joely.

"What's that?" he asked.

"All the stations have been playing it over and over," she replied.

A man wearing a motorcycle helmet approached a parked vehicle and fired into it. The vehicle was blurred out to protect the viewer from seeing violent images, but Callaway could easily surmise the occupant had not survived the barrage of bullets.

The image of the shooter froze on the screen. The news anchor came on and said, "This man is a suspect in the death of Isaiah Whitcomb. Anyone with any knowledge as to his identity should contact the Milton Police Department."

Holt must be devastated at the sight of his nephew being gunned down like that, Callaway thought. *I can't blame him. I would be too.*

SEVENTY

Mainsville Penitentiary was a federal prison in New Jersey. It housed over two thousand of the most dangerous criminals in the state. The jail was surrounded by twenty-foot-high concrete walls topped with barbed wire. Surveillance cameras captured every inch of the structure, and close to two hundred trained guards monitored the inmates around the clock.

Cosimo went through a metal detector and a physical search. He was made to fill out a form and was then escorted down a narrow corridor. Instead of going to the visitors' area where family members and lawyers met the prisoners, however, the guard took him to another part of the prison.

Cosimo's visit was pre-planned. A huge sum of money had already been distributed to all the guards involved and their supervisor, a man more corrupt than most people Cosimo had worked for. The part of the prison he was going to had suffered a mysterious "camera malfunction" lest the warden know his most famous inmate was receiving a visitor, and Cosimo had provided the guards at the entrance with one of the several false identifications he utilized.

There was still the possibility the guards and their crooked supervisor could turn on him. Even if no one had been able to pin them on him, Cosimo was still behind half a dozen killings. His arrest would be a giant score for the authorities. But even the bent supervisor and his corrupt underlings knew the reach Cosimo's employer had in the outside world. If they chose to renege on their deal, the retaliation would be swift. A car bomb. A hail of bullets during a quiet walk. Or worse—the abduction of a loved one.

His employer had lost significant control when he was arrested, but he still had money stashed away that no federal agency could find or touch. Money was power, and it could compel people to do horrible things.

The guards and their immediate supervisor were aware of this. But even then, Cosimo took no chances before arriving at the prison. He had surveilled the corrupt men's places of residence. He had photographed their children, wives, mistresses, mothers, and anyone else who held value to them. He then sent copies of these pictures to each man. The message was clear: *If you get any smart ideas, someone you know will get hurt.*

The guard who walked next to him also received a package of photos, and his contempt for Cosimo was palpable. But Cosimo could care less. His freedom was at stake, and he would do just about anything to stay free.

They moved down a corridor and came to a stop at a heavy door. The guard unlocked the door with a key that was hooked on his belt and then held the door for him.

He understood. *The guard will go no further.*

Cosimo entered and realized he was in the prison's laundromat. The industrial washers and dryers were on one side, and bins filled with laundry were on the other. The area was hot and stuffy and smelled of detergent.

The room was also empty.

This meeting's going to be private.

Cosimo spotted a man sitting next to a table with clothes neatly folded on it.

He walked into the room and approached the inmate.

The man was short, balding, and he had on thick prescription glasses. His face was without a wrinkle, which made him look much younger than he was. He had a cross tattooed on his right arm and a tattoo of a dagger on the left. The images were symbolic. He was both good and evil. Religious and feared. Peaceful and dangerous.

Paolo Beniti stood up and extended his arms for an embrace. Cosimo walked over and let the man hug him, and then Beniti kissed Cosimo on both cheeks.

"It's good to see you, Cosimo," Beniti said, smiling like he was greeting an old friend. Cosimo had only met him once, and that was for a job. "Thank you for coming," he said.

I didn't have much choice, Cosimo thought. "Anything for you, Don Beniti," he said in reply.

"I wish we could have met under different circumstances." He looked around the laundromat with disdain. "But it is what it is."

"I cried when they sentenced you to life," Cosimo said. His thoughts, however, were different. *I could care less about what happens to you, old man. It was your hubris that was the end of you.*

"Thank you," Beniti said as if the comment touched his heart. "I am sure you have seen the video of the young athlete in Milton being murdered."

"I have," Cosimo said.

"It seems that after all these years, the man who put me in this wretched place has finally shown himself."

Cosimo could not help but take a jab at Beniti's mistake. "It seems that way, but if you had hired me in the first place all those years ago, you would not be in this situation, Don Beniti."

Beniti shrugged. "It was an error I am paying dearly for. I wanted to keep it in-house, but I should have contracted the job out to someone with your special capabilities."

Cosimo almost smiled. *Good that you know you are to blame for your predicament.*

The old man's eyes glowed with pure hatred. "I want you to go to Milton and find him," Beniti said. "I want you to make sure he knows I sent you. I want you to make him pay for his betrayal."

"That's what I'm good at," Cosimo said with no emotion.

SEVENTY-ONE

Fisher entered the bar and looked around. The time was midday, but even then, the place was half full.

Don't people have jobs? she wondered. *I doubt their bosses would let them drink during work hours.*

While Fisher was still on duty, she was not here to indulge. She wanted a quiet spot to clear her mind. She was hoping to find a booth in the corner, but they seemed to be all taken.

I should go to the coffee shop across the street, she thought.

She was about to turn around and head back out the door when she spotted a familiar man sitting in one of the booths.

She smiled.

"Why am I not surprised to see you here?" she asked as she walked up to him.

Lee Callaway grinned. "I could say the same to you. You're not working today?"

"I am," she said.

"So, if you're not here to drink, then I'm guessing you are here to talk to me."

"I am not here for you."

He raised an eyebrow, but he kept grinning. "You sneaky girl. You are going to drink on the job. What will your poison of choice be? I'm buying."

She shook her head. "I just needed to get away."

"Let me guess, you need to get away from Holt?"

"It's not always Holt I need a break from. We're not a couple that needs time away from each other every so often."

She took a seat across from him.

He leaned over and winked. "*We* could have made a beautiful couple, you know."

Callaway and Fisher had dated once—and only *once*. She always reminded him of this whenever he brought up the subject. They were two different people. She was focused on a career and maybe a family down the road. He was focused on whatever caught his fancy, and he still had issues to sort out from his previous marriage.

Fisher strongly believed, even if Callaway vehemently denied it, that Callaway still harbored feelings for his ex-wife. She was the one he compared all his relationships to. In Fisher's opinion, Patti was the best thing that ever happened to Callaway, and he was an idiot to give up on their marriage. He would look back one day with regret, but by then, it would be too late. People like Callaway were more interested in new shiny objects than paying attention to the object already in their hands. They were always searching for happiness in the distance when they did not realize it was already under their feet.

Fisher shook her head. She could not believe she was getting philosophical just thinking about Callaway. Maybe Callaway held potential in him to be a better husband, father, and person. If he only knew how to get out of his own way, perhaps he could do it.

"You okay?" he asked.

She blinked.

"You look like you are in a galaxy far, far away."

"Sorry, I was just thinking."

"What'll you have?" he asked.

"Sparkling water," she replied.

He got up, walked over to the bar, and returned with a glass. He sat back across from her.

"Thanks," she said.

"I saw the video of the shooting on TV," he said. "I bet it was Holt's idea to release it to the media."

She took a sip and sighed. "I tried to talk him out of it, but he is eager to find the person who murdered his nephew. I can't blame him, though. This is the first big break we've had since we started our investigation."

"Any potential leads?" he asked.

"The phones are ringing off the hook back at the station. Why do you think I needed to get away? It's mostly people trying to settle a score with someone."

"What do you mean?"

"I had one caller say it was his neighbor. He rides a motorcycle, so he had to be the shooter. When I pushed the caller, he confessed his neighbor would ride his motorcycle at all times of the day, and he wanted to scare him into stopping." She took another sip from her glass. "I doubt any of the information will be useful."

"You can't be certain," Callaway said.

"The shooter was covered from head to toe. It could be anyone. It could even be a muscular woman."

Callaway thought for a moment. Fisher was right. There was not much to identify who the killer was.

He took a gulp from his glass. The scotch burned the back of his throat. *Why am I drinking when I'm on the job as well?* he wondered.

"Any new cases?" Fisher asked.

It was his turn to sigh. "Yeah."

"As complicated as the Paul Gardener case?"

"Far more complicated than the Gardener case."

Fisher checked her watch. "I'm in no hurry to go back to the station. You wanna tell me what it's about?"

"Sure, but if you want a drink afterward, it's not my fault."

She smiled. "I'll take my chances."

SEVENTY-TWO

Special Agent Ed Schaefer of the Federal Bureau of Investigation parked his rented Buick outside a falafel shop. He could not believe he had to come all the way to Milton.

Schaefer was in the middle of an investigation in Florida involving casinos and organized crime. The view was great, the weather was perfect, and the women were nice and tanned.

When he saw the news, he knew he had to get on the first available flight out. He made some excuse to his superiors about needing to deal with a personal matter. They were not pleased. The investigation had been ongoing for months and had cost the Bureau a good chunk of their budget. But they agreed to let him take some time off, as Schaefer knew they would after all the positive exposure the Bureau had gotten from his last major investigation.

Schaefer was tall and wiry. His skin was weather-beaten and wrinkled, his eyes were gray and hollow, and his teeth were stained from years of smoking.

He reached for a pack in his suit jacket but decided against a smoke. He had an urgent matter to attend to.

He entered the shop, making the door chime. He looked around and spotted his man in the corner.

The man was wearing a checkered shirt, cargo pants, and work boots. A painter's cap covered his dark hair, which was once a golden color. He had stubble on his cheeks, and his eyes were black.

The first time Schaefer had looked into those eyes, he almost shivered. He saw no soul in them. They belonged to a killer. Schaefer knew the moment he made a deal with him. There was no turning back. He was shaking hands with the devil.

Schaefer looked around the falafel shop. The owner was behind the counter. He was more interested in what was on the TV, which was playing a Middle Eastern program.

Good spot for a private meeting, Schaefer thought.

He approached the man and sat across from him. He slid a plate with shawarma on it across to Schaefer.

"No thanks," Schaefer said. "I'm not hungry."

The man was not offended. He pulled back the plate and bit into his shawarma. The man's real name had not been spoken in years, and Schaefer was not about to use it either. He feared someone might hear it. The man was known to the world as Kevin Brogdon.

"I saw the video," Schaefer said. "Everyone did."

He expected a response, but he got none.

Schaefer leaned closer. "What were you thinking? He was a state basketball star."

"He should not have been there in the first place," Brogdon replied without emotion.

"And what about the woman?"

"It's been taken care of."

"Are you sure? Or am I going to find another video?"

Brogdon was silent.

Schaefer gritted his teeth. "The deal was, you keep your head low, and you follow the law. I did not say you could kill people."

Brogdon leaned in closer. "I kept a low profile just like you told me, but I got bored, okay? I wanted to have some fun. I had no choice in what I did. The woman would have exposed me." He pointed a finger at Schaefer. "She would have exposed *you*."

Schaefer tried to keep his emotions in check. He did not want to cause a scene. The falafel shop was still relatively empty, but he had seen a customer or two glance in their direction.

Schaefer felt self-conscious in his black suit. He missed wearing golf shirts, shorts, and loafers. But Milton was cool and breezy, not sunny and balmy. He had no choice but to wear his business attire.

"Just make this go away," Brogdon said.

Schaefer's eyes widened. "Make this go away? Who do you think I am? The president? I am not supposed to even be here. I came because you messed up."

"You came to protect yourself," Brogdon said. "Because of *me*, Don Beniti is in prison. I gave him to you on a silver platter."

Schaefer was silent.

Brogdon gave Schaefer a menacing and arrogant smile. "I heard the FBI gave you a medal for your exceptional work."

Schaefer's jaw clenched. A part of him wanted to get up and walk away. Brogdon was not his problem anymore. He had held up his end of the bargain.

"I should let the Beniti family find you," Schaefer said. "Guess what they do to rats?"

Brogdon stared at him.

It was Schaefer's turn to smile. "Oh wait, you do know what they do to those who betray the code. It was your job to make an example of those who did, wasn't it?"

Brogdon moved his tongue over his front teeth and snarled. He said, "You owe me for the time I spent in prison for you." He pointed again at Schaefer. His finger was inches from his face. "Don't you ever forget that, got it?"

Schaefer held his stare and then sighed. "I'll see what I can do. In the meantime, you keep your head down and don't do anything stupid. You've already caused enough damage for both of us."

Brogdon smiled. "Sure, whatever you say. You're the boss."

SEVENTY-THREE

Callaway was on his way to his apartment when he received a call. Mason had information for him. Linda Eustace's photo was on a website run by a man named Glenn Maker.

"What kind of website?" Callaway inquired.

"What do you think? It's for escorts," Mason replied.

Elle's sister was an escort? Callaway thought. *That explains how she was able to pay for all those overseas trips.*

"How do I find Glenn Maker?" Callaway asked.

Mason was silent. It was his negotiating tactic. He would not give up the address unless Callaway handed over more money.

Callaway said, "Listen, I paid you a grand to find me information on Linda Eustace *and* Bruno Rocco. What about him?"

"I asked around, but no one's heard of him," Mason replied.

"Then, I guess I'm owed a refund."

"I don't do refunds," Mason shot back.

"Our deal was, you find information that I can use, and you get paid. Glenn Maker's name I can use, but unless you find something useful on Bruno Rocco, I will be in your office to collect my five hundred bucks."

"Okay, okay, slow down," Mason said. "I'll tell you where you can find Maker."

Callaway jotted down the address. After hanging up, he thought about calling Elle. She deserved to know what he had found. *It might not be a good idea just yet*, he thought. *If Katie's working as an escort, Elle will be devastated. Better I first confirm Mason's findings and then gently break it to her.*

He did not know how she would react to the news. She was already dealing with the knowledge of her sister's false identity. This new revelation would be a double whammy.

He would visit Glenn Maker without her lest she get overwhelmed.

He drove to the address. For a second, he thought Mason had pulled a fast one on him. Instead of finding a seedy-looking property, he was in front of a decent house on a residential street. There was even a park with a playground across the road. Parents and their children were visible from where he sat in the Impala.

He pulled out his cell phone to give Mason a piece of his mind, but intuition stopped him.

Why don't I go up and knock on the door? he thought. *What's the worst that could happen? I'm already here.*

He got out, approached the front door, and rang the doorbell.

SEVENTY-FOUR

As Callaway waited, he scanned the street again. It was quiet except for a woman walking her dog. She looked like she was heading toward the park.

He was about to ring the doorbell again when he heard a man's voice. It was coming from an intercom next to the doorbell. "Who is it?"

"I'm looking for Glenn Maker."

"Who wants to know?"

Callaway spotted a camera above the door. Maker appeared to take security very seriously. Callaway considered telling him the truth, but something told him Maker would not open the door to just anyone. He was running a website for escorts, after all, which made him sort of a pimp. He would have to try a different approach.

"My name's Gator Peckerwood," Callaway claimed. He pulled out the card with his alias on it and waved the card at the camera fast so Maker could not catch the lettering. "I work for A to Z Delivery." Callaway had spotted several cardboard boxes from A to Z stacked next to a garbage bin. "We have become aware that our customers' packages have gone missing, and we want to speak to you to see how we can make your deliveries more secure." Callaway knew that in some cities, mail theft had become such a big issue that delivery companies were considering installing large boxes to hold packages outside people's houses.

"Finally, you guys are taking it seriously," Maker said over the intercom. "I've had a dozen packages go missing. I've caught people on my camera pulling up to my house, parking their car, grabbing my package, and driving away."

"That's why I am here, to make certain that this doesn't happen to you again, sir," Callaway said. "I've got a few documents that require your signature. This way, I can have everything set up for you."

"Give me a minute."

Callaway waited.

The door swung open. Callaway was half-expecting a man with a fur coat, top hat, and a gold cane. Maker was wearing a t-shirt, baggy shorts, white socks, and he had a smartwatch on his wrist.

"Where do I sign?" Maker asked eagerly.

Callaway shoved his way into the house.

"What're you doing?" Maker demanded, sounding confused.

Callaway pulled out Katie's photo and said, "I'm looking for this woman. Tell me where I can find her."

"How would I know?" Maker claimed.

"She was on your website, which either makes her a client of yours or a client of someone else's. Her name is Katie Pearson, but she might be going by the name of Linda Eustace."

"Are you a customer?"

"No, I'm a private investigator hired to find her."

Maker suddenly looked emboldened. "Get out of my house before I call the cops."

Callaway crossed his arms over his chest. "Go ahead, and what will you tell them?"

"I'll tell them that you forced your way in."

"With what? I don't carry a weapon. And I didn't threaten you."

"My camera will tell the truth."

"It will show you opening the door for me, and me going through it."

Maker thought for a moment. "You have to leave."

"Why?" Callaway asked. He caught sight of a framed photo hanging on a wall in the hallway. Maker was dressed in a tux next to a woman in a wedding gown. "So you're married," Callaway said with a smile. "Does your wife know that you're a pimp?"

"I'm not," Maker said, his eyes wide with horror.

"Does she know you run a website for escorts?" Callaway said. "I bet she doesn't. Why don't I wait for her and tell her myself?"

Callaway walked over to the sofa and took a seat.

Maker came over. He had broken into a cold sweat. "Listen, man, you gotta leave or else my marriage will be over."

"Tell me what I need to know, and I'll go."

Maker stared at him. He sighed. He took a seat across from Callaway and said, "I recognize the name you mentioned, but I've never met her."

Callaway frowned. "You're a pimp who's never met his girl?"

"I told you I'm not a pimp. I'm a coder."

"A what?"

"I sit at home and write codes for computer programs."

"Is that what your wife thinks you do?"

He lowered his head, looking ashamed. "Yes. I lost my job at a tech company a year and a half ago. To pay the bills, I created the website. Its main purpose was to handle payments between the girls and their customers in a secure and confidential way."

It's good old prostitution for the twenty-first century, Callaway thought. *What will they think up for the twenty-second?*

"So how does it work?" he asked.

"The girls post their profiles on the website. If a prospective client is interested, he contacts the girls through the online system. If she accepts his offer, I set up the transaction and handle all the payments."

"So you must have the clients' names?" Callaway asked.

"No names. They all use aliases."

Callaway was confused. "But if you handle the payments, then you must have their credit card information."

Maker smiled, looking proud of his creation. "That's what makes my website so different. The client is guaranteed that none of his information is stored anywhere."

"How's that possible? There is always a trail in any transaction."

"The client pays in digital currency, which I convert and transfer to the girls in US dollars."

Callaway thought for a moment. "How do these clients purchase this digital currency?"

"I never ask where they get them, and they never tell me in order to protect their privacy. On the website, I direct them to various websites that sell digital currency. There are even people who will meet you in person, exchange money, and then transfer the currency digitally to you. It's pretty sophisticated."

Callaway mulled this over. "Are you able to see an address where the clients meet the girls?"

"No personal information is ever exchanged on the website. It's to protect the clients."

"What about the girls? Who protects *them*?" Callaway asked, putting an edge on his last word.

"I considered that *before* I set up the website," Maker replied, sounding defensive. "I'm a married man. I even have a young daughter. So I do value these girls' safety. We have something in place to protect them."

"We?"

Maker opened his mouth but shut it. He stood up. "You have to go before my wife shows up. I've told you everything I know."

"Give me something I can use to find Linda," Callaway said. "*Please*."

Maker stared at him. He sighed and said, "I can't tell you anything about the clients because even I don't know much about them, but what I can tell you is that Linda was referred to the website by a friend."

Callaway's eyes widened. "Give me the name."

SEVENTY-FIVE

Holt and Fisher were at the motel across the road from the furniture store. Cassandra Steven's phone call to Isaiah had pinged from a cell tower not far from the motel. They believed the call could only have come from there, but it raised a question: Why did Cassandra not ask Isaiah to meet her at the motel parking lot instead of the furniture store's? Was she setting him up for his eventual demise? They needed answers.

They found the owner in his cramped office. He gave Fisher another gap-toothed smile and said, "Welcome back, Detective. How can I help you?"

Fisher pulled out Cassandra's photo and held it up for the owner. "We believe this woman was staying in one of your rooms."

The owner squinted and said, "Yeah, I remember her. She was here a couple of nights ago."

Fisher looked over at Holt. *That's around the time Isaiah was killed.*

"Was she with someone? Perhaps with a tall African-American man."

The owner shrugged. "She came alone and paid cash. Like I told you the last time you were here, we charge by the hour, and we don't ask any questions. I'm guessing she might have met a customer later in her room."

"She's a hooker?" Fisher asked.

"That'd be my guess. Why else would she be here?"

Fisher looked over at Holt. His face was drawn.

Isaiah was in contact with not just a stripper but also a prostitute.

"Can we see the room she paid for?" Fisher asked.

The owner checked his ledger and said, "It's on the top floor. I'll take you up myself."

They moved to the elevators.

Fisher asked, "Is it safe?"

"It is if you are not underage." The manager cackled at his joke. "Nothing will happen, Detective. You have my word."

Right now, your word means very little to me, she thought.

The ride up was bumpy, but they emerged from the elevator in one piece. The owner escorted them to a room that had a bed in the middle, a sofa on one side, a TV across from it, and a bathroom next to it. A strong odor hung in the air that made Fisher pinch her nose.

She was walking around the room when she noticed a dark brown stain on the carpet. "That's blood," she said.

"I tried to clean it up as best as I could," the owner said.

Holt glared at the owner and said, "You saw blood, and you didn't report it to the police?"

The owner suddenly looked defensive. "Listen," he said, "the people that come here don't want the police showing up and asking questions. My clientele involves hookers, drug dealers, crack addicts, and pimps. I am used to seeing blood in my units. I once had a fight break out where one renter smashed a mirror over another guy's head. I had never seen that much blood in my life. I made the renter pay for the mess, but even then, it was impossible to clean up the blood entirely."

As Fisher and Holt stared at the stain on the carpet, they could not help but wonder, *Did Cassandra meet the same fate as Isaiah?*

SEVENTY-SIX

Cosimo entered the suite and took in his surroundings. The room had a king-size bed, a stocked fridge, a plush leather sofa, a fifty-inch flat-screen TV, and a Jacuzzi hot tub. Cosimo did not care for any of the amenities. He was not going to use any of them.

The five-star hotel was selected for its location across the street from a convention center. For the next three days, the construction industry was holding its annual fair. Companies from all over were vying for people's attention and their money. Cosimo, a stranger from out of town, would blend right in.

He provided a different name and ID when he checked in, one he had used numerous times. He had thought about retiring the alias, but he did not have time to get a new one made on short notice. The call from Don Beniti had caught him by surprise. Cosimo had just returned from a job in Montana and was not actively soliciting any new contracts. But Beniti's offer was too enticing and lucrative to pass up. He was paid in cash, all up front.

The target had surfaced after years of hiding. There was no telling when he would disappear again. Maybe he already had, but Cosimo doubted that. The target had no idea Beniti had sent someone to snuff him out.

He had the target's photo from years ago, but he was certain his appearance had been altered to make him unrecognizable. Even so, Beniti had contacts everywhere. They also believed the target was in Milton, but he was not just going to take their word for it. He would know the target was there when he saw him with his own eyes.

The basketball player's murder had alleviated any doubts in his mind. Even though the shooter's face was never seen on the video, Cosimo knew he was the target. He could tell from the way the shooter walked up to the car and the way he fired his gun.

You could change a person's appearance, but it was hard to change the way a person moved or held their weapon.

And the motorcycle helmet, black leather jacket, and black pants and boots were a dead giveaway as to who it was.

You just made a grave error, Cosimo thought. *It will now cost you your life.*

SEVENTY-SEVEN

Holt and Fisher were making their way to the police station's entrance when a black sedan parked in an open space they were passing. The driver's window rolled down, and a man asked, "Detective Holt and Detective Fisher?"

Holt's eyes narrowed. "Can we help you?"

The man got out and said, "I'm Special Agent Ed Schaefer of the FBI."

He showed them his credentials, and then he shook their hands.

"What can we do for you, Agent Schaefer?" Holt asked.

"Call me Ed."

"Okay."

"I want to make it clear that I'm not here on federal capacity," Schaefer said. "I am visiting Milton on my own time. I heard about the Isaiah Whitcomb murder. I heard he was your nephew."

"Yes, he was."

"I'm so sorry for your loss," Schaefer said.

"Thank you," Holt said.

"I want to offer you my assistance."

Holt looked over at Fisher and back at Schaefer. "We appreciate your offer, but we can handle it," he said.

"I am in no way saying you can't," Schaefer said. "I just want to say that your nephew's murder has caught a lot of people's attention. It's all over the news."

Holt's eyes narrowed. "Agent Schaefer, with all due respect, if the FBI is only interested in the shooting because of the headlines or how good it will make them look when the shooter is caught, then you're wasting your time. I don't care who gets the credit. I only care that the person responsible for my nephew's murder is in prison."

Schaefer blinked and then said, "I think you may have misunderstood me. I have no intention of stealing anyone's credit. I am here as a fellow law enforcement officer. I have family too, and your nephew's death has affected me. I just felt an obligation to reach out to you. That's all."

Holt stared at him and then relaxed. "I apologize, it's personal for me."

"No apology necessary. I completely understand," Schaefer said.

"How can you help us?" Fisher asked.

"I can run background checks on any suspects you might have. I can follow up on any leads you need looking into. I can be an extra pair of eyes and ears for you." He paused for a moment. "I heard the shooting was drug-related. Is that true?"

Holt shook his head. "They were planted at the scene by the shooter. Isaiah was not involved in drugs of any kind."

"That's good to know," Schaefer said, looking relieved. "But what about the person who called 9-1-1? Could he have a hand in what happened to your nephew?"

"Are you referring to Bo Smith?"

"Yes."

"He's clean. We thoroughly vetted his statements. He took the drugs from the Chrysler my nephew was driving, but he had nothing to do with his death."

"Isn't he a drug dealer?"

"A very low-level one."

Fisher added, "Smith doesn't have any priors for violent behavior. He doesn't even own a gun."

Schaefer mulled this over. "Well, that's good to know. I also heard a woman might be involved in what happened."

Holt nodded. "Cassandra Stevens was seen at the motel across from the furniture store where the shooting occurred."

"Have you located her?"

"Not yet, but we are actively looking."

Schaefer pulled out a business card and handed it to Holt. "If you need to bounce off any theories, or you need my assistance in any way, please don't hesitate to contact me. My cell number is on there."

"Thank you," Holt said as he pocketed the card.

SEVENTY-EIGHT

After picking up the rental, Cosimo drove straight to the Milton Police Department. He knew that in order to get close to his target, he would have to follow the detectives who were working on the basketball player's murder. Their investigation would lead him straight to his target.

He pulled into the department's parking lot and spotted the two detectives. He had seen their photos in the local newspapers, so it was easy to recognize them. They were talking to someone, and when Cosimo looked carefully, his eyes widened in disbelief.

Special Agent Ed Schaefer!

Cosimo had never met the FBI agent, but his reputation was well known in organized crime circles. Schaefer had brought down the Beniti Family. Don Beniti had been personally cuffed by Schaefer. The photo of Beniti being led from his luxurious estate into a waiting government vehicle was plastered all over the newspapers. The look on Schaefer's face was that of a man who had just caught the biggest fish in the sea.

Cosimo had quietly rejoiced at the sight of Beniti looking shocked and confused. Beniti never thought something like this would ever happen to him. He was careful in his dealings, but above all, he was feared. He did not hesitate to kill those who showed a hint of disloyalty. Even their families were not safe.

But the betrayal had not come from anyone who worked for Beniti. The betrayal had come from someone Beniti never guessed would snitch on him.

Everything would have gone accordingly, but the target had made serious errors in his execution of a contract of his own. Those errors were exploited by FBI Agent Schaefer.

If Cosimo had been the hired gun, he would have completed the contract without a hitch, and Beniti would still be free to run his now-defunct empire.

Beniti was not the only one who was betrayed years before. Cosimo also felt he was betrayed. He had earned his reputation after years of completing contracts to his clients' specifications. If a client wanted someone to disappear, that person vanished as if into thin air. If a client wanted to make an example of someone, their fates sent messages loud and clear to the intended recipients. No job was too big or small for Cosimo. He took pride in his work.

He believed there was another reason Beniti had not hired him. Cosimo's services did not come cheap, and his fee was non-negotiable. If you wanted him for a job, you better have the money to see it through and pay all the bucks up front. Cosimo didn't do half up front and half later.

There used to be a code among criminals, but in his experience, the code was only valued by the older generation. The newer generation only cared about money, power, and notoriety. They did not appreciate the service Cosimo provided. They would renege on their agreement if they saw fit. If that happened, Cosimo would have to take the drastic step to teach them a lesson. It was messy, and the blowback was always harsh, but Cosimo was a professional hitman. You did not mess with a man who lived and died by a gun.

Cosimo watched as Agent Schaefer handed one of the detectives his business card. He then got in his black sedan and drove off.

Cosimo knew that if Agent Schaefer was in town, the target was not far behind.

He decided to follow the agent.

SEVENTY-NINE

Jennifer Paulsingh lived on the top floor of a row house. Callaway got her name from Glenn Maker.

According to Maker, Jennifer was best friends with Linda Eustace. Callaway thought about calling Elle to give her an update, but he again vetoed the idea.

He did not like having someone tag along during his investigations. He never knew where his search would lead him. He had found himself in dangerous situations before, but somehow, he always found a way out.

Elle would only slow him down. In fact, he had accomplished quite a bit without her. Obviously, when it came time to fill her in on what he had found, he had to tell her everything. She had every right to know what was going on in his investigation.

At the moment, though, he was enjoying the freedom to move about without being encumbered.

He knocked on the door. It opened an inch. A bolt chain lock prevented it from opening further. A face appeared between the opening, and it took Callaway a moment to realize it was the same woman he had seen posing with Linda in a photograph they had found in Linda's landlady's garage.

"Can I help you?" she said.

"Are you Jennifer?" he asked.

"Who are you?" she replied.

For a second, Callaway thought she would slam the door shut. He quickly pulled out his business card and said, "I'm looking for Linda. I was told she was your friend."

She stuck her hand out and snatched the card from him. "You're *really* a private investigator?" she asked, staring at the card.

Why are people always surprised to find out that we exist? he thought.

"Yes, I am. Can I ask you a few questions?"

"Why are you looking for her?" she demanded.

"Someone hired me to find her."

She eyed him suspiciously. "Who?"

Callaway was about to tell her it was Elle, but he stopped. Linda did not want anyone in Milton to know of her previous life. He doubted Jennifer knew who Linda really was or that she had a sister. Back at the landlady's garage, they had found no photos of Elle in Linda's personal items. Linda Eustace was an identity Katie Pearson had created to live a life she may not have been proud of. Most escorts did not want their families to find out the profession they were involved in.

Until they found Katie, Callaway was not going to destroy the alternate life she had worked so hard to create for herself.

"Her family has not heard back from her in months," he said, trying not to be too specific. "They are worried about her."

Jennifer's features relaxed. She unlocked the bolt chain and came out into the hallway. She had dark curly hair, hazel eyes, and a brown complexion. She was wearing a sweatshirt, sweatpants, and no socks.

She crossed her arms and said, "It took them long enough to send you to find her."

Callaway detected the bitterness in Jennifer's words.

He could not tell her how Katie's lies had prevented Elle from searching for her sooner.

"Do you know where Linda is?" he asked.

"If I knew, I wouldn't have filed a missing persons report with the police."

"You did?" he asked, surprised.

"Of course, I did. She was my best friend."

Callaway paused and then got to the point. "You introduced Linda to the escort business, is that correct?"

Jennifer looked away. "It was a mistake," she said, her voice full of shame, "but Linda needed the money. I did too. That's how I got into it in the first place. It was only supposed to have been a few times. I didn't like doing it, so I quit. But Linda liked the money. She was able to afford things she didn't have before."

"I saw the photos from all the trips she took," Callaway said. "She liked to share them on social media."

Jennifer shook her head. "I didn't agree with what she was doing. The money from escorting was supposed to pay for her schooling. She wanted to become a fashion designer, you know?"

"I do," he said.

"I did it to pay for my paralegal certificate," she said. "I never finished it, but I ended up getting a job doing data entry for an insurance company. The money isn't great compared to what I made as an escort, but at least it's a steady and stable job."

"When I spoke to Glenn Maker, he alluded to the fact that the girls were protected. What did he mean by that?" Callaway asked.

"Before agreeing to take on a client, we met them at a specific location."

"Specific location?"

She nodded. "Glenn's not really a pimp. He's more of a programmer. This whole setup was like a business transaction to him. But Carl was the one who watched over us when we met the clients."

"Carl?" Callaway asked.

"Carl Goodwin. He owns an art gallery where we met the clients. He was protective of us girls. There were many times he would end a meeting if the girls felt uncomfortable or wanted to end the transaction."

"Do you know where I can find this Carl Goodwin?"

"I'll give you his address."

EIGHTY

The building was old and decayed. The white exterior paint had turned yellowish-brown. The windows were boarded up with plywood, and the lawn surrounding the property was covered in weeds and tall grass.

When the call came in, Holt and Fisher rushed over. They drove around to the back of the building. They spotted a police cruiser and parked next to it. A string of yellow police tape was already in place to secure the scene.

A uniformed officer stood before the tape. He was surrounded by three young men. The officer saw the detectives and came over.

To Fisher's pleasant surprise, the patrolman was Lance McConnell.

"Dispatch notified me about twenty minutes ago," McConnell said.

"They called it in?" Holt asked, nodding in the direction of the young men.

"They did."

"Show it to us."

They followed McConnell through the police tape and across the building's parking lot. Fisher estimated it had space for around thirty vehicles.

"What was in the building before it was abandoned?" Fisher asked McConnell.

"They used to print labels for products. I think it was owned by two brothers, but after one died, the other sold it. The new owners had no idea about the labeling business. It soon went under. I think they used to employ close to fifty people at one time."

She was not sure why she had asked him, but she liked hearing his response. *What is it about him that is making me blush?* she thought.

She quickly shook the thought away. They were here for a reason that did not involve getting googly-eyed over someone she really did not know.

Next to the parking lot was a small lake. The water was black and still.

There was an object by the water's edge. They walked up and realized the object was shaped like a body. It was covered in several garbage bags secured with nylon ropes. A pale white limb was sticking out from a corner of the bag.

A long piece of wood lay next to the body.

Holt and Fisher quickly pulled on latex gloves and carefully approached the corpse. From his jacket pocket, Holt removed a switchblade and gently cut the bag open.

He grimaced as a strong odor hit his nostrils. Fisher covered her nose with the back of her hand. McConnell took a step back.

The body was a woman with flowing blonde hair, but that was all they could tell about her.

Her cheeks were purple, bruised, and swollen. Her eyes were puffy and shut tight. Her lips were red and cut up.

Whoever she was, she was almost unrecognizable.

EIGHTY-ONE

Callaway entered the restaurant. He spotted Joely behind the counter. She nodded to a booth at the far end.

Elle was sitting at the table with a cup before her. Joely had called Callaway and told him Elle had been waiting for him for close to an hour.

He sat across from her. She sensed him and turned her head toward him. "Lee?" she asked.

"Yes," he replied.

"I went to your office, and I thought about waiting for you there, but then I decided to come here."

"You could have called me," he said.

"I did not want to do it over the phone."

His back tensed. "Do what?"

"Apologize to you for my abrupt disappearance."

He relaxed. "That's okay."

"Along with a lot of other issues, I also suffer from severe anxiety attacks." Elle lowered her head. "I haven't left my apartment since the last time we spoke."

"Oh," he said.

"I kept thinking something bad might have happened to Katie, or that I will never see her again. These thoughts paralyzed me, and I worried I would go down a deep, dark hole that I won't be able to come out of. Fortunately, my doctor prescribed me something that has lifted the cloud off. This was another reason why it took me three months to get the courage to come down to Milton and search for Katie."

"I appreciate you sharing this with me. I know it must have been difficult for you," Callaway said.

She nodded. "While I was away, did you find anything on my sister?" she asked.

He was not sure how he could break the news to her, especially after what she had just told him about her condition. "I've made some progress," he slowly replied.

She smiled. "And do you know where she is?"

"Um… I… it's just that…" he stammered.

Her smile disappeared. "Tell me what you found."

There's that determination in her voice again, he thought. He found it reassuring.

"You might not like it," he warned her.

"I want to know."

"Katie was working as an escort."

Her silence spoke volumes as to how shocked she was.

He was not sure how much time had passed when she asked, "Are you certain?"

"Unfortunately, yes," he replied. "It was how she was supporting her lifestyle in Milton."

He was met with more silence. She slowly reached for the cup, found it, and moved it toward her lips. She stopped short and said, "Do you think that's why Katie didn't want me to come to see her?"

"It could very well be," he said. "She was likely ashamed of what she was doing."

Elle put the cup down. "When I came to Milton, I never expected I would end up going on this emotional roller coaster. Every time I think I understand my sister, she blindsides me with something else." She looked away to collect her thoughts. "But this doesn't change anything," she said. "I still love my sister. She's the only family I have left. I want to know where she is."

"Good," he said with renewed hope. He worried she might give up her search. He would hate to abandon it without knowing the truth. For the past couple of days, all he had thought about was Katie Pearson and what might have happened to her.

EIGHTY-TWO

The youths who had found the body were Mike, Joe, and Will. The standout aspects of their attire was that Mike wore a hoodie, Joe sported a baseball hat, and Will had a gold chain around his neck. All three were still in high school.

"What were you doing here?" Fisher asked.

Mike shrugged. "We were skateboarding in the parking lot."

"You skateboard here often?"

Joe nodded. "Yeah. It's a quiet area. No one bothers us."

Will jumped in. "It also has stuff we can use for obstacles."

Fisher had seen a plywood sheet propped up next to a metal garbage bin for use as a skateboard ramp. Wooden crates were placed strategically in order to jump over them. There was a ramp, handrails, and lots of steps for the young men to perform their stunts on. And the empty parking lot allowed them to skateboard freely.

She could see the building's attraction. The place was private and almost secluded.

It is also a perfect location to dump a body, she thought.

She looked at her partner. Holt was still by the body. He was looking for any clues that would help him identify her. Fisher knew that would not be easy. The woman had been badly disfigured and likely tortured.

She turned to the three youths. "Tell me how you found the body."

Joe said, "I was doing a flip when I lost grip on my board and it flew out of my hands. It ended up rolling toward the lake."

Mike said, "I was closer, so I chased it down. When I finally got to it, I saw something floating in the water. I didn't know what it was, but I knew I hadn't seen it there before."

Fisher raised an eyebrow. "When was the last time you were here?"

"We came yesterday."

"And you didn't see anything in the lake?"

"I mean…" Mike said, trying to backtrack his comment. "I don't really pay too much attention to the water…"

Will said, "We usually keep away from the lake. We tried playing ball hockey here a couple of times, and we lost a bunch of balls in the water."

"What made you pull the victim out of the lake?" she asked.

Joe replied, "We didn't know what it was at first, but there was something not right about it."

"Like what?" Fisher asked.

"We saw rope tied around it."

Mike said, "I watch a lot of crime shows on TV, so I had a bad feeling it might be a body."

"He didn't want us to touch it," Joe said, pointing to Mike.

"I wanted to call 9-1-1 instead," Mike shot back.

"We eventually did call, you know," Joe replied.

Fisher did not want the questioning to get derailed. She said, "So how did you get it out?"

"We used the four-by-fours over there." Will pointed at a pile of wood on the side of the building. "We found one that was eight feet long. We used it to guide the body toward us. We pulled it ashore, but when we saw the foot, we dropped everything and called 9-1-1."

"You did the right thing by calling us," she said.

"Is it a guy or a girl?" Joe asked, curious.

"It's a woman," Fisher said. There was no point in hiding it from them. They would end up finding out through the media anyway. Plus, there was a good chance they would be interviewed for a story. They were the ones who had found the body, after all.

"What happened to her?" Mike asked.

Something terrible, Fisher wanted to say, but instead, she replied, "We don't know yet, but we're looking into it."

EIGHTY-THREE

Andrea Wakefield used a blade to cut the rope that held the garbage bag over the body. She then tore open the plastic garbage bag. The smell was even more intense. Holt and Fisher grimaced, but the medical examiner did not even flinch. She was rarely surprised or taken aback by what she saw.

Wakefield opened the garbage bag further. The victim was still clothed. She was wearing a black top, white skirt, and stockings, but no shoes. She wore a necklace, and there was a watch on her wrist. The watch was still ticking.

Her wrists and ankles were duct-taped.

"Why use the duct tape when there was already a rope to secure her body?" Holt said.

Fisher said, "It might have been used prior to the garbage bag."

"What do you mean?" Holt asked.

"She might have still been alive when she was brought here. The duct tape would come in handy so that she didn't run away."

"But why not have it over her mouth?" Holt said. "It would prevent her from calling out for help."

"That's not true," Wakefield said. "The victim's mouth was taped at first. If you look carefully, you can see residue from the glue around the edges of her lips."

"Then why was it removed?" Holt asked.

"Maybe her assailant wanted information from her that she was unable to provide," Fisher suggested.

"It would explain the condition of her face," Wakefield said.

"Is that how she died? From her injuries?" Fisher asked Wakefield.

"No, she died from a single gunshot." Wakefield turned the victim's head to the side and moved her fingers over the back. She parted the victim's hair, revealing a hole the size of a penny.

"She was shot from behind?" Fisher asked.

"That would be my guess," Wakefield replied.

Holt narrowed his eyes. "More like executed."

Fisher noticed a piece of rope around the victim's ankle. The end of the rope was split. "Is that how her body was submerged?" she asked.

Wakefield nodded. "It was likely tied to a heavy object. From my understanding, there are jagged rocks at the bottom of this lake. My guess is, when the body started taking in water, it began to float to the surface. Even with the garbage bag wrapped around it, it was not watertight. It took a couple of days for the rope to get severed by the rocks as it fought to come up."

Fisher liked throwing ideas and questions at Wakefield. She was the best in her field. There was not much that got past her.

Fisher said, "Do you believe she was shot at the back of this building?"

"Why do you ask?" Wakefield said.

"If she was, then we should scour the area for shell casings."

"In that case, I would have to say yes."

EIGHTY-FOUR

The art gallery was wedged between a bar and a pet food store. The space was confined, but the bare white walls and bright lighting made the gallery look spacious.

There were no paintings hanging on the walls. Instead, there were large computer tablets propped up on clear plastic stands all around the space.

Callaway was confused about why a so-called "art gallery" would not have any art displayed. Elle was next to him, and he wished she could see what he was seeing. He never understood nor cared much for art, but even he knew you had to have something for people to admire.

Maybe I'm supposed to appreciate the white walls? he thought.

A man appeared from behind another wall. He was dressed in a white turtleneck, beige pants, and brown loafers. He had wavy hair, a soul patch beard, and he wore round spectacles.

"Is there anything, in particular, you are looking for?" he asked with a smile.

Callaway said, "Are you Carl Goodwin?"

The man paused and stared at them for a second. "You're the private investigator Glenn told me about," he said.

"Yes, I am." Callaway pulled out Linda's photo and held it out for him. "We're looking for her. She's been missing for three months now."

"Glenn told me that too," Goodwin said.

Callaway turned to Elle. "This is Linda's sister. She's the one who hired me to find her."

"I had no idea Linda had a sister," Goodwin said.

Callaway did not want to explain that Linda was really Katie. "Linda's best friend said the last conversation she had with her was right before she was to meet a client." Callaway looked around the space. "It is my understanding they meet...*here*?"

"Yes, they do. We have a seating arrangement behind that wall for the girls and the men to meet before they decide to go on their way," Goodwin replied.

Callaway scratched his head. "I'll be honest with you, this is a highly odd way for a John to hire an escort." He regretted using the word "John" in front of Elle, but she showed no reaction, so he continued. "Usually, you find the girls roaming the streets, or you find them in the back of a newspaper, or you find the pimp who'll hook you up with the girl."

"I'm afraid those methods are still going on to this day," Goodwin said. "We wanted a new approach to what is the oldest profession in history." He paused to collect his thoughts. "I'm not sure how much Glenn told you, but he and I worked at the same software company. When we were laid off, we began searching for employment. After months of no offers, Glenn created the website, and I cashed out my pension and started this gallery."

Callaway rubbed his chin. "Speaking of the gallery, I don't see any art."

Goodwin smiled. "Let me show you." He took him to a computer tablet. He tapped the screen and swiped through the various displays. "We're not really an art gallery per se. We are more like an art creator."

"Art creator?"

"Instead of buying paintings or designs created by artists with their own tastes and aesthetics, *you* become the artist. When you come into the gallery, you select a painter's style. Picasso. Rembrandt. Van Gogh. We have over a hundred artists to choose from. You then use the tools in our software, and you paint your masterpiece. Once you are done, that's when the magic happens. Follow me."

Goodwin took Callaway behind the back wall. There was a robotic machine with arms. Callaway saw paintbrushes of all shapes and sizes, and paints of every color imaginable. A blank canvas was in front of the arms.

Goodwin said, "The software feeds the information into the robot, which then mimics the artist's brushstrokes and creates a painting in the artist's style. It's quite fascinating how accurate these machines are."

"Doesn't that lead to people creating forgeries of priceless art?" Callaway asked.

"We've had people come in and recreate masterpieces, but the materials we use are contemporary," Goodwin replied. "It would take an expert only a second to know it's not an original piece of work. A good forgery can take months or years to create. This takes less than twenty minutes."

"Amazing," Callaway said, feeling astonished.

Goodwin walked him back to the open space. He found Elle waiting for him. In all the excitement, Callaway had forgotten about her.

He coughed and said, "Coming back to Linda. We believe she might have met a client here and perhaps not made it back home."

"That's not possible," Goodwin said. "When Glenn approached me with the idea, I agreed to let him use the gallery as a meeting spot. Safety is our number one priority. If the girls got a wrong vibe from the client, I'd come in and end the meeting."

"Did the clients ever get aggressive?"

"Sure they did, but once I threatened to call the police, they'd quickly leave. A lot of them have families and good jobs. The only reason they go through the site by purchasing digital currency is because they want complete anonymity."

"But, *you* see them."

"I do, but I don't know their names or anything about them. If anyone asked, they were here to create art. Also, the girls are young and mostly students. They seem to like the way it's set up."

Callaway thought of something. "But once the girls leave with the clients, you don't know where they are going or what's happening with them."

"Glenn and I discussed this, and to make it even safer for the girls, we book a room in a fancy hotel under the website's name, so there is no record of the client ever staying there. We get a good rate at the hotel. The girls don't mind having a percentage taken out of their fee to pay for it. The hotel has great security, and it's clean. Not like the back of a car or a grungy motel."

"Can you give us the address of this hotel?" Callaway asked. "The security cameras might have caught Linda with the client on the night we believe she disappeared."

"It won't be necessary."

"Why not?"

"These girls are young and tech-savvy. On their smartphones, the girls sign in to the website with a password only they know to confirm the transaction. Once they are done, they sign in again to tell us the transaction is complete. If they don't do that, they don't get paid. This also lets us know something is not right if we don't hear back from them. It has never happened, but if it does, we have footage of them meeting the client, and we'll take it straight to the authorities. We have no issues with working with the police. We will tell them the girl is a friend of ours and we saw her at the gallery with a man. As we have not heard back from her, we are concerned for her safety."

"You and your partner have thought this through," Callaway said.

"We have," Goodwin said with a smile.

"Can you show us the footage of Linda from the day she disappeared?"

"I would, but I don't keep records going back that far. Why would I? If nothing happened, I don't see a point in storing that much data."

Callaway turned to Elle. She had not said a word, but he was certain she had heard everything. She must be thinking the same thing he was.

We hit another dead end.

"And Linda sent you the confirmation that told you she completed the transaction?" Callaway asked.

"She must have, or else I would have gone straight to the police," Goodwin replied. "Plus, there is no girl that has any outstanding balance with us, which means they completed the transaction, and they were all paid."

EIGHTY-FIVE

The media had converged like vultures on a carcass. They surrounded the building, hoping to get a shot of the lake behind.

The medical examiner had already removed the body, but Holt and Fisher still extended the police tape to block off the site. It was still an active crime scene.

Members of the crime scene unit were still scouring the area for shell casings. Fisher doubted they would find them. The killer had planned this out. The building had no security cameras of any kind. The place was a perfect spot to dump a body. Had the rope not severed, releasing the victim to the surface, her body would have likely decomposed underwater. They had also caught a lucky break with how the body was found. If the young men who hung out here to skateboard had chosen to go elsewhere, there was no telling when the body would have been discovered.

Holt approached Fisher with an intense look on his face. She knew he had been thinking hard about something.

"You come up with any theories?" she asked.

"I might have, but I'm not sure."

"It's better than what we know already, which is nothing. So what's on your mind?"

"The killer used garbage bags, duct tape, and a rope, right?"

"Sure."

"Without a receipt of some sort, we don't know where the killer could have purchased those items, but the killer had also used something to weigh the body down."

"Okay," Fisher said, trying to follow his thinking.

"I checked the property, but I saw nothing that could be used as an anchor."

"What about the four-by-fours or the wooden crates?" she asked.

He shook his head. "Wood expands in water. Any of those items would float up to the surface in no time. I was thinking more like large rocks, bricks, or concrete blocks."

Fisher's eyes narrowed. "You think the killer may have purchased something to use as an anchor?"

"Yes."

"But we don't know what that could be until we get a team of divers to go into the lake and retrieve whatever might be down there."

"That'll take time," Holt said. "On our drive over here, I remember passing by a large hardware store. I think we should go check it out."

EIGHTY-SIX

Cosimo was parked in the hospital parking lot. Cosimo had followed Agent Schaefer's Buick all the way to the hospital. He was not sure what the agent was doing there. He had considered following him inside, but he knew that would be too risky.

Agent Schaefer would recognize him the moment he saw him. All of Don Beniti's associates had become a target for the FBI, including him. He had eluded capture due to his various aliases. He had seriously considered leaving the profession and moving to some island nation with no extradition treaty with the United States. He could spend the rest of his life sipping margaritas on a beach somewhere. But being a hitman was the only trade he knew. The moment he had turned fourteen, he quit school and joined a local gang. He started off by stealing cigarettes and moved his way up to robbing liquor stores. When he caught the eye of a mob boss, he was promoted to being an enforcer for him. If someone needed to be taught a lesson, he was the man. But he did not like the job very much. First, he was not very big or strong. Second, he did not like inflicting unnecessary pain on others. Torture was not his thing.

What he was really good at, and what he truly enjoyed was eliminating people. Hits required a certain level of skill. He could blend in easily and disappear without a trace after a kill. Also, the jobs were clean. He rarely got his hands dirty. One bullet between the eyes and the target was dead.

He had used other methods as well, but nothing compared to a gun in his hand. Guns gave him an advantage other methods did not. He could eliminate the target from a distance.

He checked his watch. He was in no hurry. Patience was key to survival in his profession. That and having a ready plan. Even now, he had a plan, having scoped out all the exits and where the security cameras were. If he had to make a quick getaway, he already had one mapped out.

He kept his eye on the hospital entrance. He saw Agent Schaefer walk out. The agent made his way to his Buick and drove away.

Cosimo started the car and followed after him.

He kept a few cars back as the Buick changed lanes. He was not worried about losing Schaefer. While the agent was in the hospital, Cosimo had placed a tracking device underneath the vehicle. On his smartphone, he could see a moving red dot that told him the direction the Buick was headed.

He followed for another twenty minutes.

The Buick pulled into the parking lot of an apartment building.

Agent Schaefer got out and made his way to the front entrance. Cosimo debated waiting for him, but then a thought occurred to him.

What if the target is inside?

He quickly got out and hurried to the front entrance. He paused outside and looked into the lobby. Agent Schaefer was waiting by the elevators. He had not spotted him. Cosimo pulled out his phone and made it look like he was deep in conversation. After Schaefer boarded an elevator, Cosimo rushed inside.

He watched as the elevator stopped on the fourth floor.

He dashed for the stairs and raced up two steps at a time. He stopped on the fourth floor's landing and stuck his head into the hall. He saw Agent Schaefer standing by the door of an apartment. He looked like he was speaking to someone inside. He had his credentials out, and he waved it whenever he needed to emphasize something. The conversation lasted a good ten minutes before Agent Schaefer turned and moved to the elevator.

When he was out of sight, Cosimo pulled out his weapon and headed to the apartment. The tracker would tell him where the agent was headed next, so he was not concerned about losing him.

What mattered was who was in the apartment.

He knocked on the door and moved aside. He could see a shadow in the peephole. He knocked again.

The door swung open.

"Hey man, I told you I don't know nothing," a male voice said.

Cosimo made himself visible. He saw that the speaker was a black man.

The man quickly froze at the sight of the weapon. "Who are you?" he asked.

"You and I are going to have a long talk," Cosimo said as he pushed his way in and slammed the door behind him.

EIGHTY-SEVEN

The hardware store manager was surprised to see two detectives in his store. He had not yet heard the news about a dead body being found not too far away from his location.

The manager was short, stocky, and he had on a green vest. He frowned and said, "You want to know if we sell concrete slabs?"

"Concrete slabs, cement blocks, patio stones, bricks, anything that can be used as weights," Holt replied.

The manager pondered this odd question. "Sure, we have a landscaping section."

Fisher said, "Can you find out if someone purchased any of those items?"

The manager's mouth nearly dropped. "We ring up thousands of sales each day. I'm not sure how we can find out who purchased what."

Fisher and Holt were silent.

The manager asked, "What day were these items purchased?"

"We don't know," Holt replied.

The manager almost laughed. "Then it's like finding a needle in a haystack. I'm sorry, but it can't be done."

Holt grunted and began to make his way to the exit.

Fisher said, "Can you ask your staff if someone came by in the last couple of days and asked where the landscaping section was? Or maybe asked where they could find a rope or duct tape?"

The manager stared at her, unsure if he should oblige her request.

"It's important," Fisher added. "If it wasn't, we wouldn't be here."

The manager sighed. "Okay, let me find out." He left them.

Holt said, "Why did you ask him that?"

"We have to assume whoever dumped the body did not know the area too well. If they did, they would have known the lake's floor was covered in jagged rocks. This means they must have come to the hardware store for the first time and asked for help locating whatever they were looking for."

Holt shook his head. "That's a long shot."

She gave him a stern look. "But it's *worth* a shot. We don't have anything to go on right now."

A moment later, the manager returned with an employee. "Herb," the manager said, "tell them what you told me."

Herb was tall, rail-thin, and he had acne on his face. "A guy came in and asked me where we kept our cement," he said.

"What else did he ask you?" Fisher said.

"He was also looking for a sturdy rope."

Fisher shot a glance at Holt.

"What did this man look like?" Fisher asked.

Herb shrugged. "I dunno. He was wearing a checkered shirt, I guess."

"What else?"

"Um…" He searched his mind. "I remember he had paint stains all over his shirt and pants."

"He was a painter?"

"I'm not sure."

"When was this?"

"Um… I think it was two days ago."

"Do you remember the exact time?"

For a second, Fisher thought Herb would tell her how absurd her question was, but instead, he said, "I kind of do remember. It was right before my smoke break."

With this information in hand, the manager took the detectives to his office. A security officer was seated behind a set of monitors. The manager told him exactly what he was looking for.

The security officer began to rewind the footage on one of the screens. A moment later, he played the footage at normal speed.

The image was black and white, but it was sharp and in high contrast. The hardware store's automatic doors slid open, and a man came in. He was tall, wearing a checkered shirt, cargo pants, and work boots. His hair was dark, and he walked with purpose.

He stopped by the entrance and looked around. He was searching for the signs atop the aisles. He then spotted an employee and waved him over. It was Herb. They exchanged a few words, and the man turned right and headed toward the other side of the store.

He disappeared from view.

"Can you follow him?" Holt asked.

The security officer quickly punched a key, and the screen flickered to another image. The man was walking down the aisle. He stopped at a section. He grabbed a bundle of rope and looked at the price. He put the rope back, grabbed another one, and did the same. He did this a few times until he was satisfied with one. He slung the bundle of rope over his shoulder and headed in another direction.

The image flickered as the security officer punched another key.

The man was in the landscape section now. He looked around and then picked up a piece of concrete block. The block's weight bowed him down as he made his way to the checkout.

Fisher watched with bated breath. They could see the time stamp at the bottom of the screen. She prayed the man paid with credit or debit instead of cash, making it easy to pull up the transaction and find out the man's name.

The man pulled out some bills and handed it to the cashier. He grabbed his change and receipt and left the store.

Fisher sighed.

"Do you have cameras in the parking lot?" Holt asked.

The image flickered again.

The man was leaving the hardware store. Fisher's back tensed. The moment the man entered his vehicle, they would have his license plate.

The man continued walking. He moved farther and farther away from the camera. He had parked at the far end of the lot. There was no way to distinguish the make and model of the car he was driving.

Holt turned to the security officer, "Can you find the clearest picture of this man?"

"Sure," the officer replied.

"We want a copy of it."

EIGHTY-EIGHT

"What do we do now?" Elle asked Callaway. They were walking down the street toward the Impala, which was parked a block away from the art gallery.

Callaway felt like he was spinning his wheels. Nothing made sense to him anymore. How could a simple search turn into something so complicated?

He knew the answer all too well. Katie had lied to her sister. She told Elle what she wanted to hear. Behind her back, she lived a life that was reckless and possibly dangerous.

The life of an escort was anything but glamorous. Linda's social media posts about her visits to all those countries was not indicative of the profession's sordid truths. Most girls got into being escorts because they saw no other option to earn a living. Some were forced into the trade. Sex trafficking was a massive economic concern for most governments. The amount of money the traffickers made off the girls was staggering. And then there were the social implications of prostitution. These girls were ostracized and considered worse than lepers by the general population. Most people did not understand why someone would sell their bodies for money.

No matter how Glenn Maker and Carl Goodwin sugarcoated it, prostitution was dirty and ugly.

Callaway felt a strong migraine coming on. His nose throbbed with pain. The swelling had subsided, and he did not need to put a new bandage over his nose, but it was still not healed.

"How do we find my sister now?" Elle asked as they walked.

He had no idea. He felt terrible for Elle. The moment they saw a glimmer of hope, it was cruelly taken away from them.

"We will not stop until we know what happened to her," Callaway replied, trying to sound positive. But deep down, he was feeling doubtful himself.

He stopped and pulled out his cell phone.

"What's going on?" Elle asked.

"I know someone who might be able to help us," he replied.

"Who?"

"She's a reporter in Fairview. I worked with her on a case there."

"Are you referring to Echo Rose?" Elle asked.

Callaway looked at her. "How did you know?"

"I told you I did my homework before I hired you, remember?"

"I do."

He turned back to his cell phone. "Linda's best friend, Jennifer Paulsingh, last spoke to her before she was supposed to meet a client."

"Okay," Elle said.

"Maker and Goodwin have set up a system to protect the girls. What if someone—maybe a client—forced Linda to punch her password into the website so Maker and Goodwin would think everything was all right with her? If we find out when that reply was made, maybe it can tell us the exact time of her disappearance."

Callaway quickly messaged Echo.

"And you think Echo Rose can help us in this regard?" Elle asked.

"Echo is one of the best hackers I know, if not *the* best. She can hack into anything, even Glenn Maker's website."

Callaway hated to bother Echo, but he was at the end of his rope.

After he sent the text, something flickering in a storefront window caught his eye.

Several display televisions were relaying the news. Callaway could not hear the audio, but the scroll at the bottom read WOMAN'S BODY DISCOVERED IN LAKE BEHIND ABANDONED BUILDING.

His heart sank, and he was again grateful Elle could not see what he was seeing.

He quickly scrolled through his contact list and speed-dialed a number.

EIGHTY-NINE

Fisher spotted the Impala as it pulled into the parking lot and found a spot. Callaway had called her, and she had driven to the morgue after speaking to him. She did not tell Holt where she was going. Holt was somewhat possessive with the cases he worked on, and there was no way he would allow a private investigator to become privy to his investigation. Plus, Holt and Callaway had a history. Callaway had made Holt look foolish on another case. If Holt found out she was speaking to him, he would blow his top.

Callaway approached her. Next to him was a woman with a walking cane.

"This is Elle Pearson," Callaway said, introducing her.

"Nice to meet you. I'm Detective Dana Fisher," she said. She then got right to the point. "Lee told me your sister is missing."

"Yes," Elle replied.

Fisher turned to Callaway. "Can you describe her to me?"

"I can do better." He stuck his hand in his jacket pocket and pulled out the Polaroid. He handed the photo to Fisher.

Fisher's eyes narrowed. "How long has she been missing?"

"Three months," Callaway replied.

"And you said her name is Katie Pearson?"

"Yes."

Fisher stared at him. "But she might be going under the name Linda Eustace?"

"It's a long story," he said.

Fisher nodded and said, "Come with me."

They followed her into the building. They took the elevator to the basement and walked down a tiled hallway.

They went through a heavy door and approached another. Fisher stopped and turned to Callaway and Elle. "I must warn you the body has suffered severe trauma."

Callaway knew the warning was not for Elle but for him. He took a deep breath and nodded.

They entered a sterile room and found the medical examiner standing before a body lying on a table. The cadaver was covered with a green sheet.

"Andrea Wakefield," Fisher said, "this is Lee Callaway and Elle Pearson."

The medical examiner gave them a nod.

She pulled off the sheet.

Callaway nearly threw up on the floor. He covered his mouth and looked away.

"It's not a pretty sight, I'm afraid," Wakefield said.

Callaway turned back, but he did not move his hand away from his mouth.

The woman looked like she had been beaten to a pulp. Her face was swollen, puffy, and purple.

"Who would do this?" he asked.

"That's what we are trying to find out," Fisher replied.

Elle stood where she was. She said, "My sister has distinguishing marks on her body. Would that help to identify if this is her?"

"Absolutely," Wakefield replied.

Elle provided her the details.

Wakefield checked the body. She shook her head and said, "It's not her."

Fisher frowned. "Then who is it?"

NINETY

Elle was seated on a chair outside the examination room. She wept as Callaway tried to comfort her.

"It's not Katie," he whispered to her. "Isn't that a good thing?"

"Every time they find a body, I can't help but think it's her." She heaved a sigh and said, "I can't keep doing this."

Callaway sighed. This was taking a toll on her and him. She was right, though. When Callaway saw the news, his first thought was that the police had found Katie. A part of him wanted this search to be over, but another part of him did not want it to end with a dead person. Elle deserved closure, but she also deserved a happy ending.

The longer it took for them to find her sister, the less hope he had that she was still alive. He understood why they could not find Katie Pearson, but he could not fathom what happened to Linda Eustace.

Is she on the run from someone? Is that why she took on a new identity? Callaway wondered.

Fisher joined them. "The medical examiner has started the autopsy. There is no point for you to stay here."

Elle sniffled and said, "Do you know who hurt that woman?"

"We have a suspect."

"You do?" Callaway said, feeling curious.

Fisher paused for a moment before she said, "Holt would kill me for telling you this, but the victim was found wrapped in a garbage bag. Her ankle was tied to a concrete block so it would stay underwater."

Elle gasped and said, "Oh my God."

"How did you find the suspect?" Callaway asked.

"The suspect had gone to a nearby hardware store and purchased the concrete block and the rope used to drown the body." She pulled out her cell phone and held the screen up for Callaway. The image was black and white, but it was clear that the man was standing by a cash register.

Callaway's eyes narrowed. "He looks awfully familiar," he said.

"He does?" Fisher asked, surprised.

"Yeah. I've seen him someplace."

"Where?" she asked eagerly.

He rubbed his chin in deep thought. His eyes suddenly widened, and he stuck his hand in his jacket pocket to pull out another photo. "We found this while we were searching for Elle's sister. It was in one of her sister's personal effects."

Fisher examined the picture. "I can see the similarities, even though the hair is a different color and style."

"We think his name might be Bruno Rocco," Callaway said. "Before her disappearance, Elle's sister mentioned she was seeing someone by that name."

"That's good to know," Fisher said.

"Could the same person be responsible for what happened to that woman in there and also for Elle's sister going missing?" Callaway asked.

"It could very well be," Fisher replied. "I'll ask Holt to run the photo through our facial recognition software. Hopefully, it will confirm the name you just gave us."

NINETY-ONE

Holt was making his way through the police department's parking lot when a familiar Buick pulled up in front of him.

Agent Ed Schaefer rolled down his window and smiled. "Detective Holt, do you have a minute?"

Holt nodded. "What can I do for you, Agent Schaefer?"

"I just heard on the radio that you guys pulled a female body from the lake. Is that true?"

"I'm afraid so."

"Do you know who she is?"

"Not yet, but we'll know soon enough."

"Do you believe this is related to your nephew's murder?"

Holt's brow furrowed. "How so?"

"I mean, I'm only speculating based on what I've read, but didn't your nephew go to meet a woman at that furniture store?"

Cassandra Stevens!

Holt had a suspicion it could be her. Cassandra had blonde hair. She was five-three, and she weighed around a hundred pounds. The woman found in the lake had blonde hair. She was also around five-foot-three, but her weight would be impossible to match due to the body's decomposition. And her killer had worked her face over. Holt doubted they would be able to ID her via her face. But the department had numerous tools at their disposal. A DNA sample taken from her hair. A print from one of her fingertips. Even dental records could be used to identify her.

Holt said, "We don't know yet if it's the same woman."

"But it could be, right?" Schaefer prodded.

Holt studied him and said, "That is a possibility."

"I just want you to know my offer is still on the table," Schaefer said. "I want to help you find the person who is responsible for your nephew's murder. He was a promising athlete, and it would be a shame for his death to never be solved."

"I would not let that happen," Holt said.

"If you feel comfortable, I would love to know how far you have progressed in the investigation."

Holt paused to think this over. *What's the harm in letting him know what we've found?* he thought. *He is a federal agent, after all.*

"We haven't made much progress in Isaiah's case," Holt conceded. "But if the body belongs to Cassandra Stevens, then we might be able to solve both cases."

Schaefer's eyebrow rose. "How so?"

"We have a suspect on our radar."

"You do?" he asked, sounding shocked.

"Yes." Holt pulled out his cell phone and displayed a photo for Schaefer. "This was taken from a security camera at a hardware store. The suspect purchased items that were used to dispose of the body."

Schaefer stared at the picture in silence. He swallowed and said, "Did you trace the payments to a name? That's what I would do if I were you."

"The suspect paid with cash, but it doesn't matter." Holt put the phone away. "We know what he looks like, and soon we will know who he is."

Schaefer checked his watch. "Well, I wish you the best of luck. I hope you find what you are looking for. If you ever need my assistance, don't hesitate to contact me."

He drove away.

NINETY-TWO

Callaway dropped Elle off at a bus stop. She looked visibly ill. The thought that her sister might have drowned in the lake was too much for her. Even though it turned out not to be Katie, Callaway understood how mentally draining the experience was for Elle. It was close to torture.

Each time they felt like they were taking a step forward, they ended up taking two steps back.

Elle had declined his offer to drive her to Mayview. "I need some space," she had told him. "I've got a lot to work through."

He respected her independence, and at the moment, even he was not in the mood to make the drive. The pain in his head was pounding like a sledgehammer. He needed painkillers and a shot of alcohol in his system—preferably the latter.

He debated whether to go straight to a bar and get drunk, or go home and take medicine and pass out.

He decided against either of the options. He doubted he would be able to fall asleep any time soon, and the alcohol would only make the headache worse.

What he needed was to keep his mind preoccupied. The only way to do that was to go back to the office and try to come up with another plan.

The search for Elle's missing sister had also been a drain on his finances. The five thousand Elle had paid him was running out fast. Soon he would have to ask her for more money, which he did not want to do. He felt it was crass for him to worry about money when the poor girl was no closer to knowing the truth.

He let out a long sigh. *Why did you agree to take on this case?* he thought. *You know better than most people how difficult missing persons cases are to solve.*

The answer was simple. He was having a horrible day when Elle showed up out of nowhere. And her visit was fruitful on all accounts.

Earlier that day, he had messed up by sleeping with his client's wife. The client punished him by breaking his nose, damaging his beloved Charger, and making him return the fee with some cash on top.

Elle's case had come at a time when he was desperate. At first, the case was like a gift from the heavens, but then it had turned into a nightmare that he was not sure would end any time soon.

How long was he going to chase someone who may never be found? It could not be forever, he knew. Sooner or later, he would have to stop his search.

He just was not sure how he would break that to Elle.

He was suddenly parched. His tongue stuck to the back of his throat.

I'll have one quick drink and then I'll head straight to the office, he thought.

NINETY-THREE

Schaefer was in the falafel shop with a can of soda in his hand and shawarma on his Styrofoam plate. He was not hungry, but he could not sit there without ordering something. Not placing an order would attract attention to himself.

The shop was busier than the last time he was there. Two students were sitting in a corner, laughing at something only they thought was funny. A woman in a burqa sat at the other table, talking on her cell phone. Three people were lined up at the counter, waiting for their orders.

Maybe this wasn't a good idea, Schaefer thought. *We should have found a more private location to meet.*

But time was running out, and when he called Brogdon, his reply was to meet at the same spot.

Schaefer and Brogdon never spoke longer than thirty seconds over the phone. Schaefer was well aware that cell phone conversations were never as secure as people thought they were. The government was always listening in. Schaefer had done that many times and without a warrant too. Federal agencies and government departments broke the law all the time, which was not uncommon. Civil liberties be damned. The moment they mentioned national security to a judge, they were free to do whatever they wanted.

He glanced at his watch. The longer he sat there without touching his meal, the more suspicious he looked. The suit was already making him stick out amongst the patrons.

The door chimed, and a man entered the restaurant. The hood of a sweatshirt covered his head, and sunglasses covered his eyes.

He made his way straight to Schaefer's table.

As he sat down, Schaefer said, "You have to get out of town. The detectives are on to you."

Brogdon did not pull off his sunglasses, but Schaefer could still tell he was surprised. "How?" he asked.

"They have footage of you inside a hardware store."

Brogdon's jaw tightened. "I'm going to need another identity."

Schaefer was ready to blow his top. "This is the third ID I've supplied you with. You remember what happened in the previous town?"

"The man was drunk, and he was rude to me."

"He lost one eye because of you."

Brogdon was silent for a moment. "Just get me another ID, okay?" he said. "I'll start a new life somewhere far away from Milton."

"I can't promise you anything."

Brogdon leaned closer. Schaefer could almost smell his breath. "You will do whatever I ask you to do. I took responsibility for crimes I never committed."

"You murdered two people before I caught up with you," Schaefer reminded him.

"One I planned to kill, and the other was at the wrong place at the wrong time," Brogdon said.

"Is that what happened to Isaiah Whitcomb and Cassandra Stevens? You planned to kill Stevens, and Whitcomb was at the wrong place?"

"It was something like that," Brogdon admitted.

Thick tension hung in the air between them.

Brogdon said, "I lied before a judge so that you could get the verdict you were looking for. I told them I was Don Beniti's hired gun and that I murdered all of Beniti's enemies at his behest. The truth was, until the last contract, I had never done a single job for Beniti. I lied for *you,* Agent Schaefer, and I got twelve years for that."

Schaefer was seething. "When you killed those two people at the café, you should have gotten life, but because of me and our agreement, you only got twelve years, of which you only served half. So don't get smart with me."

Brogdon stared at him.

Schaefer took a deep breath. "You pack whatever you need and meet me outside the city. There is a gas station with a giant donut sign on the roof. You can't miss it. You don't go in the station because it'll have security cameras. You meet me by the side of the road half a mile from the gas station. I'll get you the new IDs, but you've used your last favor. After tonight, you are on your own. In fact, if I find out you hurt another person, I'll put a bullet in your head myself. Got it?"

Brogdon grinned. "I got it."

Schaefer did not like the smile, but since this murdering thug could get him in big trouble if he talked, he had no choice but to help him one last time.

NINETY-FOUR

Cosimo was parked across from the falafel shop.

Earlier, Cosimo had seen the agent speaking to the detective at the police department. Soon after their conversation, the agent drove off in a hurry. Cosimo followed after.

The agent cut in and out of traffic at speeds well above the speed limit. Cosimo could not risk being pulled over if he did the same. He was not a federal agent that a traffic cop would bow to. He was a hitman who had been eluding the authorities for years.

Cosimo was not worried about losing the agent, though. The tracker on the agent's car would lead him back to him.

When the agent went inside the falafel shop, Cosimo had a feeling he was there to meet someone. He was willing to bet all the money Don Beniti had given to him that it was the target.

He stared at the shop.

A man appeared from the corner of the shop. His head was covered by his hoodie, and he had on dark sunglasses. Cosimo's eyes narrowed. He focused on the way the man walked. You could disguise a person, but you could not disguise their walk.

It's the target!

Cosimo opened the glove compartment and pulled out his weapon. He scanned his surroundings. There was no one around him. He carefully screwed the silencer over the gun's muzzle and placed his weapon in his jacket pocket.

He got out.

A police cruiser pulled into the shop's parking lot.

Cosimo cursed and sat back down.

The cruiser stood still for what felt like several minutes, but then it moved forward toward a metal garbage bin in the lot. The officer behind the wheel leaned over, stuffed a paper bag in the bin, and drove off.

The cop was throwing out the remains of his lunch!

Cosimo cursed again. He was about to get out again when he spotted Agent Schaefer exiting the shop.

The agent stomped over to his Buick and drove away.

Cosimo waited a few seconds. As he expected, the target walked out of the shop's front doors. He quickly turned right and disappeared around the corner.

Cosimo bolted out of the car. He crossed the street and hurried past the shop to where he had seen the target go.

He saw him up ahead about half a block away. The target was walking casually. He had no idea he was being followed.

He gripped the gun in his pocket. The moment he was close enough, he would pull it out and fire three bullets—one toward the target's head, another toward his chest, and the last toward his stomach. Even if one hit the target, they were all lethal shots.

The target headed into an alley. Cosimo quickened his pace. He was not about to lose his prey. He reached the alley and saw the target was already at the other end of it.

He went into a jog.

At the end of the alley was another road where a white van was parked. The target was now getting into the driver's seat.

He took three long strides and pulled out his weapon. He aimed at the driver's side window.

A loud honk startled him.

He turned and saw a Nissan sedan in the alley. The driver honked again. Cosimo was blocking the exit. He hid the gun behind his back and moved aside. The driver quickly sped away.

Cosimo watched as the white van pulled out of its parking spot and drove away. Cosimo raced to the road and saw the van in the distance. It was too far to get a shot.

No matter, he thought. *I now know the make of the vehicle and its license plate number. I'll catch up to it in no time.*

NINETY-FIVE

Fisher was behind her computer. Holt was seated next to her. She did not tell him Callaway had provided her the name "Bruno Rocco," or that she had met him at the morgue. It would lead to more questions, and she was in no mood to answer them. He was her partner, and he would have to trust her as she ran the name through an online search engine. She got over two dozen results. She clicked on the first link.

She squinted and said, "Bruno Rocco did time in Foxworth Prison for the murder of Anthony Carvalho and a waitress named Katherine Woodward. Carvalho was going to snitch on Paolo Beniti, a crime boss with deep roots in New Jersey. During a shoot-out with Carvalho at a restaurant, Rocco was hit badly. He somehow rode his motorcycle to a nearby hospital. Any time a patient comes in with gunshot wounds, stab wounds, or wounds due to a violent interaction, the hospital staff is required to contact the authorities."

Holt frowned. "And you believe this Bruno Rocco is the same person we saw in the hardware store?"

"Give me one second," she said.

She clicked on another link. An image popped up on the screen. It was the same photo Callaway had shown her earlier.

Holt's eyes narrowed. "I see the resemblance, but I still don't see what this has to do with the imprisonment of a mob boss?"

Fisher scrolled through another article. Her eyes went wide. "You won't believe this."

"What?"

"When Rocco was in the hospital, he cut a deal with the feds. Guess who the agent was?"

Holt's face turned pale. "Don't tell me. Special Agent Ed Schaefer."

"Bingo! And because of Rocco's testimony, a lot of bad people went to prison. And after serving the minimum required time, Rocco was put in the Witness Protection Program…"

"…And now he is in Milton living as someone else," Holt said, finishing her sentence.

They were silent for a moment.

"Do you think Agent Schaefer is not entirely truthful with us?" Fisher asked.

"I think he knows more than he's letting on," Holt replied. "In fact, he caught me returning to the station. He was eager to offer his assistance."

"Something doesn't feel right to me," Fisher said.

"I know exactly what you mean."

Fisher squinted at the monitor and said, "Hold on. Someone has posted a video of the shooting online."

She clicked the link.

A video popped up. The camera was aimed at the patio of a restaurant. A large man was seated at a table. At another table, a blonde waitress was taking orders from a couple.

A motorcycle rolled up to the patio entrance. The rider was dressed in black from head to toe, and his face was covered by a motorcycle helmet. The rider jumped off the motorcycle, pulled out a gun, and fired at the large man. The first bullet hit the man, and he quickly took cover behind a table. People screamed and ducked for cover. As the rider turned to run, the large man pulled out a gun and fired in the rider's direction. The bullet hit the rider in the back. He stumbled, and without looking back, he fired a burst. One of them hit the target, and another hit the waitress as she ducked for cover. The rider jumped back on the motorcycle and disappeared from view. People quickly huddled around the fallen woman. The large man let go of his weapon, and his body went limp. The entire video was less than a minute long.

Holt and Fisher sat in utter silence.

Holt gritted his teeth and said, "If Bruno Rocco is the man in the video, then he is the one who murdered Isaiah."

"And if Bruno Rocco is responsible for dumping that body in the lake, then we have to assume she is none other than Cassandra Stevens, the woman Isaiah had gone to meet that morning."

"We have to find this person," Holt said with determination.

Fisher's cell phone buzzed. For a second, she thought against picking it up, but she did. She listened and hung up.

"Guess what?" she said.

"What?"

"They found another dead body."

Another one? Holt thought.

NINETY-SIX

Callaway stumbled into his office with a severe hangover. His one drink had turned into many. His brain was foggy as he dropped onto the sofa. The bar was only a block away. The trek normally took him less than five minutes, but that night, the walk took him twice as long.

He shut his eyes and cursed at himself. He should not have gone to the bar. He should have stayed in the office and worked on Elle's case. Getting drunk was not going to help him find her sister.

His eyes welled up as a strong wave of emotion overcame him. He was using alcohol to self-medicate. The possibility that Elle's sister was still alive was nothing more than a fantastic dream. He had to face the hard truth. Elle's sister was long gone, and no matter where he looked or how hard he looked, she was not coming back.

How am I going to face Elle? he thought. *How am I going to tell her I can't work on her case anymore? I'm not cut out for this kind of work. I chase cheating spouses.*

Callaway wanted to curl up and fall asleep. Maybe when he woke up, this nightmare would be over.

He heard a buzzing noise. His eyes snapped open.

"What the hell?" he wondered aloud.

He looked around, feeling dazed and confused. He realized the buzzing came from his jacket pocket. He shoved his hand inside and pulled out his cell phone. He checked. There were several text messages. He blinked a couple of times to clear the blur from his eyes.

The messages were from Echo Rose. She had emailed him the information he was looking for.

That was fast, he thought.

He turned on his laptop, and while it booted up, he rubbed his eyes. He grabbed a bottle of painkillers and downed two pills with some water. He clicked her email, and as he went through it, he was even more confused.

He took a screenshot of the information with his phone and left the office. He went straight to a variety store. He bought coffee from a vending machine. The brew tasted like motor oil, but it was strong. After finishing the coffee, he could feel the fog lifting from his head.

He could confirm what Echo had sent him later, but he needed answers now. They would eat away at him otherwise.

He got behind the wheel of the Impala and somehow made it to his destination without hurting someone or killing himself.

He raced up to the door and found it was still open. He entered the art gallery and was immediately welcomed by Carl Goodwin.

"Mr. Callaway," he said with a smile. "Are you back to create your own masterpiece?"

Callaway blinked. His head began to spin as blood rushed to his brain. He shut his eyes tight to make it go away.

"Are you okay?" Goodwin asked.

"I'm fine. I just ran too fast." He opened his eyes and pulled out his cell phone. "Can you explain this to me?"

Goodwin frowned and took the phone. He looked at the screen and said, "I'm not sure what I'm looking at."

"It's the messages from your website."

"How did you get them? They are password-protected."

"I had someone… never mind. You said that once a girl agreed to take on a client, they sent a confirmation message."

"Yes."

"And once the transaction, as you call it, was complete, they sent you another message to say that it was."

"Yes, that's true."

"If you look at the screenshot on my phone, on the day Linda disappeared, she agreed to take on a client, but she never completed the transaction. You said all accounts were paid up, but according to this, Linda's account was still open until she or someone else manually closed it *today*. How is that possible?"

"I'm not sure," Goodwin said, staring at the screen. "Have you shown this to anyone?"

"Not yet." Callaway shook his head a little too wildly. He was still plastered. "I wanted to ask you first before I took any actions, you know."

Goodwin smiled. "Thank you for bringing this to my attention. I'm sure there is a reasonable explanation. Let me make a call and find out for you."

"Okay, good," Callaway said with a smile.

Goodwin disappeared behind the back wall.

Callaway turned to one of the computer tablets displayed around the gallery. He swiped his hand over the screen, and it came alive.

His smile widened. *I can be a master artist too*, he thought. *Look out, world. Here comes Lee Callaway, renaissance painter extraordinaire.*

He chuckled.

He felt movement behind him. He turned to see who was there.

Something hit the back of his head.

He fell to the floor and blacked out.

NINETY-SEVEN

Bruno Rocco drove away from Milton in his white van. The sun had started to set, and the roads were relatively clear. He had stuffed everything that was important to him into a duffel bag. Rocco could not wait to leave Milton. He should have done so the moment he killed those two people.

Cassandra Stevens and Isaiah Whitcomb.

No one would miss the stripper, but he had no idea Whitcomb was related to a police detective. This had put a big target on his head.

He had met Stevens at the Gentlemen's Hideout. She was a nice girl, but she was also willing to make extra cash on the side. She offered her services to him. One night at his apartment, after they had done the deed, she decided to steal from him. When she went through his stuff, she stumbled upon his real ID. He was not Kevin Brogdon, but Bruno Rocco. She figured he was a lowly criminal on the run from the law and that she could squeeze him for money. As a painter, he would be scared and fork up the cash the moment she made a threat to go to the police.

If she had done her homework, she would have known how dangerous he really was.

They agreed to meet at the motel. He chose the location because he knew it had no surveillance. She was so dumb to show up by herself. She underestimated what he was capable of. The moment she was alone, he attacked her. He beat and tortured her for hours. He wanted to know if she had told anyone of his real identity. She denied it, but he did not believe her. As the night progressed, he went to the bathroom to take a leak. He thought, mistakenly, that she was unconscious, but when he came back out, he caught her talking to someone on her phone. He took the phone from her and made her tell him what she told the person on the other line. He now had another problem on his hands. If that person appeared at the motel, it would lead to more questions.

Across the road was a furniture store. It was dark and vacant. He texted back to the telephone number Stevens had just called. He told the person to meet her at the furniture store's parking lot.

He then knocked Stevens unconscious and duct-taped her hands, feet, and mouth. He then watched from the window as a car pulled up at the furniture store.

It was early in the morning, so he knew he had no time to waste. He had driven on his motorcycle, so it was fitting that he would execute Whitcomb in the manner he was accustomed to before he went to prison and then wound up a protected witness.

He approached the car from behind and shot the young man behind the wheel three times. He then took his cell phone. He did not want his phone to be linked with hers. He also placed a bag of heroin in the glove compartment.

The painting job was a façade for the U.S. Marshals, who were tasked to administer the Witness Protection Program. He had only met the marshal in charge of his case once when he was first relocated. The marshal was a man who was overworked and underpaid. After providing Rocco with his new identifications, he never once checked up on him.

Rocco was not too worried. He had Agent Schaefer to keep an eye on him. Or was it the other way around?

He smiled at that thought.

After killing Whitcomb, he still had to get rid of Stevens. The police would quickly link the two deaths if they were within the same proximity, and he could not transport Stevens on a motorcycle.

He left her back at the motel and returned to his apartment. He changed into his work clothes and drove his white van back to the motel. By then, the police had already arrived at the furniture store. Someone must have stumbled upon the body. He later saw on the news that it was a junkie named Bo Smith. Fortunately for him, the police were too busy with Whitcomb's body to pay too much attention to him.

He snuck Stevens's body out of the motel and loaded her into his van. As he was leaving, a police officer stopped him. He thought he was surely going to jail. But he played it cool. He asked what had happened, and the officer told him it was a homicide. The road was blocked, so the officer redirected him to another street. After that, he was gone.

He purchased the materials from a hardware store, which he now realized was a big mistake, and then shot Stevens in the head and dumped her body in the lake. After that, he destroyed the young man's cell phone so it did not provide the police with a lead.

Everything was going smoothly until it suddenly fell apart. The detectives were looking for him, and he had to get as far away as possible.

He would be relieved once this was all behind him. Agent Schaefer would come through in their agreement. He always did. He did not have much choice.

He spotted the giant donut sign in the distance. The sign was hard to miss. A thousand light bulbs illuminated the donut, like a heavenly sign.

He slowed down and pulled the van to the side of the road. He shut the engine off and waited.

He checked his watch. He still had lots of time. He thought about going into the gas station and buying something to eat. He was hungry, but he was not going to risk getting caught on the surveillance cameras. He had already made that mistake at the hardware store.

When he was a good distance away from Milton, he would stop for a bite.

He saw a flash of light in the rearview mirror. A car had pulled up and parked behind him.

Agent Schaefer's early, he thought.

The headlights blinded him as he waited for the agent to come out and hand him his IDs.

After several minutes passed, he got out. He walked over to the car and found the engine still running.

He checked the driver's seat.

No one was behind the wheel.

What the...? he thought.

He turned and suddenly froze.

NINETY-EIGHT

Callaway tried to lift his head up, but it hurt like nothing he had experienced before. The pain was ten times worse than a hangover. For a second, he did not know where he was. He blinked some more when he saw the figure standing before him, and he remembered what had happened.

Carl Goodwin had his arms crossed over his chest and a solemn look on his face.

The room they were in had a low ceiling and no windows.

"Where am I?" Callaway asked, wincing.

"You're in the basement of the art gallery."

Callaway looked down and saw he was sitting on a chair with his arms tied behind his back. His legs were also restrained with rope.

Goodwin sighed loudly. "You should not have come here. You realize what I have to do now, don't you?"

Callaway took a deep breath. He tried to make the throbbing in his head go away, but it would not. He said, "What did you do to Linda? Did you kill her?"

Goodwin shut his eyes, acting as if it troubled him to even think about her. "You wouldn't understand."

"Try me," Callaway said. "I've spent countless hours looking for her, so I think I deserve to know what happened to her."

Goodwin stared at him and then sighed. "I never meant to hurt her. I liked her. I *really* liked her. I had seen her many times at the gallery when she would come to meet the clients. I would talk to her before the client's arrival. She was smart, funny, and she knew quite a bit about art. I hoped one day she would work at the gallery with me. But she had other plans in her life. She wanted to travel the world. She wanted to fly first class. She wanted to dine at the fanciest restaurants out there. She wanted to buy the nicest things money could buy. She wanted a life other than the one she had. I thought it was a bit shallow of her, but I figured she was still young. I asked her out a couple of times, but she turned me down. She wasn't interested in dating *me*."

He looked away like it stung to even speak of her disinterest in him.

"I finally got fed up, and I offered to pay for her services. When she came, I had converted this basement into a private restaurant. I had spent all day cooking something delicious for her. I opened a bottle of wine I had kept for special occasions. I even picked out some romantic music for us to enjoy. I hoped after she saw all the work I had put into the night, she might change her mind about me paying to be with her."

He grimaced, and his lips curled into a frown.

"I hated it when she went with the other men. It was a cold transaction and nothing more. I was willing to offer her love, comfort, and security."

He balled his fists. "Instead of realizing how lucky she was that *I* had shown interest in her, she laughed in my face. She said it was sweet, but I still had to pay her for her time. I don't know what happened, but I snapped, and I hit her with a wine bottle. She fell to the ground and went limp. I thought she had passed out, but when I checked, she was dead."

His eyes brimmed with tears. "I'm not a murderer. I used to be a computer programmer. I never meant to kill her. I wanted to give her all the happiness in the world."

Goodwin put his hands over his face, pushed his glasses up above his eyes, and wept like a little boy.

"Where's Linda's body?" Callaway asked.

Goodwin composed himself. His eyes moved toward a door in the corner of the room. He wiped his face and stood up straight. "Like I said, you shouldn't have come here."

He walked over to a shelf and picked up a bottle of wine. He looked at it and smiled. "It's the very bottle I hit Linda with. I think it might still have some of her blood on it."

He gripped the bottle tight and moved toward Callaway.

"Don't do this," Callaway said.

"I have no choice."

"The police are waiting outside."

"No, they aren't."

"I'm friends with Detective Dana Fisher. She knows I'm here, and she's waiting for my call."

"No, she isn't. When you came here, you were drunk. You had no idea I had even killed Linda."

So much for that bluff, Callaway thought.

Goodwin began to raise the bottle. "I'm so sorry for this," he said.

Sure you are, Callaway thought. *What an idiot I was to let you get the drop on me…*

Goodwin got ready to swing the bottle.

A gut instinct seized Callaway.

He rocked himself onto his right side.

Goodwin's swing was clumsy. He had put too much weight on his right foot.

He missed Callaway and stumbled.

Callaway willed himself to roll over, chair and all.

Goodwin tripped over him and flew across the room head first.

Callaway heard a loud crack, followed by the sound of a bottle hitting an object and then the floor.

He glanced over.

Goodwin lay on the floor, out cold.

The wine bottle lay next to his head, still perfectly intact.

Callaway laughed, then he winced as pain stabbed his head.

Scumbag got hit with his own murder weapon!

"Are you all right?" a woman asked.

Callaway's eyes widened.

Jennifer Paulsingh was on the basement stairs. She had a can of mace in her hand.

"I'll live," Callaway replied, "but could you give me a hand here?"

She pocketed the Mace and quickly untied him. Callaway scrambled to his feet and checked on Goodwin. He was unconscious but still breathing.

He took the rope from the chair and tied Goodwin's hands and feet.

He rushed to the door in the corner that led to a small kitchen, which had a sink, microwave, and a fridge.

He pulled open the refrigerator door.

He covered his mouth with his hand, his eyes wide with horror.

Stuffed inside the fridge was the body of Linda Eustace.

NINETY-NINE

Schaefer picked up a new set of IDs for Bruno Rocco. Schaefer had earned a good reputation amongst his peers at the agency. Even then, it took some IOUs to get it done fast. He checked his watch. He was running late.

Rocco was likely already at their meeting spot. If he hurried, he might get there in half an hour. Afterward, he would take the first flight out of Milton and head straight back to sunny Florida.

He could not wait to get back on the golf course and leave this mess behind him. He was serious when he told Rocco this was the last favor. He could not be his get-out-of-jail ticket. There was only so much goodwill he had left before his superiors began asking questions.

He exited the government building and made his way to his car.

He abruptly slowed.

Standing next to the Buick were Detective Holt and Detective Fisher.

"In a rush to be somewhere, Agent Schaefer?" Holt asked.

Schaefer approached them with a smile. "You know how it is in our line of work. There is always somewhere we need to be."

"I'm afraid we'll need a bit of your time."

"What is this about?"

"We would prefer it if you came down to the station with us."

The smile on Schaefer's face evaporated. "Is something wrong?"

"We need to ask you a few questions."

"You can ask me here. Unless you are willing to read me my rights." Schaefer was not going to be pressured into doing something he was not willing to do.

"It's about Bo Smith," Fisher said.

Schaefer blinked. "Who?"

"Smith was the one who found the drugs in the Chrysler Isaiah Whitcomb was driving."

"Okay, but what does that have to do with me?"

"Smith was found dead with a gunshot to the head."

Schaefer's mouth dropped.

Fisher said, "You were seen at the hospital asking questions about Smith. There are also witnesses who saw you in Smith's apartment building the day he died."

Schaefer was speechless. "I… I didn't shoot him…"

He reached for his weapon.

Holt and Fisher pulled theirs and took aim. He quickly pulled his hand away. He raised his hands. "You can run ballistics on my gun. You'll see I never fired it."

Holt studied him. "I'm going to need your weapon."

"Am I under arrest?"

"Should you be?"

Schaefer paused to think.

He nodded.

Fisher removed his weapon from his holster.

"Tell us what's going on," Holt said.

"I have no idea."

"Help us make sense of this. I'm asking you out of professional courtesy and nothing more. You came to us offering your assistance. We gave you information on Bo Smith. Then we find out he is dead. It seems more than a coincidence, don't you think?"

"I had nothing to do with what happened."

"Did you go speak to him?"

"Yes."

"What did you talk about?"

Schaefer hesitated.

"You better be straight with us. So far, you've given us no reason to trust you.'"

"I wanted to know what he knew about Whitcomb's murder."

"And?"

"He knew only what he had already told you guys."

"Then what happened?"

"I left."

Holt stared at him.

"I swear," Schaefer pleaded. "When I left, he was still alive."

"What do you know about Bruno Rocco?" Holt asked.

Schaefer turned pale. "Bruno Rocco?"

"Yes," Holt said with a clenched jaw.

Fisher's phone buzzed. She answered and hung up. "You wouldn't believe this," she said to Holt.

He sighed. "Don't tell me. There is another dead body."

"Okay, I won't." She turned to Schaefer. "I think you better come with us. This will interest you."

ONE-HUNDRED

Bruno Rocco lay on the side of the road with a bullet between his eyes. His white van was parked twenty feet away from him. A truck driver on his way to the gas station had spotted the van and pulled over. The moment he saw the body, he called 9-1-1.

The police had blocked off the road and surrounded the area with yellow police tape. Holt and Fisher walked around the scene with looks of utter confusion on their faces. Schaefer was in the back seat of Holt's car. He, too, was shocked and dumbfounded by what he saw.

Fisher's face, illuminated by over half a dozen flashing police cruiser lights, said, "What was he doing in the middle of nowhere?"

Holt frowned. "I have no idea, but I think someone might know."

He stormed back to the car and pulled Schaefer out by his jacket collar. "You better start talking before I take you back to the station in handcuffs."

"I don't know," Schaefer said. "I'm as surprised as you."

"You knew Bruno Rocco. You had cut a deal with him. We know all about that," Holt growled. "And now he's dead. What the hell is going on?"

Schaefer looked at his jacket pocket.

Holt shoved his hand inside and pulled out a plastic baggie. Inside was a driver's license with Rocco's photo, a Social Security card, and a folded copy of a birth certificate. But the license read *Marco Keswick*.

Holt's eyes blazed with fury. "You knew he had killed my nephew, and you were helping him escape!"

Holt punched Schaefer across the face.

Schaefer fell on the gravel and spat blood from his mouth.

Holt cocked his fist again.

Fisher restrained him.

"Why?" Holt roared at the agent. "Why would you protect a murderer?"

Schaefer held up his hands to protect himself in case Holt took another swing. "I had no choice. Rocco had a recording of me feeding him lies to tell the judge. If it got out to the public, my career would have been ruined. Not to mention the verdict against Paolo Beniti and his associates would have been thrown out. Years of hard work went into putting Beniti behind bars, and if Rocco spilled what he knew, our hard work would have been for nothing."

"He was my nephew," Holt said and stormed away.

Fisher gave Schaefer a hard look. "You will answer for this mess, Agent Schaefer."

Schaefer lowered his head.

ONE HUNDRED-ONE

Police officers arrived at the gallery the moment Callaway made the call. They were followed by the crime scene investigation unit and two detectives whom Callaway had never met before.

Holt and Fisher are likely busy investigating Isaiah's murder, he thought.

The detectives took his statement and also Jennifer Paulsingh's.

Goodwin was arrested and charged with Linda's murder. The detectives believed Goodwin would spend the rest of his life inside a prison cell.

Linda's body was removed from the fridge, and by the looks of it, she had died from blunt force trauma. The wine bottle was tagged and taken as evidence.

Callaway was checked by paramedics on the scene. The lump on the back of his head was not life-threatening, but he was advised to go to the hospital for x-rays. He declined. All he needed was a couple of painkillers and a good night's rest.

He spotted Jennifer in the back seat of a squad car. He walked over to her, and an officer let him get in next to her. She was crying hysterically, and a part of him wanted to reach over and comfort her.

"I can't believe Linda is gone," she said. "I knew something bad had happened to her, but until I saw her like that, I never truly believed it."

"At least now we know the truth," he said.

They were silent for a moment.

"How did you know I was at the gallery?" he asked.

She looked up at him. Her eyes were raw and swollen. "I didn't know you were here. I came to collect the money Carl and Glenn owed me. They were terrible at paying the girls on time. I found the gallery empty. I think Carl had forgotten to lock up. I searched for him, and I heard noises coming from downstairs. I went to check, and that's when I heard the entire confession."

"Did you ever think it was Goodwin?" Callaway asked.

"No, not in a million years. I never got a negative vibe from him," Jennifer replied.

Callaway nodded.

He realized there was someone he had to call. *Elle.* She needed to know that they'd found... *Katie.*

He pulled out his cell phone and sighed. "We should let Linda's sister know we found her."

"Sister?"

"Yeah, I should have told you the first time we met," he said. "It was Linda's sister who had hired me to find her.'

Jennifer looked at him like he was crazy. "Linda doesn't have a sister," she said.

"Sure she does," he said with a short laugh. "And... her name is not Linda. It's actually Katie Pearson."

"No, it isn't," Jennifer said. "I should know. I've known Linda since grade school."

Callaway opened his mouth but then shut it. He quickly dialed the number Elle had given him and waited.

An automated message told him the number was no longer in service.

He stared at the phone in utter silence.

He got out of the squad car. "I have to go," he said to Jennifer, and he rushed away.

ONE HUNDRED-TWO

Agent Schaefer gave a statement at the Milton Police Department. He confessed to helping Bruno Rocco access new IDs, but he vehemently denied helping Rocco in the murder of Isaiah Whitcomb or Cassandra Stevens. His flight itinerary confirmed that his arrival in Milton was after their deaths. Schaefer also took no responsibility for Bo Smith's death. He held firm that Smith was alive when he left him at his apartment.

Schaefer's weapon had already been sent to the lab. A bullet from his gun would be matched to the bullet found in Smith. They would know soon enough if he was telling the truth.

Fisher and Holt now believed Rocco might have had something to do with Smith's demise. Smith was at the scene of Isaiah's murder. Rocco may have wanted to tie up all loose ends before he left Milton for good.

An officer knocked on the door. Fisher left the interview room. When she returned, she said, "Agent Schaefer, do you know a man by the name of Cosimo?"

Schaefer's eyes narrowed. "Yes, I do."

"Who is he?"

"He worked as a hitman for Paolo Beniti. We've been looking for him ever since we arrested Beniti and his associates."

Fisher said, "We got an anonymous tip that Cosimo is in Milton. He was seen at a falafel shop earlier today."

Schaefer's eyes widened. "I was there today."

"With Rocco?" Holt asked in a harsh voice.

Schaefer did not respond. But his silence told them he was.

Fisher said, "Does Cosimo have aliases?"

"Of course he does," Schaefer replied. "That's how he's eluded us for so long."

"Do you know any of them?"

"Sure, I guess."

Fisher took down the names and began checking them on her phone. After a few minutes, she said, "Nothing."

"If he had used any of them, the airlines would have flagged them," Schaefer said.

Fisher mulled this over. "What's Cosimo's full name?"

"Cosimo Castigiano."

Fisher checked. "There is an Enzo Castigiano who landed in Milton yesterday on an American Airlines flight from New Jersey."

"Enzo Castigiano is his father's name," Schaefer said. "He died a long time ago. Cosimo must be using his ID as a cover."

"And you wouldn't believe this," she said. "He just booked a return flight for later tonight."

"You have to get him before he leaves Milton," Schaefer said. "When Beniti found out Rocco had cut a deal with us, he put a bounty on his head. I'll bet every penny that Cosimo finally caught up with Rocco and completed the hit."

ONE HUNDRED-THREE

Callaway drove like a madman. It was bad enough he was nursing a hangover. He now also had to contend with a lump on his head.

He should have gone to the hospital. *What if I've suffered brain damage?* he thought.

He shook the absurd thought away. If his injury was serious, the paramedics would have taken him away in an ambulance.

He took a deep breath to calm himself. Nothing was making sense. His thoughts were all over the place.

What Jennifer Paulsingh told him had shaken him to the core. He was now on his way to Mayview to find out the truth.

He found a parking spot and raced into the apartment building. He took the elevator up and banged on Elle's door.

"Elle!" he said. "It's Lee. Open the door!"

He waited and banged his fist again. A neighbor popped his head out. He looked at Callaway suspiciously.

"Do you know if she's in?" Callaway asked, pointing at the door.

The neighbor shook his head. "I don't know. I was at work all day. Maybe you can ask the superintendent."

"Where can I find him?"

"I'll give you his number."

After calling the superintendent, Callaway waited impatiently in the front lobby. A Hispanic man stepped out of the elevator. The man's face was twisted into a scowl. He did not like being disturbed this late in the day.

Callaway explained that Elle was not answering her phone. He was worried about her health.

The superintendent took him back up to her floor. After knocking on the door a few times to make sure Elle was not asleep or bathing, he unlocked the door.

Callaway pushed past him and rushed inside. The living room was as he had last seen it. Clean, organized, and with nothing out of place.

He checked the bedroom and saw something on the bed. He picked it up and realized it was a black burqa, a piece of clothing used by Muslim women to cover themselves.

What the hell? he thought, utterly confused.

He checked the closet and saw a walking stick. He grabbed the stick when he noticed a pair of sunglasses and gloves on the floor. There was nothing else in the closet.

He went back out and found the superintendent standing in the apartment's front hall. "Everything okay, sir?"

Without answering, Callaway moved away from him. He was in a daze as he went to the living room and dropped onto the sofa. His head was reeling when he put his hands over his face.

Things were now beginning to make sense. There was a reason he had never seen any photos of Linda with Elle.

Linda didn't have a sister.

There were no text messages between the sisters, either.

Linda had never even met Elle.

The first landlord had never heard of Katie.

Katie did not live there.

Her co-workers did not remember her at the fast-food restaurant.

Katie never worked there.

No one had heard of Katie.

Katie did not exist.

Linda Eustace was not Katie Pearson.

He realized he was still holding Elle's gloves in his hands. He always thought it was odd that someone who saw with their hands would keep them covered. He now understood why. There would be no fingerprints in the apartment—nothing to lead them to the woman who had lived here.

He pulled his hands away and looked up at the ceiling. A thought circled his mind, one that would preoccupy him for a long time.

Who was Elle Pearson?

ONE HUNDRED-FOUR

Cosimo placed his belongings in his carry-on and quickly scanned the hotel room for the last time. He did not have time to unpack much. There was no need, really. He was only supposed to be there a few days. But there was always a concern that something left behind could lead back to him.

He was not going to take any chances. He had already wiped the room clean. No fingerprints, hair fibers, or items containing his DNA would be found.

All the news channels were talking about the death of Bruno Rocco. His body had been found by the side of a road. His death had been called suspicious, which was another way of saying it was a homicide.

Don Beniti will be pleased, he thought. *Beniti doesn't need to know all the details, only that Rocco's finally dead.*

Cosimo did not have time to plan this trip. Beniti's call came out of nowhere. The video of the basketball player's shooting had caught everyone by surprise, but it confirmed Bruno Rocco was still alive and living in Milton.

Cosimo would not want to walk away from the contract. This required him to use his father's identifications to create a new one for himself on such short notice. It was a risky move, but he doubted the police had been able to put things together. By the time they did, he would be long gone.

He checked his watch. There was still some time before his flight out of Milton. He went to the balcony and lit a cigarette. The air was cool as he let out a thick cloud of smoke. He was taking another drag when something caught his attention.

Two police cruisers suddenly pulled up to the hotel's entrance, followed by an unmarked police car. A man and a woman emerged from the car. Cosimo recognized them as the detectives investigating the Isaiah Whitcomb murder.

Cosimo was certain they had not seen him. He stubbed out the cigarette and placed the butt in his pocket. He was not going to leave the cigarette for someone to analyze later.

He went back inside the room. He checked his gun to make sure it was loaded. He grabbed his carry-on and left the room.

Instead of taking the elevator, he took the stairs. If they were here for him, they would block off all entrances and exits, including the elevators.

The stairs were still not the best option, but he had no choice. He had to get to the garage somehow.

He hurried down the steps two at a time. He reached the basement level and peeked through the door. His rental was at the far end of the garage. He had parked it there for a reason. It was further away from the cameras near the elevators.

He walked briskly through the garage.

He spotted a burly man standing by his vehicle. The man looked like one of the detectives.

Cosimo prepared to turn back.

Their eyes met.

The detective reached for his gun. Cosimo pulled out his and fired at the detective. The bullet hit the rear windshield, shattering it. The detective rolled on the concrete and returned fire. The car next to him shook as bullets penetrated the exterior.

Cosimo dropped the carry-on and ran in a full sprint in the opposite direction.

How did the detective know where my car was parked? he thought.

The only logical answer was that the detectives had contacted the hotel well in advance of their arrival. They knew which room he was staying in and how he was going to make his escape.

He raced down to the garage's lower level. He realized there was no way he could leave the building on foot. Officers were likely stationed in every corner.

He would have to force his way out.

He saw a Mustang parked in a row of parked cars. He smashed the driver's window with the butt of his gun. He wedged the gun in his belt and got behind the wheel. He jacked the car in less than thirty seconds.

He revved the Mustang out of the parking spot.

He saw a woman in the distance. He recognized her as the female detective.

She was blocking his way out.

He jammed his foot on the accelerator. The Mustang jerked forward and then raced toward her. As he got closer, he saw she was aiming her gun at him.

She fired a shot.

He tried to duck, but the bullet pierced through the windshield and lodged in his shoulder. He yelled in pain as he lost grip on the steering wheel. The Mustang spun three hundred and sixty degrees and smashed into another parked car. The alarm went off, blasting his ears.

He opened the door, got out, and fell to the concrete. He tried to get on his feet when he saw the male detective running toward him.

He drew his gun when he sensed movement to his right.

He turned and saw the female detective in a crouched position. Her weapon was aimed right at him.

He swung the gun in her direction.

A hail of bullets ripped through him.

Cosimo was dead before his head hit the concrete.

ONE HUNDRED-FIVE

The stadium was packed as thousands of students, professors, faculty members, and family gathered to honor the late Isaiah Whitcomb. The college had decided to retire Isaiah's jersey.

A special scholarship was also set up in Isaiah's name. Each year, it would be presented to a promising high school student who excelled in both sports and academics. The student should also be a role model and a good citizen: traits Isaiah embodied.

Dennis and Marjorie were in tears as they stood in the middle of the court to watch the officials raise Isaiah's jersey up to the rafters.

Holt and Fisher were in the stands. Nancy could not make it. The excitement was too much for her, so Holt recorded everything on his cell phone. They would watch it together later at home.

The body in the lake was officially identified as belonging to Cassandra Stevens.

According to Special Agent Ed Schaefer, Rocco had confessed to killing Isaiah and placing the drugs on him to send the detectives on the wrong trail. He had tortured and killed Stevens because she had found out the truth about his identity. This proved Isaiah was not a drug dealer and that he was at the furniture store to help a woman in trouble. Isaiah's relationship with a stripper had nothing to do with the fact that two young people had lost their lives at the hand of a cold-blooded killer.

Agent Schaefer was handed over to the FBI. They assured them an inquiry would be launched against Schaefer for his involvement in protecting Bruno Rocco. Holt seriously doubted anything would come out of it.

Schaefer's investigation and Rocco's statement had allowed the FBI to bring down Paolo Beniti. If the truth ever got out that Rocco had lied on the stand, their entire case against Beniti would fall to pieces. The FBI would never let that happen. Schaefer would most likely be forced to take early retirement.

There was a twist in the case. Cosimo's gun was matched to the bullet found in Bo Smith. Schaefer was telling the truth when he insisted he had no idea how Smith had died. But Cosimo's gun did not match the bullet found in Bruno Rocco. Cosimo may have disposed of the murder weapon prior to the police arriving at the hotel, but this was something they would likely never know.

Holt smiled as Marjorie waved and blew him a kiss.

Isaiah was no longer with them, but his spirit would live forever.

ONE HUNDRED-SIX

One month later

The house was surrounded by a large garden and had a pine tree on the front lawn. The street was lined with mailboxes and white picket fences. The neighborhood looked like it had come straight out of a postcard.

He rang the doorbell and waited. A woman answered the door. She had gray hair, wrinkles around her neck, and deep brown eyes.

"Are you here to take her away?" she asked, a look of concern over her.

"I'm not sure," Callaway replied.

He had called before coming, so his arrival was not unexpected.

"She's a good girl," the woman added. "I'm her mother, and she did it for me."

"Can I speak to her?" he asked.

She studied him for a moment, trying to discern his intentions.

"She's waiting for you in the solarium," she said.

Callaway walked through the house to a room in the back. The room was covered in glass. There were pots and plants in each corner. In the middle was a small table with two chairs.

A woman was seated in one of the chairs. Her dark shoulder-length hair was showing roots of natural blonde. Her shirt was snug on her slim body, and her sharp green eyes were staring directly at him.

"Hello, Elle," he said.

"Lee," she replied.

"You look… *different*," he said.

"I'm sure I do."

He took a seat across from her.

"How did you find me?" she asked.

"It's not difficult when you know where to look," he replied. "I had to go back to the beginning. I had to strip away everything I knew or thought I knew."

"And what did you know?" she asked.

"That you were looking for your sister," he said. "But in reality, all along you were looking for someone else."

"Who was I looking for?" she asked, quizzing him.

He smiled. "Bruno Rocco."

She nodded.

"He had come up in our search for your sister, when in fact, he had nothing to do with her disappearance. The moment I knew this, everything started to make sense. Rocco had been hired by Paolo Beniti to take out Anthony 'Fatboy' Carvalho. Carvalho was going to snitch on Beniti to the FBI. How ironic that in the end, it was Rocco who ended up snitching on Beniti to the feds. The hit was supposed to have been quick and clean. Drive up to the restaurant where Carvalho was having his meal and put a bullet in his head. I saw the video. Rocco ended up bungling it royally. He gave Carvalho the opportunity to return fire. A waitress ended up being killed in the shoot-out." Callaway paused and slowly added, "Her name was Katherine Woodward. She left behind a father, a mother, and an older sister. That sister's name was Eleanor Woodward."

Elle nodded again.

"It made sense that you chose names that were easy to remember," Callaway continued. "'Katie' for Katherine, and 'Elle' for Eleanor. It allowed you to keep your story straight when you arrived in Milton. It also allowed you to manipulate me for your own purposes."

He gave her a hard stare.

Silence hung in the air between them.

"I know you must have a lot of questions for me," she said.

"I do."

"Now that you are here, why don't you ask them?"

"Why the charade with the sunglasses and walking stick? You are not blind."

"No, I am not." She sighed. "I'm sorry for the way I used you, but I had no choice."

"We all have a choice."

She paused. "Yes, we do, but I didn't."

He waited for her to explain.

"You're right when you said I came to Milton not to search for my sister but for Bruno Rocco." Her voice turned hard. "Rocco killed my sister, and all he got was twelve years, of which he only served six before he was a free man. He cut a deal with the government so that he would get leniency. But what about us? What about the family that had lost a sister and a daughter? My father died a broken man. After Katie's death, he was never the same. He had always believed the system protected the weak and provided justice to all. Those who were guilty were given a punishment that fit their crimes. But that's not what happened with Katie. She had a full life ahead of her. The six years Rocco got would never be enough to compensate for that loss. The system is corrupt and controlled by those in power. The FBI wanted a big catch, and Paolo Beniti was the biggest in New Jersey. A lot of people at the FBI received awards and promotions, including Special Agent Ed Schaefer."

She paused to control her emotions. "I had met Schaefer a couple of times. On each occasion, I grilled him as to why the government would go so easy on a convicted killer. People had been given far longer sentences for selling pot, and this was premeditated murder. Rocco had gone to the restaurant with the intention of shooting and killing another person. My sister had gone to the restaurant to earn money to pay for her tuition. She was going to college, and she planned to get into medical school one day."

Elle paused and looked away. The memory of her sister was too strong.

Callaway did not push her. He knew she would tell him when she was ready.

She gritted her teeth. "I could not allow Rocco to roam free when my sister was robbed of her life. I had to find him and make him pay for what he did to her... for what he did to *us*. I spent every waking hour obsessing about him. I searched for any information on him. It was difficult. The FBI and the U.S. Marshals are extra protective of individuals placed in the Witness Protection Program. I knew Rocco had been given a new ID, but I did not know what it was. I changed my appearance and began making moves on a young FBI agent. He was straight out of Quantico, so he was eager to prove himself. I got intimately involved with him. I'm not ashamed to say I used him. But he gave me valuable information on Rocco. I did not know the ID Rocco was living under, but I was able to find out he was living in Milton." She took a breath and continued. "This led to some challenges. I knew if I came to Milton asking direct questions about Rocco, it would catch the attention of the people protecting him. It would also spook Rocco. He could go deeper into hiding, and I might never get this close to him again. People knew the real Katherine Woodward had a sister and that she was not blind. Elle Pearson became the ideal alter ego to accomplish this task."

"Then how does Linda Eustace play in all of this?" Callaway asked.

ONE HUNDRED-SEVEN

"I first needed a reason for my arrival in Milton," Elle said. "While I was researching a cover story, I found out a woman by the name of Linda Eustace had been reported missing only three months before."

"Linda's best friend, Jennifer Paulsingh, had filed the report with the police," Callaway said.

"Yes. It's not that difficult to get information from a missing persons report. It tells you quite a bit about the person. The moment I had a name, I was able to construct my story."

Callaway put his hand up to stop her. "I still don't understand why you chose to be blind."

"There were two reasons for that: One, I had to create a persona that would allow me to get close to Rocco without arousing a lot of suspicions."

"And the second reason?"

She lowered her head. "That was for you. I knew you would not ask too many questions if you knew I had a handicap."

Callaway looked away. He was seething. *She was right*, he thought. *I didn't question her even when my senses told me something was not right, and only because I thought she was blind.*

"Again, I am sorry for the way I used you."

"As sorry as you were when you used the young FBI agent to find Rocco?" he shot back.

She opened her mouth but shut it. She smiled. "My relationship with him was intimate, so I guess we used each other. But you only cared about finding my sister."

"That's what I was hired to do."

"Yes, but the five thousand dollars was not nearly enough for the amount of work you did. You would have kept going even when the money ran out. Your strong sense of justice is what made me choose you in the first place. I wasn't lying to you when I said I had heard about the Paul Gardener case."

"It seems like a lot of people have." He paused and then said, "I checked with Mayview PD, and you had never filed a missing persons report for a Katie Pearson."

She nodded. "The one I gave you when we first met was false. You wouldn't believe what you can do with a little knowledge of graphic design."

"Is that what you do? I mean, as a profession?"

"I have a degree in art and philosophy. Not very helpful if you want a high-paying job. But I counsel families who were hit with violence, in how to get through their loss."

Callaway gave her a hard look. "And do you advise them to put on a disguise and get revenge on those who hurt them?"

"Ouch," she said, but then smiled. "No, I don't, but by speaking to them, I realized the pain never goes away. It festers until it becomes all-consuming. If Rocco was still in prison, I would have never taken any actions. But knowing that he was walking the streets, living his life without a care for the pain he had caused my family, ate away at me to the point I had no choice but to do something about it."

Callaway then said, "And that's why it was not Cosimo Castigiano who killed Rocco, it was actually *you*."

ONE HUNDRED-EIGHT

"Yes, I killed him, and you know what?" she said boldly. "Seeing the look in his eyes when I told him who I was and why I was there was worth all the trouble in the world."

Her tone carried the same conviction he had heard before. Joely was right when she had said Elle may have looked weak, but there was a quiet intensity to her.

Callaway said, "There are still some things I don't understand. And I'm curious to find out the answers."

"You already know what I did, so you can ask me whatever you want."

"When we went to the house where Katie was supposed to have lived, how did you know the basement apartment had yellow wallpaper?"

"When I was constructing my story, I searched online and found properties that were available for rent. I went—not disguised as Elle—but as me, and I got a tour of the basement apartment. I knew people would deny knowing Katie Pearson—after all, she was not real, so I had to make sure the details were accurate so that *you* could believe she existed."

"And what about the people at the fast-food restaurant? You knew quite a bit about them."

"I became friends with one of the employees via a social networking site. You wouldn't believe how much people gripe about their work, co-workers, and their bosses. I was able to dig out information on almost everyone at the restaurant. When they failed to remember a Katie Pearson, I was able to use the information to prove I wasn't lying."

He pondered her answer. "Okay, but what about the apartment you were living at? Whose is it?"

"The apartment belongs to a professional. He travels most of the year, so he rents it out on a bed-and-breakfast site. The unit came with all the furnishings, so I didn't have to do much to set it up except move the television and some personal items into the storage locker. A blind person has no use for a television, you know." She lowered her voice. "At the apartment, when you had tea with me, you told me a lot about yourself and your family. I can say that it was one of the times I wanted to tell you the truth. Here you were so forthcoming about your life, and I was deceptively feeding you half-truths."

"Half-truths?" he asked.

"Not everything I told you was a lie. The story of my sister getting lost in the woods when we were young was not made up. And I do have a cousin who went blind at the age of fourteen from chickenpox. I used things from my life to create a character that was believable."

Callaway paused and then said, "I still don't understand how Linda Eustace played into all of this."

"I knew a woman had gone missing, and because of her profession as an escort, the police were not making an effort to find her. I even went to the Milton PD and inquired about her case, and the response I got was, 'She's an adult and she can choose to go wherever she wants.' I figured, in the course of getting close to Rocco, I might be able to help find out what happened to her."

"Is that why you kept leading me to Rocco in our search for Linda? You were hoping I would start looking for him as a suspect in her disappearance?"

"Yes. When we were going through the box with Linda's personal items, I snuck Rocco's photo in there to make it look like I had found it."

"And did you know the box belonged to Linda when we went to her landlord's house?" Callaway asked.

She shook her head. "I had no idea Linda was a diving champion in high school. It caught me by surprise when you mentioned it. I just needed the opportunity to introduce Rocco in her story, so I took it. Unfortunately, each time I mentioned Rocco as a person of interest, you pushed him aside."

"I could not find a link between someone with mob connections in New Jersey to the disappearance of an escort in Milton."

They were silent again. There were a lot of facts for Callaway to digest, but there was still more he needed to know.

"What about the anxiety attacks you claimed you were suffering from? What purpose did they serve?" he asked.

"When I saw the video of the Isaiah Whitcomb shooting on the news, I knew my time was running out. Whitcomb was related to one of the detectives, which meant the police were not going to stop looking for Rocco. I feared they were going to find him before I did. I needed an excuse to get away from you and expedite my search…"

"…Because I wasn't really looking for him."

She nodded. "I had no idea Rocco had committed the additional murders. Had I known, I would not have involved you. I would have tailed the detectives instead."

"But you did, and we found the person who killed Linda."

She smiled. "I guess some good came out of me hiring you."

He gave her no reply.

She said, "When that woman's body was found in the lake…"

"Cassandra Stevens?"

She nodded. "When we went to the morgue to identify her, I had to shut my eyes after seeing what Rocco had done to her face. I almost threw up in my mouth, but I knew if I did, my mask would have come off. But some good did come from our visit there. When Detective Fisher showed you the photo on her cell phone from the hardware store, I knew I was close. I made some excuse to you, and I began trailing Detective Holt. To my surprise, at the Milton PD, I saw Detective Holt speaking to Agent Schaefer. If Schaefer was there, then Rocco was close by. I began following Schaefer instead, and he led me straight to him. It was at a falafel shop. I wore a burqa…"

"I saw it in the apartment."

"No one pays attention to women in burqas. They are invisible to the general public," she said. "I was able to get a table next to them. I overheard their entire conversation. When I was leaving, I saw a man who looked familiar."

"Cosimo Castigiano?"

"Yes. His name had come up in my research. He worked for the Beniti Family. I knew he had come to kill Rocco as I had. I could not let that happen. At the falafel shop, he followed Rocco to his van before I cut him off in an alley. I allowed Rocco to walk away unscathed. But I knew I did not have much time. I made an anonymous call to the Milton PD. I told them Cosimo was in the city and that he was looking for Rocco. I knew where Rocco was meeting Schaefer. And when I caught up with him, I put a bullet between his eyes."

Callaway almost shivered at how coldly she recounted the deed. She was a murderer, but he understood why she had done it. Rocco had brutally killed two innocent people in Milton. He had also killed two people in New Jersey, one of them being Elle's sister. Elle would now spend the rest of her life as an only child to her mother. Her father had never gotten to see justice done for his youngest daughter.

Elle said, "You now know the whole truth, Lee. So, where do we go from here?"

He stared at her for a long time.

He leaned closer to her and said, "Detective Holt believes Bruno Rocco killed Isaiah Whitcomb and Cassandra Stevens. He also believes Cosimo Castigiano killed Bruno Rocco. Carl Goodwin was charged with murdering Linda Eustace. I think justice has been served."

Callaway stood up.

"Goodbye, Elle," he said. "I hope now you can finally move on with your life."

Elle stared at him. Her eyes moistened. She then choked up and mouthed, "Thank you."

He walked out of the room, leaving Elle alone in the solarium.

He knew he would never see her again. He also knew her secret would go with him all the way to his grave.

Visit the author's website:
www.finchambooks.com

Contact:
finchambooks@gmail.com

Join my Facebook page:
https://www.facebook.com/finchambooks/

LEE CALLAWAY SERIES

1) The Dead Daughter
2) The Gone Sister
3) The Falling Girl
4) The Invisible Wife
5) The Missing Mistress
6) The Broken Mother
7) The Guilty Spouse
8) The Unknown Woman
9) The Lost Twins

THOMAS FINCHAM holds a graduate degree in Economics. His travels throughout the world have given him an appreciation for other cultures and beliefs. He has lived in Africa, Asia, and North America. An avid reader of mysteries and thrillers, he decided to give writing a try. Several novels later, he can honestly say he has found his calling. He is married and lives in a hundred-year-old house. He is the author of the Lee Callaway Series, the Echo Rose Series, the Martin Rhodes Series, and the Hyder Ali Series.

Made in United States
Orlando, FL
06 May 2023